LANDOOBREY DAZE

Karla Smith

*With love and thanks to all
who've helped this book happen.*

https://www.landoobreydaze.co.uk/

https://www.facebook.com/landoobrey.daze

CHAPTER ONE

"Landoobrey," Eric said again, waving his father's handwritten directions. "I'm just trying to get to Landoobrey."

The man took no notice.

Talk about peeing in the wind, thought Eric, which was all he'd been trying to do in the first place. Safe enough, he'd assumed, halfway up a breezy Welsh mountain in the middle of the night.

He'd barely unzipped himself when a voice very close to the zip had said, "You can put *that* away, Sonny Jim."

And hadn't he just? Trying to zip up and zip off at one and the same time, tripping, stumbling and cursing the intermittent moonlight all the way back to the van. Finally hurling himself into the driver's seat and locking the door.

The outline of the man had grown larger with every measured step. Dressed in combat gear and night goggles and toting a machine gun, he was easily the scariest thing Eric had ever seen. Until the tank turned up, thinly disguised as a gorse thicket, blocking the road ahead.

Surrounded, Eric had then remembered his directions to Landoobrey. Proof, surely, that he'd bona fide business here? Wherever "here" was. A fat lot of good it had done him, though, waving them and shouting at the soldier who was at the van window now making hands-up gestures with his gun.

Eric didn't need telling twice and thrust both hands into the air with such force he snapped a thumbnail on the long-defunct interior light and bent the fingers of one hand right back.

Putting his thumb in his mouth he waggled his other fingers checking for breakages. Too late, he realised how this might have looked to the soldier, who danced a bit then said, "Right, chummy, that's enough. Open up."

Eric lowered his window, dodging the encroaching foliage as the camouflaged head of his pursuer popped in.

"What's your game, then?" said the soldier, close enough now for Eric to count three stripes on his upper arm.

"It's no game," Eric assured him. "I'm lost. I just want to go here."

He angled his piece of paper towards the night goggles, which turned this way and that like a confused owl as the wearer sought to focus. Eric sighed. Surely a torch would have done just as well? About to make some waggish remark about sledgehammers and nuts, he spotted a row of implement handles sticking out of a nearby ditch. It wouldn't do, he thought, to go giving anyone ideas.

Eventually the sergeant admitted defeat, withdrew from the window and removed the goggles. Patting down the resulting dishevelment in his fronds, he put out a hand for the piece of paper.

The owl motif was stronger now and Eric suppressed a nervous giggle at two pale brown circles in the bootblack face. It was hardly smart, he realised, to laugh at a man clanking with weaponry and already annoyed. Pulling himself together he handed over his piece of paper, all limp now and blurred with sweat.

"See?" he said. "That's where I'm headed."

The sergeant took the directions and began to examine them by the thin beam of a little torch. "Name, Sir?" he asked.

"Eric Bagnall."

"And what do you do, Mr Bagnall?"

"I'm an artist," mumbled Eric.

He still felt uncomfortable calling himself that in spite of his debut piece, *A Deep Depression in Driftwood,* having somehow ended up in the Tate Modern. Still, perhaps there were times when his new found fame might do him some good? He looked up at the sergeant, but it seemed neither his name nor his occupation had cut any ice there.

"And what's in the skip, Sir? Oh, sorry, I meant to say 'van'."

The answer, thought Eric, was his life. The more portable bits of it at least. Having no requirement for furniture where he was going, the little Escort was doubling as a removal van. Bursting with boxes and black bags carefully packed and labelled back at the flat.

"My luggage," he said. "Well, my belongings really. Everything I possess."

"Right," said the sergeant. "And what's at Landoobrey?"

Eric forbore to lean out of the window and tap the give-away words at the top of the paper ("Directions to holiday cottage at Landoobrey"). Instead he replied, "My house." Then, in the interests of accuracy, he added, "Well, my parents' house originally. A holiday cottage where we came every year when I was a boy. But mine now."

My sanctuary, he whispered to himself. Recalling the way press and public alike had hounded him since his rise to fame. The former even going so far as to camp out in the back garden of his flat. He defied them to find him at Landoobrey, though; given the trouble he was having finding himself there.

"And your parents?" enquired the sergeant.

"Gone to The Guardians of Eternal Peace," said Eric, sadly.

"Very sorry to hear that, Sir," the sergeant replied.

Eric realised there'd been a misunderstanding but he hesitated to put it right. The latest peculiar sect to ensnare his parents had required them not only to renounce all material possessions, including the holiday cottage, but also to march with them for the universal disbanding of armed forces. These were not, he felt, the sentiments to share with a tank regiment on exercise.

"Er, thanks," said Eric, "but it's thirty-five years since I last visited the village. I can't seem to find it for love nor money, not even on a map."

"No such place, that's why," the sergeant surmised. "Least, not to my knowledge. Jones," he went on, turning to a copse of trees alongside the lane. "You 'eard of Landoobrey?"

One of the trees detached itself from the group and paced jerkily towards the Escort, hampered by the greenery festooning its six-foot trunk and a backpack practically the size of the van.

"No, Sarge!" said the soldier standing smartly to attention, the sudden movement causing an autumnal moment in his camouflage. "I could ask Binks, Sarge?"

"Do that, Jones."

The soldier rustled off, making for the tank blocking the narrow lane.

At his knock the top hatch flew open and a head shot out, crowned by the obligatory vegetation. Silhouetted against the night sky it reminded Eric of a charcoal sketch he'd seen once of Carmen Miranda. Again, he held his tongue.

"Landoobrey?" echoed the tank driver in the tone of one who might've put a pondering forefinger to his lips were it not for the confines of the hatch and a certain regard for his image. "No, Sarge! I could ask Mellden?"

"Do that, Binks," the sergeant said, and the tank driver sank without trace.

Eric sighed. With an estimated fifty or so further trees to consult plus however many soldiers there might be crammed into the belly of the tank, it looked like being a long night.

"Sarge!" The tank driver popped up again, his mudpack cracking under his smile of triumph. "Mellden says there's a village-come-small-town on the lower slopes of this mountain. Would that be it?"

Eric nodded, not having the vaguest idea. But even if it wasn't Landoobrey, he reasoned, there might be a B&B there, where he could put up for what was left of the night.

"Thanks ever so much," he said. "Village-come-small-town, eh? That's exactly what I'm looking for. I'll be on my way then, shall I? Let you all get on?"

The sergeant held up a hand. "You can be on your way, Sir, for now, but just bear in mind this is MOD territory. Best not come driving over here next time, eh?"

"No, no of course not," Eric agreed, not at all sure how he'd managed to do it this time. "Really helpful of you, I must say," he added, starting his engine and watching the gorse thicket shudder as its driver did the same.

He was about to drive off when he was struck by something he'd seen earlier in his journey. "Actually, I'm sure that *is* the village I want," he said, "because they'd be gearing up for their annual Carnival round about now."

The sergeant looked baffled. "Gearing up for a Carnival, Sir? What makes you think that?"Eric let in the clutch as the tank finally cleared the narrow lane. "The flags," he explained, calling backwards out of his window. "All along this road. Big red ones. Didn't you see them?"

***

There was no road sign at the entrance to the village, only a large portion of open hillside between two tall, rusty poles. But that didn't matter. As soon as Eric had rounded the last hairpin bend he'd known he was in the right place.

Cradled in the lap of the surrounding mountain, the sprawling, overgrown village looked as if someone, possibly God, had picked up the leftovers from a dozen other settlements and simply chucked them. They'd landed, Eric thought, in the sort of disarray he'd always associated with Landoobrey. The tall Georgian houses of its centre and Victorian villas of its outskirts, interspersed by the humble cottages of a bygone age and the afterthought of bungalows. Its narrow streets, twisting and turning, clambering ever-upwards, bound for peripheral farms and hamlets almost as old as the mountain itself.

A mountain, breathtaking in the soft light of a new day. Its ridges and folds, peaks and gullies dropping like a curtsey to the river, pounding the valley below.

Crossing the cattle grid, Eric pictured his parents sitting side by side in the family three-wheeler, holding hands over the handbrake and telling each other they were "home". Calling into the cramped back seat where their only child languished under the luggage, wishing himself anywhere but here:

"Eric, we've arrived. Landoobrey at last."

Landoobrey, at last, he repeated to himself, steering carefully up the high street, heading for the other side of town where his new home was the last in a row of small detached cottages.

It was funny, he thought, how anxious he'd always been *not* to come to Landoobrey in his younger days. Never so pleased as in the summer of his fifteenth birthday when his parents had allowed him to stay home alone.

The place had been geared exclusively to drinking back then, with fourteen pubs in a population of two thousand largely sozzled souls. Two thousand and two, if you counted his parents embarking on day one of their holiday bender before they'd even unpacked the car. In fact, practically the only inhabitants of Landoobrey who hadn't been three sheets to the wind had been himself, the latest clutch of village babes in arms and the ardently teetotal Chapel Brigade. A small but vociferous minority on a similar hiding to nothing as The Guardians of Eternal Peace.

7

Still, things were bound to have changed by now he told himself. No village-come-small-town could resist the passage of time forever. Not even Landoobrey. And this, Eric felt, could only be a good thing. Potentially, there would be fewer pubs, enabling the residents to finally take charge of their lives and ...

"Shit!" he yelled, gripping the wheel at the sight of a prostrate figure in the middle of the road, pressing an ear to the tarmac.

Slewing to a halt, he watched the figure, wearing a Stetson, a tank top, purple lederhosen and plimsolls, climb unsteadily to its feet.

The woman approached the open window of the van.

"Knew you was coming," she said, leaning a beefy forearm on the Escort roof and belching out alcohol fumes of such purity that Eric feared combustion with the glowing tip of the roll up clamped between her lips. "Heard you, see?"

Slowly, Eric unclenched his fingers from the steering wheel and passed a trembling hand over his face. "What the hell," he asked, "were you doing lying in the road like that?"

"Listening," said the woman, as if that much should have been obvious.

"What for?"

"Holiday traffic. Time of the year when we might get some, April."

"But it's May," Eric couldn't resist pointing out.

"Really? Oh well, it's late then. 'Part from you, stranger. Just passing through are you?"

Fleetingly, Eric wondered whether this mightn't be such a bad idea.

"Actually," he said, "I'm not a stranger. I know the village quite well. I used to stay at the holiday cottage here years ago. With my parents."

"Polly and Mick!" The woman slapped her lederhosen like a Bavarian folk-dancer limbering up. "Your mam and dad's Polly and Mick?"

"Well, yes, as it happens."

"So you must be young Eric?

"Er, yes. That's right." He glanced down at his touch of middle-aged spread, resting on the belt of his jeans. "Not so young these days, I'm afraid."

Leaning into the van, the woman followed his glance, her gaze coming to rest in his lap. "Phew," she said. "You've grown a bit that's for sure. What brings you here, then? Holiday is it?"

"No," said Eric. "I've come here to live."

"Have you, now?" The woman finally shifted her focus from his lap to his face. "Well, that *is* good news."

Nose to nose with an intruder, for the second time that night, Eric felt her eyes roaming his features. He was confident she'd find him little changed over time. His face unremarkable as ever but barely lined in spite of his forty-nine years of age. Mild blue eyes, as yet unencumbered by glasses. Hair only lightly dusted with grey. All testament, in Eric's book, to a healthy and abstemious lifestyle. That and going to bed early every school night of his twenty-five years as a woodwork teacher. A career he'd cheerfully abandoned when fame and fortune had come knocking.

"Phew," said the woman again. "You've aged a bit, too. Don't suppose you remember me, do you? Hetty the Hart?"

Anything less like a hart was hard to imagine but Eric found he did remember her, only too well. Landlady of the White Hart pub and one-time mayoress of Landoobrey, she'd tended to wear hot pants in the old days in place of the lederhosen and had occasionally thrown a smartish jacket over the tank top for civic duties, but otherwise …

"Of course I do," he said. "Well, well … how's the pub trade, these days?"

Hetty touched her dog end with the tall, blue flame of her petrol lighter, which she often told people cost more to run than the average family saloon.

"Pretty dire." She gestured up a side road, where the White Hart lay between the Blue Bell and the Red Lion. "Only a dozen or so regulars in again this evening."

Eric glanced at the clock on his dashboard. 4.30 a.m. Was there anywhere else in the world, he wondered, where practically dawn counted as "evening"?

"That's why I came out here," Hetty went on. "I can often drum up a bit of business from the ones that stop after swerving to miss me. Flog 'em a nip of brandy, if nothing else, for the shock."

She raised an amused eyebrow at Eric and finally he got it.

"You weren't really listening for traffic, were you?" he asked.

The Stetson shook vigorously. " 'Course not. Think I'm daft?"

"What were you doing, then?"

"Giving an ear to the *Ffrwd Wyllt*."

Eric searched his memory, recalling that *Ffrwd Wyllt* was Welsh for "wild stream" and that one such unpredictable watercourse occasionally flooded the ancient drainage system beneath the town. It had even been known, if Eric remembered rightly, to burst from the ground as a series of little springs. Causing sunbathers to think better of it and drinkers to blame one another for the odd, spontaneous trickle on the earthen floors of the pubs.

"Er … why?" he said.

"The farmers are getting tetchy about spending money. If the *Ffrwd Wyllt* runs any time afore midsummer, a good harvest is guaranteed. Gets 'em spending again, it does, when that happens."

"And is it running?"

"No, but I needn't tell them that." She grinned and jerked her chin towards the pub. "Oh, well. Duty calls. Can't tempt you, I suppose?"

He shook his head. "Some other time, perhaps."

Hetty snorted. "Believe that when I see it, young Eric. You never did approve of my pub, did you?"

Eric blushed, realising he might have been a bit of a prig in his younger days. Determined, perhaps, to be the opposite of his parents whose general wackiness and love of life were legendary, especially here in Landoobrey.

"I was fourteen last time I was here, Hetty," he said. "Technically, I wasn't even allowed in the pub."

"Not allowed? Who said so? I'd have served you, any time."

Eric sighed. This was just the sort of lawlessness he'd always associated with this place.

"And anyway," added Hetty. "You're old enough now, ain't you?"

"Yes," he admitted, "but I've got to get to the cottage yet and unpack. Then I reckon I'll be about ready for that lovely antique bed of Mum and Dad's. Be a nice change from the lilo in the box room I always got lumbered with as a kid."

"Mmm," said Hetty, turning away rather abruptly Eric thought. "Well, good luck with that. Look forward to seeing you around. And welcome back."

Eric sketched a wave and set off once more towards the cottage. It had been a long and trying day. Being lost had been bad enough. Being found by the army almost worse. But he was nearly there now.

***

The key was exactly where his parents had said it would be: in the front door. Pocketing it with a tut, he stepped over the threshold of his new home. A quick look round, he decided, then in with his belongings.

Flicking a light switch he peered ahead into the long, narrow passage separating his three downstairs rooms. Sitting room to the left, running from front to back of the property; parlour to the right; kitchen and scullery tacked on behind. At the end of the passage, a curved and rickety staircase led to the bedroom, box room and an antiquated little bathroom.

For a moment he felt a pang of longing for his recently vacated flat with its bright paintwork and teak-effect floors and doors. A far cry from the off-white walls and black treacle varnish of the cottage. Still, he wasn't about to look a gift house in the mouth. Not when it came fully furnished so that all he had to do was walk in and unpack. A ready made bolt-hole, in fact, where he could rest up and reflect on the media madness that had recently taken over his life.

He closed the heavy front door, fancying, as he did so, that he caught the faint murmur of voices quite close at hand. Probably only the breeze he thought as, whistling cheerfully, he began to explore.

CHAPTER TWO

The two schoolgirls camping out in Eric's garden looked at one another in dismay. Awoken by sounds of a car door slamming and a man whistling, they were now watching the lights of the cottage coming on, one by one.

"That's a bugger," said thirteen-year-old Meryl to her younger sister, Beryl. "Someone actually taking a holiday in the holiday cottage."

Beryl said nothing, her shock and disappointment being beyond mere words. It was typical, she thought, of Meryl to take it so lightly. In fact, it was typical of Meryl to take *everything* lightly. Having different dads, the girls were unalike not only physically, with Meryl being small and dark and Beryl tall and fair, but also in their outlook on life. Meryl, inclined always to see sunshine, no matter how heavy the rain. Beryl, struggling under a black cloud of impending disappointment...

She put this down to the way life had treated her up to now. Being called Beryl, for a start. All due to a mix up at her christening, when Mam had been all set to name her latest baby Cheryl. Until the vicar pointed out she already *had* a Cheryl (and an Eryl, a Deryl and a Meryl come to that.) "Better make this one Beryl, then," her mam had reportedly said. "I think her dad had an auntie called that. Or a wife."

But at least back then she'd been the baby of the family, doted on by her four older sisters. Couldn't last, could it? Not with a mam who shed babies like dandruff. Within a few years the three boys had come

14

along, christened in turn and without incident: Harry, Barry and Garry.

As the boys grew, so the tiny flat over the chip shop seemed to get smaller, smellier and noisier, with their mam's only answer to it being to throw her hands in the air, saying she was beginning to feel like the old lady who lived in a shoebox.

Beryl wasn't sure her mam had got the words of the rhyme quite right but she knew what she meant. Finally, the cramped conditions had got so bad, Meryl and Beryl had jokingly offered to camp out in the back yard of the chip shop.

Their mam hadn't needed asking twice, which Beryl thought was rather sad. After all, they were hardly the ones causing the trouble, were they? As the middle children of the family, she and Meryl were also the quietest. So quiet, in fact, that their mother often said she hardly knew they were there. Which had turned out to be truer than anyone realised, because they'd decamped days ago from the chip shop yard and so far it seemed they hadn't been missed.

Still, the old vegetable plot, behind the holiday cottage, had been a step up in the world, with the facilities afforded by the nearby house taking much of the hardship out of life under canvas. A proper bathroom, for instance, and a fully working loo. Until recently it had offered a range of other home comforts, too, the lack of which made her wonder what sort of minimalist holiday the recently arrived guest had let himself in for.

Anxiously, she turned to her sister. "We won't have to move again, will we?"

"Don't see why," Meryl replied. "We're well enough hidden here."

"Not if he decides to do some gardening," objected Beryl.

"Oh yeah. Nothing better, is there, than digging over someone else's veg patch on your holidays?"

Beryl poked her head further through the tent flap. "We're right by the washing line," she pointed out. "What if he wants to use it?"

"He's a *man*, Beryl," said Meryl. "I reckon we're safe enough."

Beryl thought for a moment. "What'll we do about … you know … the loo and stuff?"

"He's bound to go out sometimes, isn't he? To the pub at least. Everyone does. We'll just have to synchronise our bladders with when he goes for a pint."

Beryl blushed like she always did when Meryl used grown-up words like "bladder". Not that the word itself was unfamiliar because their mam used it often. But more as a describing than a naming word.

A thought struck her. "What if he takes to locking the doors?"

Meryl shrugged. "There's always the scullery window. We can nip in and out through that. It's not as if he's going to be here for ever, is it? A week, maybe. Two at most."

Beryl sighed. "It won't be the same," she whispered, her troubled eyes welling with tears.

***

Inside the cottage, Eric had troubles of his own. Starting with the discovery that his fully furnished cottage wasn't.

16

So much for his parents renouncing all material possessions, he thought, glancing again at the note left for him in the spot where his antique bed ought to have been. Apparently the hut they'd been allocated at the sect had been "simply too basic for words". They hoped, therefore, that Eric wouldn't mind them having "stopped by for a couple of bits and pieces".

"… a couple of bits and pieces," he repeated. For which read an entire houseful of furniture, including one bed, one sofa, two armchairs, a TV set and a dining suite.

And, as if all that wasn't bad enough, the shock of finding no bed to put it on had caused him to drop his box labelled "Bed Linen", which had promptly burst spilling half a packet of cornflakes, a cracked eggcup and a dustpan.

In the circumstances, of course, the missing linen was no big deal but it hinted at a serious malfunction in his labelling system. How could it have happened, he wondered, pushing his hands deeper into the pockets of his anorak. Or "blanket", as he was now resigned to calling it.

Leaving the clutter where it was, he set off back downstairs in search of a comforting mug of sweet, milky coffee.

Sadly, the bed linen soon transpired not to have been the only casualty of his packing. After a fruitless search of his remaining luggage, he had to conclude that his other kitchen box, containing milk, coffee, sugar, bread, eggs and bacon, must still be sitting on the worktop back at the flat.

As auspicious starts went, he decided, there were distinct echoes here of *Titanic*, and her near miss in Southampton Water.

***

Two hours later, Eric awoke, completely unrefreshed, on his sitting-room floor. He breakfasted on cornflakes with a splash of ice-cold water, then took a quick bath before tackling his unpacking. Anxious not only to see how far the rot went with his labelling system, but also to find some fresh clothes to put on.

Wrapping himself in a large fluffy towel, which had somehow escaped the raiding party, he opened a box labelled "Kitchen Scraps" on the basis that it might contain his bedding. It didn't. Only several back issues of *Art Now* and the remains of the plastic plant his ex-wife had once thrown at him.

A lifelong bachelor until Imogen came along, and not about to make the same mistake twice, Eric had kept the plant as a reminder that shares in marital bliss could go down as well as up. He picked up the faded cyclamen, gingerly, as if Imogen's right arm might somehow still be attached to it.

How thrilled he'd been when the statuesque PE teacher had asked him to marry her. Or rather, she'd told him to, which had turned out to be the shape of things to come. Luckily, the marriage hadn't lasted. Imogen's approach to matrimony being not so much a matter of tying the knot as of making a loose bow. One tug on a spare end and she was gone.

Eric dropped the plant and began opening his other boxes, trying to ignore the increasingly strong smell of fish and cabbage from his pile of black bags.

Finally, he opened one labelled "Jeans" and sighed. It was as he'd feared. His entire wardrobe must, even now, be sitting on the pavement outside the flat awaiting the Wednesday collection.

He added "clothes" to his ever-growing mental shopping list. Everything but the furniture, he thought, could probably be purchased in Landoobrey. It was a nuisance, though, having to go out so soon after his arrival. He'd hoped to start work today on his new piece.

***

Thinking of his new piece made Eric glance at his old one, *A Deep Depression in Driftwood.* Or at least at a framed photo of it, which he'd hung in the sitting room to cover a dark patch on the wall where, he was fairly sure, an expensive little water colour had once been.

The original of his piece was, of course, in the Tate Modern. He could still scarcely believe it had catapulted him to fame the way it had. And all by accident, really, if he was honest. It wasn't as if he'd even done much to the large chunk of wood he'd found on the beach. Or rather that had found *him,* he reminded himself.

Sticking up out of the sand, it had looked at first as if it was a person; trapped from the waist down, arms elevated, head thrown back as if screaming for help. Coming closer, he'd seen that it was in fact a piece of wood – his favourite material for sculpting – and that the grain was perfect for sanding down and polishing. Maybe to put it in the little amateur sculptor competition they were running at the library.

Eric could smile, now, at the way Fate had caused him to make such a fiasco of his first ever go at exhibiting a sculpture. All the entrants had been allocated a space but there hadn't been enough plinths to go round. Anxious to show off his piece to its best advantage, Eric had asked a friend to weld him up one and deliver it to the library for 6.00 p.m. By which time Eric hoped to have hoisted his sculpture aloft in readiness for dropping it onto its stand, ahead of the judges' visit at 7.00 p.m.

It was a good plan, Eric reflected, gazing once again at the photo. Doomed to failure, of course, when his friend's van had broken down, leaving Eric's masterpiece suspended by its wooden neck on a rope slung over a nearby beam. It had won him the competition, though. This entirely serendipitous combination of a hanging man and the title of the piece, *A Deep Depression in Driftwood.*

Eric shuddered, looking back on the furore that had followed his win. Especially after one of the national papers had picked up on it and sent a journalist to do a feature on him. The journalist having then gone completely over the top, determined, it seemed, to make the humble "teacher-turned-sculptor" into a household name. He'd succeeded, too, to the point where Eric's sculpture had begun to attract art critics and gallery owners from all over Europe, culminating in the offer of a spot at the Tate Modern.

And all the while, Eric had just been waiting for it to dawn on someone that the title of his piece owed more to a large hole, halfway up the side, than to any reflection of mood or psychological disposition.

The doorbell rang, jolting Eric from his recollections. Cautiously, he peered outside, fearing for a moment that the press were onto him. Looking again, however, at the Land Rovers and livestock trailers lining the street, he decided his visitors were more likely to provide the morning milk than the daily paper. Though why a dozen or so farmers should have congregated in his garden was a mystery. As was the fact that they appeared to have brought their own furniture with them to sit on.

Looking for clues in the crowd, Eric saw the unmistakeable outline of Hetty doing the rounds with a tray, handing out brimming pints of the local ale. He glanced at his watch. Surely 8.00 a.m. was a bit early for the hard stuff? And it was hard, too. "Slurry", they called it. Named not only for its colour and consistency but for its almost immediate effect on the consumer's powers of speech.

Curious, Eric approached the party.

"Hello, young Eric," said Hetty, ambling over and showing no trace of her excesses the previous night. "Brought you some bits and pieces. Just a few unwanted leftovers, but they might be useful."

Eric glanced at the farmers.

"Not the people, Eric, the furniture. It's from the local auction rooms. Thought it might help, being as your mam and dad stripped the cottage of pretty much every stick?"

How kind, thought Eric, accepting a pint of slurry from Hetty's tray.

"By the way," she murmured, "I've seen the boys right this morning, but that's not to say a pint or two from you wouldn't go amiss next time you're passing the pub. Reckon they deserve it for fetching and carrying this lot? They'll put it in the house for you, too, in a minute."

Eric nodded, taking a mouthful of slurry and reeling at the smell, which was somewhere between a well-rotted compost heap and the contents of an abattoir drain.

"Thanks, Hetty," he said, alarmed to hear it come out "Angzetty" on the strength of just one sip. Getting a grip on his tongue he added, "I'll drop by soon. And I do appreciate all this." He waved a hand at the furniture. "Means I can get on with my work sooner rather than later."

Hetty looked at him. "I've been meaning to ask what you do for a living."

Eric could have kicked himself. The last thing he wanted was everyone in Landoobrey knowing his business and blabbing it abroad. Potentially to the antenna-like ears of the Paparazzi.

"I meant get on with my *house*work," he said, quickly. "I've a bit of money put by so I don't actually work as such."

"Oh. Right. Well, good on you, young Eric. And welcome back – again."

Hetty shuffled off and Eric was struck by what a capable person she was in spite of last night's evidence to the contrary. Perhaps that explained why she'd regularly held the position of mayoress in the old days? An unconventional choice, he'd always thought, what with her dress sense and total disregard for rules and regulations, but she was clearly a person who got things done. Plus, her experience of breaking up fights must come in useful at planning meetings and AGMs.

Deciding he couldn't face the rest of his pint, he contrived to lose it by means of a headlong trip over a hollyhock. A trip, he realised, that he'd only partially engineered. Then he began to mingle, thanking all the farmers and assuring them of a pint each, at his expense, in due course.

Passing a large, comfy-looking armchair, he glanced down at two young girls, practically sitting on one another's laps.

"Hello," he said. "Do you live near here?"

"*Fairly* near," said Beryl, casting a covert glance towards Eric's back garden.

CHAPTER THREE

After a morning spent arranging his furniture and putting away such belongings as had made it to Wales with him, Eric decided to pop out for some essential supplies.

As he strode down the high street he was accosted by one person after another, asking after his parents. Making him wonder just how many other tourists the remote little town had ever seen.

Approaching Mrs Jenks' shop, he found the exterior virtually unchanged from when he was a boy. The large front window was still mostly obscured by dark-brown awnings and flanked by two rusty metal signs. One urging smokers to "Try Capstan Full Strength NOW". The other reminding housewives that "A Lux-y Wash Day is A Luck-y Wash Day".

How might the interior have altered, he wondered, seeing in his mind's eye the owner's early attempts at departmentalising: "Haberdashery", "Stationery" and "Book Shop" to the left, "Groceries" to the right, "Household Goods", comprising everything from a tin tack to a tin bath, out the back. The latter being reached by a narrow passageway, which itself housed "Gardening and Outdoor Leisure". Or, as Eric now recalled, a couple of sun umbrellas and a rake.

Inside the shop it was instantly clear that nothing had changed. Certainly not the proprietress, still wearing her familiar hairnet and a blue gingham overall, just like in the old days. Same carpet slippers, too, Eric was sure, with the scuffed toe of one permanently pointed, like the front paw of a spaniel, the better to scurry after the needs and wants of her customers.

Mrs Jenks, like Hetty, had worn well. In her mid-seventies by now he estimated, but as lean and fit as ever. Probably because she'd never had any truck with self-service shopping. Preferring to do the equivalent of a supermarket dash for each and every person through her door.

"Hello, young Eric," she said with a grin. "You came back then?"

He smiled. "Looks like it, Mrs Jenks."

"People do, you know. Lost count I have of the people that's come here for one reason or another and ended up stopping."

"Really?" said Eric, trying not to sound surprised.

"Oh, yes. We've got an actor now, you know, and a writer. Quite successful, in their own way and plenty of money about 'em when they first arrived. 'Course, they've gone through most of that now."

The shopkeeper allowed herself a moment of sad reflection then brightened a little. "And then there's your mam and dad, isn't there? Year on year they came. Couldn't keep away, it seemed. Something in the water maybe?"

Scotch at a rough guess, thought Eric, but he said nothing.

"Anyway, what can I get you, eh, lad?" Mrs Jenks cocked an enquiring eyebrow, fingers twitching, toe trembling on the dark-brown lino of her shop floor.

Eric reeled off his requirements and stood back. Watching the blurred figure hurtling from milk to marmalade, bacon to beans, lobbing tins and packages with unerring accuracy onto the counter.

Barely blowing, Mrs Jenks finally fetched up at the pre-war cash register. Raising both hands, she slammed down a combination of keys like a church organist at the climax of the Wedding March.

"Twenty-one forty-nine, please," she said as the drawer shot out.

Eric could only marvel at the way she'd added up his bill on the run. And that, he soon realised, was the least of her talents. She'd also converted the amount back to old money before ringing up twenty one pounds nine shillings and ten pence. LSD being the only currency catered for by the till.

She handed him his change and nodded at the shopping. "Manage, can you, with that? I can always get the boy, Arnold, to trike it round?"

"Is he still here?" asked Eric, shocked. "He must be at least … what … ninety?"

"Ninety-four," corrected Mrs Jenks, "but plenty of work in him yet."

***

As he left the shop, Eric remembered the round of drinks he was supposed to be putting in for his erstwhile removal men. He therefore took a right turn, halfway up the high street.

Approaching the White Hart, he recalled how Hetty had implied at their first meeting that he wasn't a pub person. She'd been wrong, though. In his teaching days he'd been just as happy as the next man to sip a half of shandy over a quiet game of dominoes.

Any hopes he may have had about the White Hart lending itself to such genteel pursuits were soon dashed. Putting out a hand, he'd barely made contact with the pub door when it flew open to emit a young man, somehow still clutching an almost full pint of beer, travelling at more or less head height to Eric. Somewhere behind the human cannonball, Hetty could be heard yelling, "Right, *who's next*?"

Perhaps I'll come back later, Eric thought. When it's nice and quiet.

His plan of inaction decided, he went back to the cottage where he put his shopping away. That done, he considered starting some work but his nerves were still jangling from the incident at the pub.

Perhaps what he needed was a good, brisk walk. It was such a nice day, what could be better than an exploration of parts of the village further afield from the cottage? Starting with the town square, in which the imposing façade of the council chamber and court house were to be found.

***

Arriving some minutes later on the cobbled pedestrian area in the centre of town, Eric found the buildings a little tired and shabby-looking but otherwise as serene and dignified as he remembered them.

Sadly, the same couldn't be said for a big man in an ill-fitting suit, currently engaged in kicking a smaller one. The latter, lying on the pavement spitting out teeth and singing *Private Dancer* at the top of his voice.

Catching sight of Eric, the big man turned. "Want some, boyo?"

"Who, me?"

"Of course you. No one else gawping, is there, where they've no right to be?"

Eric glanced around, finding the square all but deserted. Luckily, though, this being court day, the police were out in force, huddled in a distant doorway, primed and alert for trouble. At Eric's frantic wave, both of them threw down their playing cards, took a last drag on their fags and ambled to the scene.

"What you doing, Tony?" asked one officer, whom Eric now recognised as an older, fatter version of PC George, long-term stalwart of the local constabulary. "You're due in court any minute on two drunk and disorderlies and a GBH. Yet here you are, kicking a harmless stranger."

"He's not harmless," the man called Tony yelled back, "and unlike *him*," he stabbed a forefinger at Eric, "he's not a stranger neither." Briefly escaping the policemen's clutches and aiming another kick at the figure on the pavement, he added, "He's my bastard character witness – and just look at the state of him."

***

Temporarily losing his appetite for sight-seeing, Eric left the square. So much for the passage of time, he thought. The place was as bad now as it had ever been. But he'd done the right thing in moving here. Landoobrey being about as far from the world of art and culture as it was possible to get.

Thinking of art and culture, Eric quickened his pace towards home. A spot of lunch, he thought, then he ought to start setting up his studio.

He planned to work in the parlour because, as well as possessing good light, it was the only room in the cottage with a lock on its door. This, Eric felt, was essential, given the tendency of Landoobreyians to stroll in and out of one another's houses whenever the mood took them. He well remembered his mother, cheerfully cooking breakfast in the old days for many a house guest who hadn't been there the night before. The cottage being a useful stopover point for drinkers, incapable of making it any further towards home.

After lunch, Eric spent some time unpacking his sculpting tools and arranging them in the parlour. Then he spent some more time rearranging them and some more doing the washing up and putting his dishes away. Looking at his watch, hoping it might now be bedtime, he was dismayed to find that it was still only 4.00 p.m. There was no getting away from it. He'd have to go back to the pub.

***

Approaching the door, Eric was heartened to hear far less noise from within than at lunchtime. Which made sense, he thought. Surely even the hardened drinkers of Landoobrey couldn't keep up that sort of pace all day?

Congratulating himself on having chosen an ideal time for his visit, he stepped into the gloom. The lack of noise, however, hadn't necessarily signified a lack of people. The pub was packed.

Aware of many a bleary eye on him, Eric edged into the bar. At the counter, he found himself alongside a man dressed in leather trousers, a denim jacket and a cravat. This, Eric thought, must be the actor. A moment later, his suspicions were confirmed as the man began to demonstrate the art of picking up a cigarette packet to a bored looking blonde.

"Do you see, lovie?" he said. "I'm acting with my *whole* hand. Makes such a difference doesn't it?" Flexing his fist again, he hovered it tremulously over the packet. "And now," he added, "I'm acting scared with it."

Yawning, the blonde moved off.

The actor cast a regretful glance after her then swivelled on his bar stool in search of his next victim. Which, the way things were going, looked like being Eric. Where, he wondered, was Hetty when he needed her?

Eric read a beer mat, trying not to meet the actor's eyes, but to no avail. A tap on his arm was followed by an elegant hand extended towards him, fingers placed just so, onyx ring glinting in the dim light of the bar.

"I'm Mel Meredith," the actor said, as if this ought to mean something to Eric.

"And I'm Eric Bagnall," replied Eric, shaking the proffered hand.

As he did so he realised that, in fairness, he and the actor might have much in common. Both were artists, after all, and incomers to the town.

He was about to comment on the second similarity, remembering that his incognito status meant his lips were sealed on the first, when a girl walked into the bar. She was hardly what you'd call stunning in Eric's opinion, being at least thirteen stone, wearing a dress three sizes too small for her, a large floppy hat and baseball boots. Mel, however, seemed smitten. Perhaps it was a case of any skirt in storm, thought Eric, as his new acquaintance murmured, "Later, dear boy" and swivelled away.

Stetson akimbo, an exhausted-looking Hetty finally made it down to Eric's part of the bar. "Slurry, young Eric?" she enquired, grabbing a pint glass and tilting it at the tap. Eric looked at her, sensing challenge in her crinkled blue eyes.

"Why not?" he said, privately thinking of at least a hundred reasons. None of which, he felt, would cut any ice with Hetty.

As she poured his drink, Eric peeled off several notes from the bundle in his wallet. "I really just popped in to bring this for the farmers' drinks. Make sure they have what they want, eh?"

Hetty handed him his pint, whistling as she counted the cash. "Wow. This'll cheer the buggers up. You sure?"

"Shertain," he said, waving a carefree hand. He eyed his untouched beer. How, he wondered, could it have had this affect on him merely by proximity?

"They'll be dead chuffed. Ta. Now, I suppose I'd better fill you in on who's who, if this is to be your regular watering hole?"

"Mmm," said Eric, doubtful that water was likely to feature much in his visits to the Hart. "Good idea."

"Right," said Hetty. "Well, that big gang at the other end of the bar is my darts team. They've been on an outing today. Had a good run out by all accounts, but pleased to be back, as always."

Eric glanced at the crowd of lads, relieved to hear they didn't spend all their waking hours in the pub. And while being no great shakes with an arrow, he could do worse, he decided, than to see about joining the team. The idea of an outing now and again was appealing. Especially if the destinations included museums and sites of historic interest.

"Where did they go today?" he asked.

"The White Swan," said Hetty. "Other end of town, if you remember, up by the castle? And over there, on the banquette," she went on, "is our resident writer."

"Resident" being the operative word, thought Eric. The writer was fast asleep alongside a table, on and around which were scattered spectacles, a notebook and pen, and his slippers.

"Right," Eric said, nodding.

"And Mrs Jenks, of course, you already know." Eric followed the tilt of Hetty's chin towards a group of card players, among whom he was astonished to recognise the little shopkeeper. Having exchanged her hairnet for an eye-shade, she was in the act of laying down a royal flush. Then, parking a fat cigar in the corner of her mouth, she scooped up her winnings.

"And that," Hetty lowered her voice and indicated a man with his back to them, further along the bar, "is Tony Williams."

Eric's heart sank as he found himself looking for the second time that day at a big man in an ill-fitting suit. A quick glance at the dark, jowly profile, reflected in the long mirror behind the bar, confirmed his worst fears. "I think we've met," he said, quietly. "Outside the court house earlier."

"Might have," agreed Hetty. "I heard he was up today."

"Got off by the look of it?" suggested Eric, regretfully.

Hetty nodded. "Foregone conclusion, I'm afraid."

As if sensing two pairs of eyes on him, the big man inched himself round to face Eric.

"Know you, don't I?" he asked.

"Er, no, I don't think so," replied Eric.

"I do," insisted the man, swaying and gripping the bar, his knuckles showing white beneath the creeping hair on his fingers. "You set the law on me earlier."

Eric was saved from replying by the arrival of what he initially took to be a dustbin lid on a stick, but turned out to be a very thin man in an over-sized flat cap.

The newcomer tacked an unsteady course from the gents' door to the counter. "And this is Terry," breathed Hetty. "Tony's twin."

Eric stared. He could only conclude that nature, having lavished so much bulk on Tony, had run out of material halfway through his brother.

"Trouble, that one is," Tony jerked a fat thumb at Eric.

"Is that right?" asked Terry with a sneer.

"Aye. Trouble with a capital ..." He broke off. "A capital what is it?"

"Letter?" suggested Terry.

"That's it. Trouble with a capital letter."

Two pairs of black eyes fixed themselves on Eric, who did his best to look blandly inoffensive.

"Not the brightest bulb in the garden centre either, by the look of him," observed Terry.

"On the string," corrected Tony.

"Eh?"

"You mean he's not the brightest bulb on the string."

Terry thought this over. "No," he said. "You don't get bulbs on a string, unless, of course, you're thinking of an onion?"

Tony ignored the question and continued to stare at Eric. "On holiday are you?" he growled.

"No," intervened Hetty swiftly. "Eric's come to live at the cottage, last in the row, bottom of Bridge Street. Came there often, he did, as a boy." She laughed, lightly. "So much so, in fact, he's practically a local."

It was a nice try, thought Eric, but it evidently didn't wash with either twin.

"Local be damned," grunted Tony. "Unwanted blow in, boyo, that's what you are, or I'm the Dalai Lama"

"And I," said Terry, evidently not to be outdone, "am a camel."

Glaring, they tackled the sticky froth of their pints, their noses reminding Eric of a couple of mashed strawberries each on a bed of cream.

Deciding not to say so, he eased himself away from the Williams Twins and glanced around, seeking a change of subject. He found it in the shape of a haggard-looking man, sitting alone, gazing into a tumbler of whisky

"What's his story, Hetty?"

The landlady's face softened. "Old Tom Dunn? Poor sod, he's recently had to deal with just about the worst job in farming."

"Not a mass cull?" whispered Eric.

Hetty shook her head. "His VAT return."

CHAPTER FOUR

Some time later, Eric made his way home, surprised
and delighted to find that umpteen pints of slurry had
affected him far less than he'd feared.

"I've had a wonderful time," he told himself.
Then, for good measure, he told a lamp post, a privet
hedge and two elderly members of the Chapel
Brigade, out for a late evening stroll.

"Shelf your shute," he said, disappointed when
first the woman of the partnership and then the man
refused him a dance.

Spinning on his heel he headed for home confused,
as he drew nearer, by pub sounds from within and the
fact that his key didn't fit the open door. Gently,
Hetty turned him in the right direction and sent him
on his way.

Walking doggedly, Eric made once again for his
house, annoyed to find someone singing tunelessly
quite close at hand.

"Shut up," he shouted, putting both hands over his
eyes. "I can't smell myself talk." The tuneless voice
droned on. It was only when he attempted to square
up to the singer and give him what for that Eric
discovered it to have been himself.

At last, he saw the lighted windows of the cottage
on his left and veered towards them. It was amazing,
he thought, how unfamiliar his surroundings still
seemed. The giant gargoyles on his gateposts, for
instance, were a surprise. Not to mention the large
wooden seat, halfway up his garden path, and a
Welsh dresser blocking his front door.

The seat, however, looked inviting and he sat down.

"Psst," said a voice from the general direction of the dresser.

"Well, maybe just a bit," admitted Eric, eyeing the talking furniture and letting the night wash over him.

***

"Psst," said Terry Williams, again. "You there, Tony?"

Silence reigned in the hallway of the little terraced cottage, second from the bottom of Bridge Street. Terry scowled. It was typical of his brother, he thought, to go missing right when there was work to be done. Doubly annoying, given that sneaking into the cottage and robbing old Posh Godfrey of all his worldly possessions had been Tony's idea. Or at least, it had been Dilys Daydream's, which these days amounted to the same thing.

"Piece of piss," Tony had said. "Dilys'll let us in, then it's out with the stuff and away."

So far, however, all the graft had been down to Terry, who'd already pushed a heavy oak settle halfway down the path and was now attempting to do the same with the dresser. It was stuck fast, though, jammed up against an ornamental cannon, taking up most of the old man's doorstep.

Mentally cursing Posh Godfrey who, in downsizing from ancestral mansion to pokey cottage, had chosen to clutter up his new home with so many remnants of his old one, Terry tried again to summon help.

"Pppppssssssstttt…"

"What's up?" demanded Tony, closing the parlour door softly behind him and squeezing past a suit of armour, almost as wide as the hallway.

***

"Sorry I've been a while," he added, not sounding sorry at all. "Dilys has just been showing me something very interesting in the base of the old man's grandfather clock. Boxful of surveillance equipment, dating from his days in naval intelligence."

"Really?" Terry tapped an impatient foot.

"Mm." Tony's eyes gleamed at the memory of Dilys, dropping to her knees in front of the clock, the skirt of her uniform rising like a great, grey cloud over the crescent moons of her stocking tops as her tattooed elbows hit the floor.

"Nice to know you and Dilys have been enjoying yourselves," said Terry, cutting across his brother's thoughts and nodding towards the dresser, "whilst I've been busting a gut trying to get that thing over the doorstep."

Tony followed his glance. "Nice piece, though, isn't it?" he asked.

"Provided you don't look at her from the front," admitted Terry, grudgingly.

"True," said Tony, "but I meant the dresser. And that old settle isn't half bad either. Be just right, won't they, in the hotel? Like Dilys says, cost a fortune it would to furnish it otherwise, great big place like that."

"Like Dilys says," mimicked Terry. "Hand in surgical bloody glove you are with that district nurse."

"Just as well, too," Tony defended himself. "Been able to put some good stuff our way, hasn't she? Cleaned every stick of it for us, too. In fact, she's still at it now, giving the old man's Whatnot a good rubbing … A Whatnot," he snapped, as Terry began to giggle, "being a piece of furniture, which will also look great in our hotel."

Terry stopped laughing and cast an anxious glance at the heavy, velvet curtain over the bottom of the stairs. "As long as she's sure the old man won't miss anything?"

"Certain," replied Tony.

"What is he, then, blind?"

"Better than that, Terry, he's bedridden. According to Dilys, the only way he's ever coming down his stairs again is in his box."

Terry shuddered. "Thought he was coming down them a while ago, I did, what with him shouting was there anyone there and Dilys yelling back as it was only her, come to make sure his gas was off."

"She has got a bit of a mouth on her," conceded Tony, for whom the District Nurse's strident tones were a constant reminder of her South Wales coalfields roots. And, in particular, of the hooters signifying a change of shift. "Right," he added, walking purposefully towards the dresser. "Better get this shifted, eh?"

"'Bout time," grumbled Terry. "Be here all night otherwise."

"Mm." Tony surveyed the heavy piece of furniture. "Has to be said, though, as we'd have been done and dusted hours ago if you hadn't been so long coming out of the pub. Thought you were right behind me?"

"Ah," said Terry, skipping over to join his brother "I've been meaning to tell you about that. Got waylaid, I did, by Hetty, going on about this meeting of hers tomorrow night."

"I didn't hear anything about a meeting?"

"No, well, you'd already left, hadn't you? Matter of fact, I expect she thought we both had but I'd stopped off for the loo if you remember. Funny taste there was on that fifth pint and I wasn't sure I'd make it here."

"So, what did Hetty say?"

"I didn't tell her. All the others were fine, and it could just as easily have been the pickled egg I had with it."

Tony sighed. "No, Terry. What did she say about the meeting?"

"Oh. Just that there's going to be one. Seven o'clock tomorrow night, in the village hall, to discuss this big event she's got planned. Hopes to bring loads of people here, she does, on the big day, and keep 'em coming right through the summer."

Tony stared. "And you think that's OK, do you? Town crawling with outsiders and us with the barn crop practically ready to ship, and the hotel due to open in just a few weeks?"

"Didn't say it was OK, did I?" muttered Terry. "Just telling you, I am, what Hetty said."

"Right. Anything else said, was there, that I ought to know about?"

Terry thought long and hard. "Only that Mel and Ms Harris have already joined her, to form a committee and start planning the event. Oh, and she ended by saying that no one was to breathe a word about the meeting to 'those dratted Williams's'. Now I don't know if she meant the Penybanc Williams's or the Spencer-Williams's maybe, up at the manse ..."

"Or she might have meant us," put in Tony.

"Us?" echoed Terry. "Bloody cheek if she did."

"It's more than cheek," said Tony. "It's proof Hetty's up to something she knows full well we won't approve of. Still, forewarned is forearmed, eh?"

Terry sniggered. "Always makes me laugh, that does, although I suppose four arms could be useful if …"

"Shut up, Terry," said Tony. "I need to give this some thought. Meantime, let's get this bloody dresser out, shall we?"

***

In the garden a fitfully dozing Eric viewed the killer cupboard with concern as it broke free of the doorway and made a little dash towards him.

When the Williams Twins then stepped out from behind it, drink, fear and indignation, in that order, fuelled his response.

"What are you doing on my property?" he shouted.

" 'T'aint your property," replied a somewhat rattled Tony Williams.

" 'T'aint ours either, mind," put in Terry, earning himself a glare from his brother.

"Well there," said Eric, with dignity. "I deg to biffer. This property is mine, and was my mum and dad's before me. So, strictly speaking, you're trespassing and I'd like you to move along now, please."

"Deg to biffer?" queried Terry. "What does that mean?"

Tony shrugged. "Some smart London legal talk I expect. Latin maybe." Turning to Eric he said loudly, "It's us ought to be asking what *you're* doing, interfering with the activities of perfectly legitimate, local people?"

Terry looked confused. "Thought we were illegitimate?"

"*We* are, yes," replied Tony, forgetting in the heat of the moment that this was supposed to be a secret, "but our business activities are legitimate aren't they?"

"Well ..." Terry cast a doubtful glance at the furniture.

"Point is," Tony swept on, "being local, *anything* we do is OK. As Dad used to say, it's outsiders who want watching." He thrust his face into Eric's. "Especially you. Swanning in here with your fancy city ways, calling the cops on people, settling on our ... er ... well, on our settles."

"Stealing our women," put in Terry.

"Has he stolen any?"

"Well, he looked like getting into bed with Hetty the Hart in the pub, earlier, over that meeting I was telling you about. All for it he was."

"He was, was he?"

"Yep. And there's no telling," Terry added slyly, "what he might go around saying about this little shindig of ours tonight, given half a chance."

"He's saying nothing," growled Tony. Putting out a hand to Eric's coat hood, he lifted him bodily. "Right, boyo," he said to the slowly revolving Eric.

"You can just forget everything you've seen and heard here tonight. Got me?" Eric nodded in passing. "And whilst you're about it, you can forget all about Hetty's meeting tomorrow night as well."

"What meeting?" mumbled Eric.

"That's the way." Tony dropped Eric, who teetered back and forth for a moment like a skittle. "Catches on quick enough, don't he?"

"Mm." Terry looked about himself with a puzzled frown. "Makes you wonder, though, what he's doing here in the first place? Hetty said he lives bottom of Bridge Street. This is the bottom but one."

"Got it wrong then, ain't he? Typical bloody incomer." Tony pushed Eric towards Posh Godfrey's gate and shoved him through it. "In the wrong place you are, mate," he shouted as Eric staggered away. "In more ways than one."

"Ha," Terry smirked. "That's one who won't be showing his face at that meeting tomorrow."

Tony nodded. "All we've got to do now is find a way of stopping the rest of the town."

"We could put it about that the meeting's off," suggested Terry, "and menace anyone old and vulnerable, warning 'em not to attend?"

"Goes without saying," agreed Tony. "Won't stop Hetty turning up, though, will it, with her little committee?"

"Mm." Terry thought for a moment. "Pity we can't find some way of listening in on that meeting. Stay one step ahead of the game then, wouldn't we?"

Tony looked from his brother to the lighted window of Posh Godfrey's parlour where the shadowy figure of the grandfather clock towered in its corner, its base concealing the old man's stash of surveillance equipment. "Need to see Dilys," he muttered, setting off up the path.

"You only saw her five minutes ago," Terry called after him sulkily. "What do you want to see her again for?"

Tony turned. "To ask her help in making a bug, and smuggling it into the hall, specially for Hetty and her pals."

"You want to put a bug in the hall?" echoed Terry. "You off your head? Who's to say lots of other people won't catch it too?"

***

Waking the next day, Eric could see why his new bed had found no takers at the auction rooms. It was hard and lumpy in the extreme. What was more, he was cold.

Shivering, he turned over and tried once more to snuggle down. Then, encountering the corner of a particularly hard lump and feeling something very like a carpet burn on his cheek, he realised he was sleeping on the stairs.

He was still there, immobilised by a headache such as he'd never had in his life before, when the doorbell rang round about teatime.

He opened one eye in time to see a long envelope appearing inch by inch on the doormat. Puzzled, he tried to sit up, clutching his ears as Hetty's voice boomed, "See you at seven, young Eric. Don't be late."

"I won't," he called back. Late for what, he wondered.

***

Some time later, Eric awoke again, still puzzling over Hetty's words as she'd shoved the envelope under his door. Clearly he'd arranged to be somewhere, at seven o'clock that evening, and the arrangement could only have been made in the pub.

Taking a firmer grip on the stairs, he closed his eyes and forced himself to try to remember something – anything – of his wonderful time.

Dimly he remembered Hetty's introductions to the regulars, including the actor, Mel Meredith, who, upon finding himself abandoned by two women in as many minutes, had turned his attention back to Eric. Shrugging and flicking a thumb after the departing rear of the plump girl, he'd said, "She had to go, poor love. Something about a sick grandmother."

Over his shoulder, Eric had watched the girl walk out of the pub and into the arms of a man around half Mel's age. Eric hadn't let on, though, as he fell into conversation with the actor. Quickly discovering that they did, indeed, have quite a lot in common, including an impulse to buy each other slurry.

It was here that Eric's recollections became a little blurred. "The Hokey Cokey", he felt, must have featured somewhere in the proceedings, because he remembered rushing forwards and backwards shouting, "Oh, hokey cokey cokey". What was less clear was whether anyone else had joined in.

He was still pondering this when the mists suddenly lifted. Surely Hetty had interrupted his exhibition dance with an announcement about a forthcoming meeting? And hadn't he said, in his cups, he'd be thrilled and honoured to attend? And that he'd fight anyone who said he couldn't?

CHAPTER FIVE

On his feet at last, Eric regarded the envelope miles away on the mat. It was a pity, he thought, that the cottage didn't run to a letter box with a wire cage halfway up the door, to catch the mail. Or that Hetty hadn't seen fit to leave her missive in the outdoor postbox, screwed to a fence post, at a similarly convenient height.

Sighing, he lowered himself like a novice ballerina in plié, collected the envelope and rose again, all without moving his head. Turning the envelope over, he found a few words scribbled on the flap: "Welcome to the gang. Info enclosed. H."

"The gang," mused Eric, creeping to the kitchen, having realised that steaming his letter open would probably be quieter than ripping the envelope.

A naturally private person, he'd never been much of a one for joining "gangs". But then again, he reminded himself, he'd never been much of a one for getting plastered, forming a one man male voice choir, and sleeping on a staircase. All of which he'd somehow managed to accomplish in his first forty-eight hours in Landoobrey.

As the kettle came to the boil, Eric eased open the envelope and extracted a single sheet of paper. "MEETING TONIGHT," he read, "7.00 P.M. THE VILLAGE HALL." He nodded his approval. At least Landoobrey didn't conduct all its affairs in a pub. It would be good, he thought, to meet with his fellow townsfolk in such a civilised setting as the village hall. Which, as he recalled, had gravitas in abundance and no slurry. Keen to see what the meeting would be about, he read on, feeling a growing sense of alarm as he caught the words: "LET'S TURN THE SPOTLIGHT ON OUR TOWN!!!"

Eric's heart sank. Spotlights were precisely what he'd come here to avoid. What was wrong with Landoobrey remaining the anonymous little backwater it had always been?

In the next paragraph, he had his answer. The local economy, it seemed, was in decline. Had been for decades. Some of the locals were therefore planning a grand event: a Summer Spectacular, designed to attract people from far and wide, and administer a much-needed shot in the arm before the little town expired altogether.

Thinking back to his arrival in Landoobrey and the shabby state in which he'd found the main square, Eric could sympathise with this. Even so, his first impulse was to give the meeting a miss. Get quietly on with his life, maybe even make a start on his new piece. After all, who would miss him? Then he remembered the fuss he'd made about attending the meeting. Mightn't it look a bit odd, he wondered, if he didn't turn up?

Ten minutes later, splashing happily in his bath, Eric had decided two things. One, that his monumental hangover had gone, the other that he *would* go to the meeting, just to show his face. But that didn't mean he had to get involved, did it? Or go to the actual event, when the time came? He would simply hide away in his little cottage until life in Landoobrey returned to its normal, unspectacular self.

Towelling himself dry he was surprised to find that, against all odds, he could quite fancy a little something for his tea. There was just time if he was quick about it.

***

At about the same time as Eric began whisking the eggs for his omelette, Miranda Barton glanced at her chunky, designer watch. 6.20 p.m. London time.

She reached for her phone, deciding to try her elusive client once again. And this time, she thought, she'd better get an answer. It was one thing, Eric sloping off to the middle of nowhere to escape the pressures of his new-found fame. Quite another to ignore his agent's calls.

A multitasker from way back, Miranda dialled Eric's number while tapping a calculator and skimming through a portfolio of work by an as yet unknown artist desperate for her representation.

Hearing the ringing tone, she sat back in her chair, ruffling her thick, red hair. The rattle of her bangles adding the melody line to the rhythmic roar of traffic, far below her office window.

She was about to put the phone down unanswered for the umpteenth time when she caught Eric's cautious "Hello?"

Miranda sprang forwards at her desk, setting the bangles off again. "Gotcha," she said in her husky, Cockney voice. "Where you *bin* all day?"

For a moment, Eric was unable to answer, being too busy juggling his mixing bowl, his whisk and his parents' telephone. Finally he gave up and flicked the phone onto speaker. Thinking all the while that this had better be a real emergency, that being the only circumstance under which he'd agreed his agent might call him.

47

"Out," replied Eric, continuing to whisk quietly. Deciding not to add, "for the count" because Miranda had often told him he was one of her more respectable clients. At least in comparison to a couple of graffiti artists, also on her books, for whom the world was their canvas. Including, it seemed, the pastel walls and marble pillars of some of the smartest restaurants in town.

"Out?" squawked Miranda. "All day?"

"Yes, as it happens." Heading to the kitchen for some salt, Eric called over his shoulder, "I'm going out again soon, too. So, what's the problem? I asked you only to call if something important came up ..."

"So you did," interrupted Miranda. "And so it *has*."

Spinning round, Eric stared at the phone. "Is my piece all right?" he asked, suddenly concerned for his sculpture as a pet lover might fear for an absent pooch.

Miranda shifted in her chair. "All *right*? It's more than all right, Eric. Everyone at the Tate is raving, positively *raving*."

This of course had been Eric's private opinion all along. Even so, he couldn't resist a small grin of pride. "Good," he said. "But why then did you ring?"

"One word," said Miranda, tucking the phone under her chin and beginning to count a stack of tenners on her desk. "Merchandise."

Eric could hear the capital letter all the way down the line from London.

"Merchandise?" he repeated, sending it back again. "How do you mean?"

"I mean, Eric, that the Tate people are clamouring for something to sell in their gift shop as a souvenir of your piece."

"They've got the postcards," Eric pointed out, putting a finger in his eggs, licking it and resuming his journey to the kitchen. "What more do they want?"

"Postcards are fine, Eric, for your more run-of-the-mill exhibits – your Rembrandts and your Stubbses – but an Eric Bagnall sculpture ... well, that's different. People want to reach out and *touch* it."

In the kitchen, Eric shook a few drops of damp salt from the cellar, blushing to hear himself compared to such greats. "Well they can't," he said, returning to the sitting room and subjecting the eggs to a further pounding, "given that it's suspended fifteen feet above the gallery floor."

"Exactly," shrieked Miranda, "which is why the Tate have rather cleverly suggested miniature replicas. Hand-carved and signed by you."

Eric stopped whisking. "How am I going to sign a miniature replica?" he asked, knowing this wouldn't be the hardest part.

Miranda stacked up the tenners and consulted her notepad. "They thought autographed luggage tags attached by a little piece of string representing the rope."

"And how many do they want?"

"A box of fifty initially, just as a trial run. They'll be the limited edition handmade pieces on sale at a whopping price. Then we might have to set up some sort of manufacturing process to deliver them to the mass market. After all," added Miranda with a throaty laugh, "you'll hardly be able to sit there in your bolt-hole turning them out by the thousand, will you?"

"Er, no," admitted Eric, doubtful that he could turn them out by the one, given that he hadn't actually carved the original.

"So, what do you say, Eric? I'll tell them you'll do it shall I?"

Eric picked up his whisk and put it down again, realising there was no time, now, to cook and eat his tea before the meeting. "Sorry, Miranda," he said, returning his eggs to the kitchen and looking for his shoes, "I'm afraid I'm going to have to say no. It's just too big an ask, especially when I'm trying to get started on my second piece."

Miranda cursed under her breath. "A big ask, I grant you, Eric … but a big cheque, too, if you pull it off."

"How big?" asked Eric in spite of himself. He blanched as she told him. "Wow," he said. "That is large."

"And all for you, less my ten percent of course." Miranda thumped more buttons on her calculator and smiled. "As for your new piece, well, you'll hardly be working on it twenty-four seven, will you? Perfectly possible, I'd have thought, for you to knock out a few miniatures in your tea breaks?"

Eric was silent for a moment. He could feel the pressure mounting again with all this talk of his new piece and having to try to make fifty copies of his old one.

In the pause, Miranda glanced again at the figure on the calculator and redoubled her efforts. "Come on, Eric. Promise me you'll at least think it over?"

"OK," mumbled Eric.

"Talk it through with the gallery people themselves if you think it would help?"

"It wouldn't," said Eric, firmly. Then a thought struck him. "And don't you go giving them my number, will you, or telling them where I am. The last thing I want is a load of arty types descending on me with the press in tow."

"Your secret is safe with me," Miranda assured him, putting the phone aside and tiptoeing to her bookcase where her collection of road atlases and OS maps occupied three shelves. Landoobrey, she reasoned, oughtn't to be too hard to find. And it would be great to have a grid reference to give the people at the Tate along with Eric's phone number.

In the meantime, Eric's words continued to pour unheeded from the handset.

"Good, because that was the deal, if you remember: that I would have absolute peace to work on my new sculpture? So far, no one here has the vaguest idea that I'm Eric Bagnall, world-renowned artist ... I'd like to keep it that way."

***

The two girls, huddled at the rear of the cottage, shifted against the wall. "Wow," said Meryl. "So *that's* who he is."

It being common knowledge in the village that Eric was going to the meeting, they'd brought their night things and a towel for a quick bath in his absence. Just as they were passing the sitting room, Eric had rushed in to answer the phone. There'd been no choice but to duck immediately below the open window.

"Who is he, then?" whispered Beryl. She'd failed to follow the speaker-phone conversation as closely as her sister, being partly submerged in a climbing rose and convinced she was sitting on a slug.

"He's *Eric Bagnall*," said Meryl.

"But we knew that already."

"Yes, but we didn't know he was *the* Eric Bagnall the *sculptor* did we?"

Beryl looked sceptical. "Don't pretend you've heard of him."

"Hasn't everyone?" Hearing Eric's van starting up, Meryl scrambled to her feet. "Come on, we can slip in now for that bath. And perhaps a little look round the great man's home while we're about it."

" 'Home' being the operative word," grumbled Beryl, who hadn't got over the arrival of a houseful of furniture, signifying that Eric was no mere minimalistic holidaymaker but a new and permanent neighbour.

Twenty minutes later the girls stood in their pyjamas and dressing gowns surveying the photo of *A Deep Depression in Driftwood*.

"This must be his 'magnet hopeless'," said Meryl. Then, spotting the same wooden object depicted on a little pile of postcards on the sideboard, she scooted over to them. "And these must be the postcards he was on about."

"What's his magnet hopeless?" asked Beryl.

"It means his great work."

"Doesn't look all that great to me. Looks like a bit of wood with a hole in it."

"Well, that just goes to show, Beryl, that what you know about art could be written on a shirt button …

although … in some ways … well, you might have a point."

"Of course I've got a point," said Beryl. "And we've seen it now for what it's worth, which if you ask me isn't much, so … Where are you going?"

The question was addressed to the back view of Meryl who'd walked right up to the photo, taking Eric's new sofa in her stride.

"How hard d'you reckon it'd be," she asked, wobbling a little on the springy cushions, "to make fifty copies of this?"

"Well, not hard at all if we had a photocopier, which we haven't and …"

"Not of the picture, Beryl. Fifty miniature copies of the sculpture."

"A bit like the woman asked Eric to do, you mean?"

"*Exactly* like that, yes."

"But why?" objected Beryl. "Even Eric didn't want to do that, in spite of the woman offering him a great big cheque. Why should we?"

"For the money, of course. Our Saturday job savings won't hold out much longer." Meryl flopped down on the sofa, absently twiddling the belt of her dressing gown. "Eric wasn't keen I'll grant you but he did agree to think it over, didn't he?"

"Only to get her off the phone," said Beryl, who was shrewder than she looked at times.

"Right, but he still agreed. So this Miranda's half expecting to receive them any minute in the post. What's to stop us making them, sending them off and getting the money?"

"Whoa …" Beryl clutched her still-damp head. "As plans go, that one's got more holes in than a teabag. For one thing, we don't know where to send them. For another, wasn't there something about them being signed by Eric himself? Even if we knew what his signature looked like, which we don't, forging it'd be dead iffy."

Meryl tutted. "Trust you to look on the black side when actually it's all perfectly doable." Eyes shining, she ticked off on her fingers, "Firstly, we *do* know where to send the miniatures because the name and address of a Miranda Barton, Eric's agent, is printed on the label at the bottom of this photo. Secondly, Eric's signature is scrawled across the corner of the postcards so we can copy it. Thirdly, if we put PP in really tiny letters like a smudge on the back of the luggage tags, I reckon that'd cover us, legally, for signing his name on the front."

"But what about the money? A cheque made out to E. Bagnall's about as much use to us as a sou'wester up the Nile … or *any* cheque come to that being as we haven't got a bank account …"

Meryl thought for a moment. "How about, when we send the little sculptures off, we put a covering letter with them, supposedly from Eric, asking his agent to send the money in cash? Then all we'll have to do is get up really early every morning until the money comes, so we can visit Eric's outdoor postbox before he does."

"Right," said Beryl. "But – and this is a *big* but, Meryl – how are we going to make the wretched things in the first place?"

"Well," said Meryl. "All we need are some bits of wood, in roughly the right shape." She looked again at the photo. "And every tree you ever look at has bits like that on, doesn't it? Where two smaller twigs fork off a big one? I'm quite good at whittling. Remember when I made a barley sugar leg for the kitchen chair and Mam went off her head? Ought to be easy enough to cut some twigs, shape 'em up a bit, bung on a coat of varnish and attach a pp'd luggage tag." She waved a hand at Eric's masterpiece. "After all, like you said, it's only a bit of wood, isn't it, with a hole in?"

CHAPTER SIX

Speeding away from the cottage and fearing himself late for the meeting, Eric narrowly missed the plump woman carrying a large cardboard box who stepped off the kerb in front of him.

What, he wondered, did the pedestrians of Landoobrey have against using their own bit of the road?

Before Eric could drive on, the woman banged on his window. "You young Eric?"

"Yes," he replied, feeing a little foolish about the prefix "young". The woman, while not wearing particularly well, was a good decade or so younger than him.

"Great. Off to the meeting, are you?"

"Yes," said Eric, again. After two days in Landoobrey he no longer asked himself how everyone knew his business. They just did.

"Gi's a lift then. Gonna rain and me veins is givin' me gyp." She lifted the hem of her skirt to reveal blotched, bare legs above flip-flopped feet. "Throbbin' they are, all the way up. Get worse they do, too, when it rains."

"Right," said Eric. Peering into the bright, cloudless sky, he gave the veins the benefit of the doubt. "Best hop in, then," he offered. "Are you going to the meeting, too?"

"Not me," said the woman. "But I live not far from the hall. In the flat, as it goes, over the chip shop. Put this in the back, shall I?" With that, she put her box in the back of the van before settling herself in the front and slapping the dashboard. "Come on then, young Eric. I 'aven't got all night, even if you 'as."

Remembering that he hadn't, Eric put the van into gear and shot away from the kerb.

"I'm Sally," by the way, said the woman. "Sally Stitch." Bumping herself round in her seat, she extended a soft, fat palm towards Eric, who steered left-handed, for a moment, reaching over himself with his right. At the last moment she flipped her hand, palm downwards. "You can kiss it if you like," she said. "*And* me 'and."

A giggle rose from the depths of her belly to ooze, like a rich, sweet, chocolate fountain from her open mouth. Eric, who'd been about to shudder in revulsion, found himself trembling for a different reason. Beneath the fleshy blur of her face she was beautiful. Or at any rate, she certainly had been once.

Aware that she was awaiting some sort of response, he said, "Sally Stitch? Unusual surname." Then, remembering the tendency of Landoobreyians to call each other after their jobs or businesses, he added, "Are you perhaps a dressmaker?"

Sally giggled again and shook her dark head. "It's short for 'stitch in time'."

Eric looked baffled.

"As in 'saves nine'?" Sally prompted.

"Sorry," he said. "I'm not with you."

Sally sighed. " 'Ad an 'ysterectomy, didn't I? After me youngest came along. So, last few years I bin Sally Six Sprogs, then Sally Seventh 'Eaven, Sally Eight Mates and now I've 'ad the op, which I may tell you was … "

"Right," Eric interrupted, anxious to avoid the gory details. "I'm with you, now." Flinging the van into a tight bend, he added, "So you've eight children, eh?"

Sally looked thoughtful. "Well, I 'ave as a rule. But just lately I seem to be missing a couple."

"Two of your children are *missing*?" Eric was so alarmed, he nearly drove off the road. "Have you told the police?"

"Isn't no need for that," said Sally, comfortably. "They bin seen at school. Just missing from the chip shop yard, they are. Smelly place that was for 'em, mind, and in the line of fire, slops-wise, so good luck to 'em I say. Oh. This is me."

She rapped the dashboard again and Eric braked in front of the fish and chip shop.

"Thanks." Sally scrambled out of the van, tapped the roof in farewell and began to swagger away.

"What about the box?" Eric called, with a nod towards the rear of his van.

Sally clapped a hand over her mouth. "Bugger me, I nearly forgot the kid."

Eric blanched, remembering in the new light of his delicate cargo how badly he'd driven.

"God. I'm sorry," he said, as Sally reappeared at his window. "Will he be all right?"

"Well, he bin flung about a bit." She cocked an ear to the box and shook it gently. "But that's nothing, is it, compared to being run over in the first place?"

"*Run over?*"

"Yeah. Must 'ave got out when no one was looking and ... splat. Lucky for me he's still got one leg intact. 'Least," she added, looking reproachfully

58

at Eric, " 'e *did* have when he went into the van."
Hoisting the box further onto her hip, she grinned
broadly. "Aww ... don't take it so 'ard, young Eric.
Bound to be a bit bashed about, ain't it? Road kill?"

***

"What do you make of that?" asked an outraged
Terry, watching Eric's arrival at the village hall from
the Land Rover, parked at the kerb.

"He's either very brave or very, very stupid,"
grunted Tony, fighting for breath in the driver's seat.
He'd always had trouble finding a vehicle to fit him
and the Land Rover was no exception.

Terry wriggled in his own seat, where, as he put it,
there was room to swing a catamaran. "Better hope
it's not catching, then. Waste of time warning people
off attending if they're going to turn up anyway."

"Hardly been a stampede for the door, has there?"
Tony pointed out. "How many's that gone in now?"

Terry counted on his fingers. "He was the fourth,
after Hetty, Ms Harris and Mel Meredith."

Tony smiled. "There you are then. Not many is it
to plan Hetty's grand event?"

"No," admitted Terry, "but if that Eric hadn't
come along, after we expressly told him not to, there
would've only been ..." He consulted his fingers
again.

"Three," snapped Tony. "There would have been
three. Still, thanks to Dilys, we'll be listening in,
won't we, to every word that's said?" He put the
Land Rover in gear. "Time to get parked up
somewhere a bit less obvious and start setting up the
kit."

"How far away do we need to be?" asked Terry,
eyeing the equipment on his lap with disfavour. The

59

news that the bug was nothing to do with germ warfare had been a relief, but he couldn't ignore the smell of the District Nurse wafting up from the antiquated radio receiver, pinched from Posh Godfrey's cottage.

"Within about a hundred yards should be OK."

"How about Bethesda Street, then? Meets this one at right angles doesn't it, and it's only a spit from the hall?"

***

Eric hit the double doors of the hall like a surgeon late for an appendectomy. He couldn't have known, he told himself later, that Hetty would be in the foyer rearranging some posters. Or that, alarmed by his entrance, she'd step backwards having clean forgotten she was standing on a ladder.

"Is your name Gethin?" she grumbled as Eric helped her up.

For a moment he wondered about concussion. "Who's Gethin?"

"Bull in a china shop, same as you. And you'd better have a good reason, young Eric," she went on, straightening her Stetson and extracting a drawing pin from her palm, "for busting in like that."

"Sorry," said Eric. "I thought I was late."

"Damn nearly *me* that was." Looking up at him, Hetty added, "You looks as pale as I feel, mind. Proper peaky, in fact. No need to ask why."

Eric had expected some sort of comment on his excesses of yesterday. Assuming a "man of the world" expression he said: "Put it down to a dozen or so pints of slurry, eh?"

"Or three," murmured Hetty.

"Three dozen?" Eric's hand went instinctively to his liver.

"Three *pints*, young Eric. Four at most."

"Oh." Feeling slightly deflated, Eric took a couple of turns around the foyer, admiring the faded Art Deco features, now partially obscured by Hetty's handiwork. It was quite a feat, he thought, to have made every perfectly oblong poster lean like a parallelogram on the patchy, pale pink walls.

"Anyway," said Hetty, smirking, "I didn't mean your *hangover* had drained your colour. Thought it might be more to do with giving a certain person a lift?"

Eric stared. "How do you know?"

"Word travels fast in these parts."

"Faster than an Escort van, that's for sure. I've only just dropped her off."

"Kind of you to pick her up in the first place."

"I had to. She was worried about her veins … in the rain."

Hetty opened one of the front doors and squinted up at the clear blue sky. "Lucky you was there, then. Looks like we could have a drop by about a week next Wednesday."

Squirming, Eric felt obliged to explain himself further. "I didn't like to say no. She was carrying this enormous cardboard box, you see …"

"Ah. And what delicacy was our Sal taking home for dinner tonight?"

"Baby goat," said Eric. "At least I hope it was. Does she do that a lot … pick up things that have got knocked down?"

"All the time," said Hetty. "Anything from a bat to a badger by all accounts. Although, just lately, she seems to be coming by a better class of carcass. There's your goat, today, and a brace or two of partridge Monday, and a nice bit of mutton, according to Sal, a week or so back. And none of it as damaged as it might be." Seeing Eric's expression, she added, "Can't blame her I suppose, with all those little'uns to feed. And they all look pretty well on it, don't you think?"

"Well, she looks OK," said Eric, remembering a vestige of bone structure and those tiger-yellow eyes. "I haven't met the children."

Hetty pursed her lips. "You have, you know. Two of her girls were in your garden, day after you arrived, sitting in a big armchair. You spoke to them."

Eric cast his mind back. "Oh, I remember." He thought for a moment. "But they said they lived quite near the cottage and the chip shop's miles away."

"Well, it was them, young Eric," said Hetty. "I'd know Sally's kids anywhere."

Eric shrugged, then, finding himself at the inner door to the hall, he put his ear to it. "Sounds pretty quiet in there."

Hetty paused in the act of dusting a glass display case with her hankie. "Mmm." She looked at her watch. "I've been giving everyone a few more minutes but I don't think we can wait much longer. I'm surprised, though, about Mrs Jenks and Arnold not turning up."

"But where's everyone *else*?" Eric protested, keenly aware that his chances of keeping a low profile were diminishing in line with the attendance level. "This is Wales, surely, land of committees?"

"No," corrected Hetty. "This is our little bit of Wales ... land of apathy." She shook her head sadly. "It's a bit odd, though, because there seemed to be a lot of support for the meeting, didn't there, in the pub last night?"

Eric said nothing, the latter part of the evening being a closed book to him.

"Makes me wonder," went on Hetty thoughtfully, "if the Twins haven't somehow found out about the meeting and been scaring people off attending."

Eric stared. "Would they do that?"

"I'm afraid so. Hardly in their interests, is it, us planning a grand event guaranteed to bring more strangers to the town, given how they feel about outsiders?"

Eric shifted uncomfortably, recalling his own run-in with the Twins in the pub.

"And, as I say," went on Hetty, "it doesn't take much to put this town off from doing anything dynamic."

Sighing, she resumed her dusting as Eric peered over her shoulder into the glass case.

"Something still inspires the populous," he observed, pointing to a photo of Hetty in her mayoral chain of office. "They've voted you in again, I see."

"Not so much voted me in, young Eric, as never bothered to vote me out." She paused for a moment, and then brightened. "Still, as regards this meeting of ours, better a handful of people, truly committed to the cause, than a hundred only along for the ride, eh?"

"Oh, yes," said Eric, blushing at his own lack of commitment. "As long as you're sure it's OK for me to be here, given I'm not a proper local?"

"*All* are welcome," said Hetty, firmly. "And if you don't contribute anything else, you've already upped the turn-out by twenty-five percent."

Eric did the sums with a sinking heart.

CHAPTER SEVEN

In the hall, the first thing Eric saw was a donkey and cart ambling across the far end. As his eyes adjusted to the light, however, the cart revealed itself to be a chariot, the donkey a horse, the amble a gallop, and the whole thing a backdrop at the rear of the stage. This, Eric presumed, was in readiness for Mel Meredith's forthcoming and somewhat ambitious production of *Ben Hur*, the details of which the actor had shared at length the evening before.

Looking around, he spotted the man himself demonstrating the art of holding a cigarette packet to a middle-aged lady with hair like a dandelion clock. He was a trier, thought Eric. You had to give him that.

"Dear boy," cried Mel, as Eric and Hetty took take their places at the table. "Fab you could make it. Don't happen to know the time do you?"

Eric went for his cuff then noticed Mel, waving frantically behind the white, fluffy head of his companion. Watching her hair trembling in the resulting breeze, Eric suppressed a chortle. As he did so, a low-pitched rumble from the other side of the table seemed to indicate Mel was doing the same.

"That's enough, boys," said Hetty, sharply. "Eric, I don't think you know Ms Harris, do you, our events secretary?"

"Pleased to meet you," said Eric, recovering his manners and walking round to shake Ms Harris's damp little hand.

"Likewise," simpered Ms Harris.

There was that sound again, thought Eric, but it no longer resembled a giggle so much as a Geiger counter. And it wasn't coming from Mel.

"Ms Harris takes the notes at all our meetings and keeps the file for us," Hetty went on, nodding at what looked like, and in fact was, a knitting bag on the table in front of the dandelion-haired little lady.

Ms Harris smote her forehead. "So I do," she said, opening the bag. Breathing hard, she flung out four balls of wool, a couple of patterns and what looked like a draught excluder but was in fact her new winter hat, dangling from a pair of needles. Finally, she took out a thick file and straightened it on the table in front of her.

The noise had reached alarming proportions by now. "Can't anyone else hear that?" asked Eric, glancing around the table.

Hetty looked up from her notes. "Hear what, Eric?"

"That humming, chattering, buzzing sound? Or is it only me?"

Hetty smiled. " 'T'isnt only you, Eric, but the rest of us are used to it by now, aren't we, Ms Harris?"

Ms Harris simpered again. "It's only my heart-rate monitor, young Eric. Had it fitted this morning, I did, by Dilys Daydream the District Nurse when she dropped in about my bunions."

Eric wrestled with this apparent anatomical discrepancy. "She fitted a heart monitor for bunions?"

"Good Lord, no. But she happened to notice I was a bit breathless. Asked me if I was excited about something and I had to admit I *was*, because of coming to the meeting tonight." Ms Harris cut a sideways look at Mel and fluttered her pale lashes. "Soon as I said that, she insisted on my wearing this heart monitor for the rest of the day. Thought it wasn't working to start with, I did," she added playfully, fluttering her lashes once again at Mel, "but it's going like stink, now."

Mel, who was beginning to look as if he might be regretting his earlier flirtation, leaned across the table to Eric. "Er, I wouldn't mind hearing some more of your views on fine art, old man, when you've a minute."

"My views on fine art?" squeaked Eric, his own heart thudding in alarm. Surely he hadn't told Mel about his sculpture? "How do you mean?"

"You know. Some more about what you were telling me yesterday in the pub?"

"What was that?"

"Can't remember, dear boy. Rather hoped you could."

"Well, I can't," said Eric shortly. "And I doubt it was important anyway."

To his relief, Hetty then declared the meeting open, adding, "So, let's get straight down to business, shall we? Perhaps we'd better fill young Eric in on our progress so far?"

There was a murmur of assent and Hetty went on. "We've had a couple of meetings already and come up with this idea of a Summer Spectacular to attract people from far and wide, and finally put our little town on the map."

Eric nodded. "Literally," he agreed, remembering the absence of Landoobrey from his Road Atlas. "In fact, I'd insist on it next time they have a reprint."

There was a baffled silence from the table and Eric shifted in his chair. What, he wondered, had he said?

"Anyway," said Hetty. "We came up with this idea and we've gone some way towards planning it." Nodding to Ms Harris, she added, "How about we show Eric the file, eh?"

"Oh, yes, yes." Ms Harris passed the bulky ring binder across the table.

Impressed, Eric opened it at the first page, which said "RAFT RACE?" It was a good start, he thought, then he discovered that was all it was. Rifling through the rest of the file he found only blank sheets of paper and the odd row of pink stars, presumably stuck on by Ms Harris for her own amusement.

"So, young Eric," prompted Hetty. "What do you think?"

Aware of expectant looks all round, Eric turned back to the first page. "Well, it's very neat," he ventured. "Very neat indeed."

The blushing writer of two words and a question mark patted her dandelion hair.

"But what do you think of the idea?" Hetty went on. "It was the first and I think the *best* we've come up with so far."

Eric was momentarily lost for words. On the one hand, a raft race alone would pretty much ensure the ongoing anonymity of his bolt hole, which suited him fine. On the other, if they were going to have the wretched Summer Spectacular at all, surely they ought to make it spectacular in some way? Remembering his newcomer status, however, all he said was, "A raft race, eh? Well, that is a good idea. On the Doobrey, I presume?"

Again, the table fell silent.

"On the what?" asked Ms Harris, at last.

"The Doobrey," said Eric, who'd always been under the impression that this was the name of the river running through the town. "The River Doobrey?"

"Ah," said Hetty. "Got you now, young Eric. Yes. On the river."

"Right," said Eric. "Well, it's a great *start* but I guess it's thinking caps on, now, isn't it? To come up with a few more ideas?"

Everyone applied themselves to staring at the table looking vacant and Eric began to see why progress so far had been slow. To break the silence he said, "Well, there are heaps of other things we could do, aren't there?"

"Umm," said Hetty, "that's just it. There *is* a lot we could do, but we're lacking a central theme. Something to tie it all together. That's why we keep coming back to the raft race. We could do that on its own, if all else failed."

"Ah, yes, but all else isn't going to fail, is it?" said Eric, more ardently than he meant to. Then, thinking off the top of his head he added, "Why don't you tie the event in with the Carnival? That was always the high spot of my holidays here as a boy. And, if I remember rightly, wasn't it held on the same date as the proposed new event? Midsummer's Day? Which, if I'm not mistaken, is on a Saturday this year?"

Hetty stared at him. "We haven't had the Carnival for years, Eric."

"Not had the Carnival? Why ever not?"

"Gethin," said Hetty and Ms Harris in unison.

"Ah," Eric smiled. "The bull in the china shop, eh? There's always one, isn't there? And what did this Gethin do that was so bad?"

"Nearly got us sued, that's what," snorted Hetty.

"Oh, dear, that is bad," agreed Eric. "Still, water under the bridge now, eh? And," he waved a hand around the table, "where's Gethin now? Not here, is he?"

"He's dead," said Ms Harris.

"Oh, I'm sorry."

Hetty shrugged. "He had it coming. And no one was as pleased as us, I can tell you, to see his no good carcass hanging in the window of Poulsons the butchers."

Eric doodled on the pad thoughtfully provided by Hetty. "This Gethin," he said, "was a real bull, wasn't he, in a real china shop?"

Ms Harris nodded, her eyes misting behind her bottle bottom glasses. "'Course he was. Ruined everything, he did, getting loose from the parade. And it was doubly surprising because, for all his faults, old man Williams was a prize stock-handler. He should never have let him go."

"Old man Williams?" queried Eric. "Not the father of the Twins, by any chance?"

"Well, yes," admitted Ms Harris.

Eric put his pen down. It was clear to him that sabotaging local events was nothing new in the Williams family. "Well, it's a shame," he said, "because there's heaps of potential, I always think, for generating revenue from a Carnival."

"What does that mean?" asked Ms Harris.

"Making money," said Hetty, thoughtfully. "And maybe young Eric's got a point. After all, the china shop went bust years ago in more ways than one. So maybe we *could* reinstate the Carnival. Join it up with the Summer Spectacular. What could we call it, though?"

"How about A Summer Spectacular and Carnival?" offered Mel.

"Wow," said Hetty. "That's good."

Mel blew on his manicured fingernails as Ms Harris reclaimed the file from Eric and licked her pencil.

Realising the meeting had turned something of a corner, Eric said, "OK, so we're all agreed. The Summer Spectacular will be run in conjunction with the Carnival. I can see it now," he added. "Lots of decorated floats and maybe a fancy dress procession going all around the town, before the main event gets underway on a nearby field, say?"

Everyone looked at him with a degree of admiration, which Eric felt was out of proportion to what he'd actually said.

"Great," said Ms Harris, writing busily.

"And we'll use the Bowen Field, of course," went on Hetty.

The events secretary's pencil skidded to a halt. "The Bowen Field?"

"Well, why not? It's ours, isn't it, to do as we wish with, thanks to the old Earl?"

"The old Earl?" queried Eric.

"Old Earl Bowen," Hetty clarified. "Last of the line, he was, when the family died out a century or more ago. Bit of a lad, too, by all accounts, prone to swilling ale and pinching wenches in the taverns of the town. Took it into his head one day to give the field next door to his house to the local people, in perpetuity. The poorer folk used to grow potatoes on it, and harvest the trees and hedges for firewood. But there's nothing to stop us using it now for the Summer Spectacular, which will benefit the whole town."

Ms Harris sniffed. "Nothing to stop us? Aren't you forgetting that the Twins have just bought the old Bowen place and all the land it sits on?"

"All the land except that field," Hetty corrected her. "That belongs to the town and I'd like to see the Twins prove otherwise." She beamed around the table. "So, that's the venue sorted. As for the Carnival part, well, that's practically planned already. We'll just do what we always did in the old days. Dress a few people up, whiz the lorries round the town and get on back to the pub."

Eric bit his lip. Although he'd said the Carnival had been the high spot of his holidays, the benchmark had been set pretty low, with a maximum of three floats ever in attendance.

He cleared his throat. "I may be wrong," he said, slowly, "but I think we're missing a trick, not making more out of the Carnival. We could encourage all the community groups to take part and each of them could put on a show or tableau, on lorries donated by local businesses?"

"Phew," said Hetty. "That'd be a lot of lorries. PC George would have to hold up the traffic for ages to get that lot across the main road."

"Yes," said Eric, "but if he's got to stop the traffic for three lorries he might as well stop it for thirteen, mightn't he? Or twenty-three?"

Hetty made a noise, somewhere between a chuckle and a guffaw. "Steady on, young Eric. I happen to know there aren't twenty-three lorries within about a forty-mile radius of the town."

"No," conceded Eric, "there probably aren't. But the lorries would only form part of the parade because it's a grand opportunity, isn't it, to tell some sort of story about this part of the world? Intersperse the Carnival floats with exhibits based on a farming theme, maybe, to promote the agricultural heritage of the area?"

Seeing Ms Harris's hand going rather convulsively to her chest, Eric added, hastily, "Not livestock, of course. Not after last time. But how about a grand parade of vintage farm machinery? Bound to be lots of bits and pieces, aren't there, lying about on local farms and small-holdings?"

"The Pugh Sisters have a pony and trap," put in Mel. "They offered it me for *Ben Hur*. Don't know if I mentioned that yesterday, Eric? My latest production? I'm going with the convention that one person can just as effectively embody a battle scene as a thousand, and ..."

"Oh, yes." Hetty intervened, swiftly. "So they have. And there's that steamroller up at Cwrt Y Bryn, isn't there? The one Moggs Morgan absent-mindedly drove home the night he got sacked by the Tarmac? We could ask him if it still goes?"

"That's the way," said Eric. "Now we're really getting somewhere. What else could we have?"

It was slow and tortuous going, but eventually they had a long list of possible feature items for the parade. A list, Eric realised, looking down at his notepad, that he'd inadvertently replicated. Well, not quite replicated, his version being devoid of the little pink stars Ms Harris seemed compelled to peel off and stick on whenever there was a lull in the proceedings. One-handedly, now, Eric noticed, the thumb and forefinger of her other hand being permanently engaged in plucking at her bosom.

"What about music?" asked Mel. "We could get some of those super little marching bands from the valleys? You know, where one girl twiddles a stick and they all wear tunics and really short skirts and blow kazoos?"

"How do you spell 'kazoo'?" asked Ms Harris.

"Doesn't matter how you spell it," said Hetty. "We're not having them."

"Spoilsport," said Mel, with a grin. "What'll we have instead, then?"

Hetty looked thoughtful. "I reckon we've enough local talent to put together a little band of our own. And, given your enthusiasm for the subject, Mel, I vote you can be in charge of that."

"OK." Mel made an entry on his otherwise blank pad. "I'll have to hold auditions, of course."

"Count me in," said Ms Harris, pitching her voice over the increasingly loud hum from her chest.

"Right," said Mel and if he was disappointed in any way by the prospect of Ms Harris in a really short skirt, he didn't show it. "And I'll need a venue for the auditions and somewhere to practise."

"You can use the Hart," said Hetty. "And before you ask, I haven't got a casting couch."

"That's a shame," shouted Ms Harris, to Mel's evident consternation. "Sorry," she added. "This thing's getting louder by the minute. Must be working, eh? Building up a good head of steam?"

She wasn't joking, thought Eric, who almost fancied he saw a little puff of vapour from her cleavage. "Well," he said, recalling himself to the matter at hand, "it's all coming together isn't it, on the Carnival side? Next we need to tackle the Summer Spectacular itself. Decide what stalls and attractions we're going to have; plan some games and other activities and maybe some demonstrations of country crafts; check what insurances, if any, we might need; organise the publicity … "

Eric looked up from the notes he was busily making to discover he was the only person still sitting down.

Hetty smiled. "How about we all go away and think about it and reconvene another time?"

"Oh," said Eric. "OK. But in the meantime we ought to start sourcing items for the vintage machinery part of the parade. Hopefully you'll find the farmers and small-holders are willing to donate things, especially if a personal visit can be made to each, so that they all feel included." He ran his eye down his list. "Starting, perhaps, with the Pugh Sisters' pony and trap. We could use that for the Carnival Queen."

"Did you say, hopefully *we'll* find people are willing?" queried Hetty. She turned to Ms Harris and Mel. "*We* can't do it, can we?"

"Certainly not," said Ms Harris, who was now fanning her front with the ring binder. "Not if we've to make a personal visit to all the outlying properties. We haven't a car between us."

"Besides which, I've got the pub to think about," said Hetty.

"And I've got the music to think about," put in Mel. Then, with a glance at the backdrop, he added, "And my play won't produce itself, either. I'm doing *Ben Hur* if you remember, Eric, which, as I may have mentioned yesterday ..."

"OK," said Eric. "I'll do it."

"That's the way." Hetty peered down at Eric's pad. "Luckily you've made a list, I see, of everyone you've got to visit. Watch yourself, though, won't you, at the Pugh Sisters' place? They live right next door to the Williams Twins and ..."

She got no further because, at that moment, there was a loud bang, followed by a small fire, in the vicinity of Ms Harris's chest.

***

In the immediate aftermath of the explosion, Ms Harris was delighted to find her ample bosom the subject of a detailed examination by Mel.

It almost made it worthwhile, she thought happily, being blown up in the first place. Especially as she'd got off so lightly. Her lucky escape being due in no small part to a new bustier, which had arrived just that morning from the catalogue. Claiming to lift, separate, elevate and enhance, it had turned out to resemble a couple of sandbags fastened with a bungee. What it lacked in looks, however, it had more than made up for in shock absorption, enabling her to sail through her experience with barely a tremor.

"Found anything interesting, Mel?" she asked, hoping he hadn't yet and might need to go back in for another look.

But Mel, it seemed, had seen enough. Gravely, he confirmed that Ms Harris had almost certainly been harbouring a bug in her heart monitor, and transmitting the contents of the meeting to a radio receiver, stationed somewhere beyond the hall. It didn't take a genius to work out who was responsible.

"Then the Twins will have heard everything," whispered Ms Harris, "and all because of me."

"Never mind," said Hetty, kindly. "You weren't to know what Dilys was up to, were you? Although I *had* heard a whisper she was starting to see a sight too much of that oaf, Tony Williams … Still," she added, "I don't think we said anything too revealing, did we?"

Ms Harris stared at her. Not said anything too revealing? Surely they'd given away each and every part of their plans for the big day? And there was no taking it back now.

"Pub anyone?" asked Mel, to a murmur of heartfelt agreement.

"I'll just pop the van home, first," said Eric. "And join you there."

***

In Bethesda Street, Terry sat with his hands over his ears, angrily surveying the radio receiver in his lap.

"Thought you said this thing was safe?" he moaned.

Tony peered across at the machine. "Well, Dilys said it was and she should know. Soldered it herself, she did, into the small hours. What happened?"

"What happened?" echoed Terry. "Didn't you hear the bang?"

"What bang?"

"In my earphones. Nearly took my bloody head off. Reckon it's blown up, I do, at the other end."

"Really?" said Tony. "That's odd. According to Dilys, the only risk of that happening would be if it got damp."

"Well, there you are then," fumed Terry. "Sweat's damp, isn't it? I doubt there's many places sweatier than Ms Harris's chest, given she was making sheep's eyes at that twerp Mel Meredith for pretty much the whole of the meeting."

"How do you know?" objected Tony. "It's a bug, not a surveillance camera."

"Heard her, didn't I? 'Ooh, count me in, Mel … Shame there isn't a casting couch, Mel …' Turned my stomach, it did. Next time – if there is a next time – you can do the listening."

"OK, OK," said Tony, "but what else did you hear? Anything from that Eric on the subject of our little removal job last night?"

Terry shook his head. "No, but that's the least of our worries. This event is going to be *huge,* Tony, with a grand parade of vintage machinery and a marching band and everything. What's more, they're planning to have it on Midsummer's Day – the very date we've got planned for the opening of our hotel – and on the Bowen Field, bang next door."

Tony stared. "But that's *our* field. Bought it fair and square, we did, along with the rest of the property."

"Not according to that lot," Terry jerked his chin in the direction of the village hall. "According to them, old Earl Bowen gifted the field to the town, yonks ago, in perpendicular … no, that's not right. Er, in perp something."

"Perpetuity?"

"That's it. Means they can use the field *for ever*, and there's not a damn thing we can do about it."

"I know what perpetuity means," snapped Tony, "but where, I'd like to know, is it written that the old Earl gave the field to the town?"

Terry considered the question. "I don't know that it is," he said, slowly. "Everyone just knows it's true."

"What people *know*, Terry, and what they can *prove* are two different things. And *we* can prove, because of the deeds, that the Bowen Field belongs to *us*."

Terry reached for his seatbelt. "Thank God for that. Let's go and slip Hetty the bad news, shall we, stop this thing in its tracks?"

Tony swung the Land Rover in the opposite direction to the White Hart. "No," he said. "Let's not."

Terry stared. "But we can't have all those people flooding into the town, can we? Sussing the barn crop, maybe, and ruining everything at the hotel …"

"No," grinned Tony. "But what we *can* do is let Hetty's committee spend a load of money on deposits, and insurances, and a mountain of useless publicity, before we finally pull the plug on the venue. Am I clever," he added, "or what?"

Terry looked at his brother. "Willy," he declared, suddenly, "is a far better word for what you are."

"Eh?" said Tony.

"It's a compliment," explained Terry, kindly. "Calling someone willy. As in willy as a fox."

***

Later that night, awash with the half pint of slurry he'd drunk, purely to settle his nerves, Eric sipped an antidotal pint of milk. It was the last in his fridge but if it did the trick, who cared? He could always nip out for some more first thing.

As he sipped, he congratulated himself on finally making it upstairs to his new bed. And very comfortable it was, too. Certainly in comparison to the floor and staircase alternatives of recent nights.

Which was just as well, because if ever he needed his rest, it was tonight. The knowledge that the Twins now knew the latest plans for the Summer Spectacular was a big worry. Particularly as they'd heard most of them from Eric's own lips. Carried away by the whole thing, he'd virtually chaired the meeting, taken more notes than the events secretary and lumbered himself with organising a grand parade of vintage machinery, all on his own.

Still, he reminded himself, finishing his milk and plucking a piece of paper from his bedside cupboard, the parade was taking shape already. He'd managed to get a set of directions, at the pub, to all the possible exhibitors on his list so that he wouldn't get lost when he visited them.

Not that being lost was always such a bad thing, he thought sleepily. After all, he'd been lost, hadn't he, when he'd stumbled across the raw material for his *Deep Depression in Driftwood*? That had been on a beach, of course, and under the impetus of Imogen, berating him for booking a three star hotel at Margate when she'd distinctly told him five stars in Mauritius.

Never one for confrontations, Eric had turned and walked away. In the wrong direction as it happened, accidentally heading for Ramsgate and a supplicant figure in the soft, brown sand.

Eric smiled now, as he snuggled down. Little could he or his wife have known that his errant footsteps were taking him towards a fortune. A fortune Imogen had unwittingly forfeited by filing for divorce the moment they got home. Ironically, on the grounds of Eric's unreasonable behaviour. Citing, among other things, his insistence on bringing a rotten old lump of wood back with them …

And who was to say history wouldn't repeat itself? That he wouldn't find the bones of his new piece somewhere on his travels this week? Because surely if there was one thing the countryside had in abundance, it was bits of wood?

Reaching to turn off his light, he caught a slurred but deeply respectful conversation outside in the street.

"After you," said a voice.

"No, after *you*," said the same voice.

Diagnosing a lone drunk on the narrow bit of pavement by the cottage wall, Eric allowed his eyelids to droop. It was a far cry, he thought contentedly, from trying to get to sleep back at the flat. There, if it wasn't sirens wailing far into the night it was traffic roaring on the bypass. And, if it wasn't either of those, it was the altogether more menacing sounds much closer to hand. Like the scratching and rustling of youngsters up to no good in his garden. Which, he realised, putting his head under his pillow, had so far ingrained themselves on his brain that he fancied he could hear them even now.

CHAPTER EIGHT

"What a night," yawned Beryl next morning, as she and Meryl waited for Eric to leave the house.

She'd spent ages, in the small hours, trying to find her way back to the tent after answering the call of nature. Finally feeling the taut canvas beneath her outstretched hands, she'd crawled in through the flap. Only to knock flying the biscuit tin containing the twigs she and Meryl had so far collected for making the miniature sculptures. The next few minutes had been agony, expecting Eric to appear at any moment and order them to decamp. "I barely got a wink of sleep," she added as Eric's front door banged behind him.

"*I* slept fine," said Meryl, leading the way through the scullery window and upstairs to the bathroom, "but that's because *I* didn't gut myself on the last of the pop before turning in."

Sensing a lack of sisterly sympathy, Beryl changed the subject. "Wonder where he's off to in such a hurry?" she said, standing on tiptoe and peering out of the bathroom window after the departing figure of Eric before padding over to the sink. "Won't be far, I shouldn't think, without his car, so we'd best get a move on."

"We've got to get a move on anyway," said Meryl, her voice muffled by her pyjama top, which she'd left hanging round her neck to save time while she washed. "Soon as we're dressed we need to go to the shop. Splurge the last of our savings on some luggage tags and a tin of varnish. Then I reckon we're almost there."

"Almost destitute you mean," said Beryl, helping herself to Eric's toothpaste, their own having run out the day before along with their soap, "and nothing to show for it so far."

"Oh, stop whinging. Every entrepreneur knows you've got to accumulate to speculate." Meryl inched her arms back into her pyjamas. "And I reckon we'll crack these miniatures over the weekend, especially as we won't have to keep an eye open for Eric because he'll be out most of the time tracking down stuff for his parade."

"Handy, wasn't it," said Beryl, searching in vain for a clean bit on her towel, "overhearing that little snippet of gossip this morning? Assuming Ms Harris has got it right, of course."

"Oh, I expect so," said Meryl thoughtfully. "After all, she was at the meeting, wasn't she? And if Eric's going to be *out* such a lot, what's to stop us being *in*? We could move our entire production line indoors, couldn't we? Give ourselves a bit of elbow room and cut manufacturing time by loads."

Beryl gave up on her own towel and plucked Eric's neatly folded one from the radiator. "Good idea," she said through a face full of purest Egyptian cotton. "And if we're going to be in the house anyway, maybe we could get some of our washing done, too? It's not as if Eric ever uses that machine of his, is it?"

***

For the first time since arriving in Landoobrey, Eric had awoken refreshed. Which was just as well, he thought, striding away from the cottage, given everything he had to do today. First there was the milk to get, then he needed to buy some new clothes before he could even think of visiting the Pugh Sisters. Such garments as he possessed were beginning to look as if he'd slept in them. Which he had, of course, twice.

He'd toyed with the idea of putting them through his washing machine but memories of his mother standing ankle deep in water and kicking it had rather put him off. Perhaps one day he'd buy a new one, he thought, passing the window of Evans Electricals where an elderly twin-tub slumbered in the sunshine. He could certainly afford to. In fact, he reminded himself, he could afford to buy virtually anything he wanted, including a new set of clothes every day of the week, if needs be.

Strolling on, Eric felt a pang of guilt concerning his bank balance. Here were the citizens of Landoobrey having to mount an event to save themselves from financial ruin, when all the time he was sitting on a fortune large enough to revamp much of the town. Not only that but a world famous name, such as his own, could make a real difference if he were to publicly declare his patronage of the event.

Even as this thought crossed his mind, Eric dismissed it. He simply couldn't face the prospect of losing his incognito status and stirring up another media frenzy.

But, he told himself, walking purposefully on, he was doing his bit for the town in other ways, wasn't he? And, if the Summer Spectacular failed to deliver the goods, he could always consider an anonymous donation at some point in the future.

***

In her shop, Mrs Jenks was engrossed in the runners and riders for the 2.30 at Haydock. Hearing the ting of the shop bell, however, she clapped the paper shut and whipped off her specs.

"Ah," she said, "young Eric. Just the person I wanted to see. What's all this I hear about the Summer Spectacular meeting not being off, after all?"

"Not off, Mrs Jenks? How do you mean?"

"I mean not off as in *on*, of course, because I was told yesterday it was off, then this morning I was told it was on and definitely not off, but nobody told me that yesterday so the last I heard until today was that it was off. Do you see?"

"Er, yes," said Eric, who didn't, "although I thought it was on all along, which is why I went."

"Hmm," said Mrs Jenks grimly. "Well, it looks like those Williams boys have been busy, then, doesn't it? Putting it about that the meeting was off when ..."

"Er quite," interrupted Eric, anxious to avoid another off and on exchange with Mrs Jenks. "But I can assure you the meeting went ahead, exactly as planned."

The shopkeeper eyed him mischievously. "Not *exactly* as planned, surely? Word is, it all got a bit heated, towards the end?"

It was an unfortunate phrase, in the circumstances, and Eric suppressed a shudder. "Just between ourselves, Mrs Jenks, it did, due to an unfortunate incident with a listening device planted in Ms Harris's … er …chest."

"Doubt her front's seen that much action for years," said Mrs Jenks, briskly. "Still, good meeting was it, apart from that?"

"Excellent." Eric dragged his thoughts back to happier things. "I think we made a great start on planning the event. Plenty left to do, though," he added. "If you feel like coming along to the next one?"

"I'll be there, young Eric. Right, run out of milk have you, lad?"

"Er, yes," said Eric. "How did you know?"

"Well," Mrs Jenks settled her elbows on the counter, "I calculated the cereal and beverages you might take in an average day, subtracted what you wouldn't have had, being comatose for most of yesterday, and factored in the pint, which you likely had last night on account of that half of slurry after the meeting."

"Wow," said Eric. "Well, as you say, I'd like some milk, please. How much would you suggest?"

Mrs Jenks pursed her lips. "How about you take three pints and come back Monday? You'll be needing some more bread by then, won't you?"

Eric nodded. It was as if she could see right into his soul, he thought. Or his larder at any rate. "Three it is then, please."

"Right you are." Mrs Jenks assembled three pints on the counter at her usual breakneck speed. "Anything else I can do for you today?"

"Well, yes, as it happens. I'm in need of some new clothes. Is there anywhere locally I could buy some?"

The shopkeeper lifted her hands and slapped them down again on the counter. "Right here, young Eric. Right *here*. Out the back."

Eric followed the jerk of her hairnet towards the passageway connecting the front to the back of the shop, via "Gardening and Outdoor Leisure". "I thought out the back was "Household Goods"?"

""Household Goods" *and* "Gents Outfitting". It's a new department, run entirely by Arnold. We thought it best, seeing as it's to do with men's things."

"Men's things?"

Mrs Jenks nodded and leant closer. "It's been years since I handled a pair of men's underpants, young Eric. I don't intend to start again now."

***

Squeezing past a job lot of compost, Eric emerged from the cramped confines of "Gardening and Outdoor Leisure" into what had been, until recently, the sole domain of "Household Goods".

His nose twitched as the peat and potash smell of the passageway yielded to a heady mix of Ajax, Jeyes Fluid, candle wax and carbolic. There was also, he noted, a woody undercurrent, identifiable as recently sawn hardboard.

Looking around, he soon spotted the reason for the latter in the shape of a hastily thrown up cubicle bearing the legend "Gents Outfitting" on its ill-fitting door.

Pushing the door open, Eric found Arnold leaning on a walking frame, skimming cellophane packets from a box on the counter onto some wonky-looking shelves. Unwittingly wandering into the path of one pack, Eric felt a cold slap on the side of his face.

"Sorry," said Arnold, " 'ain't got my eye in yet."

He could say that again, thought Eric, ducking to avoid a second missile. Turning to protest, he came face to face with Arnold, fiddling with something small and round, wrapped in a grubby hankie.

Eric went for a browse. At the far end of the tiny display area, he found three brawny mannequins modelling the latest in tweed suits, tweed caps and what looked like tweed shirts.

"Right, young Eric," wheezed the old man, tossing aside his empty box. "What can I do for you?"

Deeming it safe to return to the counter, Eric did so, saying, "I'd like some cords, please, or jeans, and perhaps some polo shirts?"

"Do they come in tweed?" asked Arnold.

"Er, not as a rule."

"We do a nice line in tweed. It's what we sell most of."

"Right. Well, I'll certainly bear that in mind for the colder months, but I was hoping for something a little lighter for the summer?"

"Summat with no sleeves, perhaps?" said Arnold, swinging over and taking a packet from a shelf.

"Well, yes, that'd be a start. What did you have in mind?"

"Nice little giblet?" Arnold lifted his glasses and peered again at the label. "Er … gusset? … Damned if I know how you pronounce it."

"I think it's a gillet," said Eric, helpfully.

"Take your word for that, young Eric." Arnold shook the garment from its pack. "Nice little tweed gillet then?"

"Umm," said Eric. "Attractive as it is, I think I'll leave that for later in the year, too. For now, though, how about we start at the bottom?"

"At the bottom?"

Eric lowered his voice, in deference to Mrs Jenks. "I'm in need of some underpants, please, and some socks."

"Ah. Got you, young Eric. Well, we keep a fair selection of pants."

"Not in tweed?" said Eric, with a light laugh.

Arnold glanced behind the counter. "*Some* of them, yes, if that's your fancy?"

"No," said Eric, firmly. "It's not my fancy at all."

"Take your word for that, too, young Eric. Now, how about you tell me what you're after and I'll tell you if we've got it?"

"Right. Well, I need some socks, as I say, made of wool for preference, and pants in cotton or a cotton lycra mix?"

Arnold scratched his nose. "I ain't read all the ingredients, but our socks is here, in the display rack and, see those shelf units over there? Our pants are in the drawers underneath. The ones marked 'Drawers'."

"Great," said Eric. "And you're sure you can't help with anything else? Those cords I mentioned, or some polo shirts?"

"Well, Mrs Jenks did order in some other items – for the younger folk, she said." Arnold looked doubtfully at Eric. "Have a poke about if you like in that big, round basket."

Eric made his selections from the sock rack and the drawers marked "Drawers", then moved on to the basket. Here he found a couple of T-shirts and a polo shirt but no cords. Then he caught a flash of blue denim. Jeans would do nicely, he decided, picking out a pair and checking the size scrawled on the pack.

About to leave "Gents Outfitting", Eric had a thought.

"Arnold," he said, "I've got to go out to the Pugh Sisters' place this morning."

Arnold nodded. "Aye, to ask about borrowing their pony and trap for the Carnival."

"Exactly. Well, the trouble is, I wrote these direction down in the pub last night." Extracting a piece of paper from his pocket he showed it to Arnold, who studied it, both ways up, for some time.

"Been learning Mandarin long, have you?" he asked finally.

"No. It's just that I had this half of slurry …"

"Say no more," said Arnold. "How's about I talk you through it, eh? Start to finish? Used to do deliveries up there, I did, for Mrs Jenks so I know it well."

"That would be marvellous. Only if you've time, of course."

Arnold narrowed his real eye. "Well, time *is* money, young Eric."

Eric took the hint, handed Arnold some cash and five minutes later the old man had described every hairpin bend and four-in-one hill on Eric's route. He also touched, like Hetty, on the proximity of the Pugh Sisters' place to that of the Williams Twins.

"Like I say, young Eric, you keep away from their farm whatever you do. Neither of them two scareaways wants meeting on a dark night."

Eric swallowed. "Well," he said. "Hopefully it won't *be* dark. I should be there and back, shouldn't I, in about an hour? As long as the poor old van can make it up all those hills."

"You wants to try the buggers on a trike," said Arnold, "with a Zimmer frame strapped on the back."

***

With his pile of packages stacked under his chin and Arnold's directions fresh in his mind, Eric emerged from the back room. His visit to the shop, he thought, had definitely been one of his better ideas.

This was an opinion not shared by Meryl, who shifted uncomfortably as Eric joined her at the counter. What, she wondered, was he doing here? It was hardly part of the plan for Eric to catch her and Beryl shopping for materials with which to forge his replicas. The luggage tags, in particular, would be a dead giveaway. On the bright side, Beryl had been ages looking for them already. Perhaps Eric would have paid and left the shop by the time she found them?

"Got 'em," said Beryl, bouncing in from "Haberdashery" and "Stationery". "Just where you said they were, Mrs … Oh, bum." Her voice tailed off as she recognised Eric at the counter. Instinctively she thrust her hands behind her back.

Mrs Jenks tapped a slippered foot. The exception to her rule of no self-service shopping was children, whose legs, she considered, had a good few more miles left in them than her own. "Let's have 'em, young Beryl," she said. "Up on the counter where I can see 'em."

"Let's have what on the counter?" asked Beryl, turning scarlet.

"Them luggage tags, of course, what you've just spent ages looking for. Though what you wants with them and a tin of varnish beats me."

"I can tell you that," said Eric, and both girls froze. "About the luggage tags, at least. Playing some sort of game, eh? Pretending you're off round the world, perhaps, on a grand adventure?"

"That's right," said Meryl, shooting a warning glance at Beryl.

Eric looked pleased. Having been out of teaching for a while he was glad he hadn't lost his touch with the younger generation.

Leaning over, he picked up the varnish. "Not so sure what you want this for," he said, turning the tin round in his hands. "Still, there are heaps of uses for varnish, aren't there? I use it a lot of it in my work."

Beryl looked at him from under her lashes. "What work would that be?" she asked. "I thought you told Hetty in your garden that you don't actually work at all?"

Eric could have kicked himself. "Er, no," he said, "and so I don't … not any more. But I used to be a woodwork teacher. Used a lot of varnish then, I did …"

"Yes, well," interrupted Mrs Jenks, her fingers hovering over the till. "Let's get these bits rung up shall we, girls?"

Reluctantly, Beryl put the luggage tags on the counter.

"There. That wasn't so difficult was it?" Mrs Jenks squinted at the price stickers, asking casually, "So, where are you two off to, now? Back home, is it, to that tent of yours in the chip shop yard?"

"Back home, yes," said Meryl truthfully. After all, the tent *was* home. Wherever it happened to be pitched.

"Funny that," said Mrs Jenks. "Someone was telling me only this morning as your mam hasn't seen you for ages."

"No change there, then," whispered Beryl as she and Meryl scuttled out of the shop.

Eric glanced after them. "Were those by any chance the missing children of Sally Stitch?"

Mrs Jenks nodded. "Mm. But they're not missing as such. Volunteered they did to camp out for the warmer months and free up some space in that flat. Did a runner, though, a few days ago. Wherever they went, they're looking after themselves mind. All washed and brushed up."

"Mmm," said Eric, catching a whiff of soap not unlike his own expensive brand on the draught from the door. "Looking after themselves rather well, too."

***

Back at the cottage, Eric flung off all his clothes and squashed them into a plastic bag along with everything else he'd been wearing for the last couple of days. Then he nipped to the bathroom for a quick wash, dismayed to find the lid off his toothpaste, and his bar of soap far smaller than he remembered.

Worse, upon reaching for his towel he found it on the floor of all places, screwed up in a ball and feeling faintly damp. "You're slipping, Eric, my boy," he told himself, returning to his room.

There, he ripped the packaging from his jeans, which, he soon discovered, weren't. In fact, the only thing they had in common with a pair of trendy denims was having two leg-holes. He put them on anyway, because they were the only clean garment he possessed. Then he fastened the shoulder straps and regarded himself in the mirror. Hoping the Pugh Sisters wouldn't mind being visited by a cross between Huckleberry Finn and a Walton.

CHAPTER NINE

"What *was* he wearing?" giggled Meryl as she piled the raw materials for the miniature replicas of Eric's sculpture onto his kitchen table.

"Dungarees, I think," replied Beryl, throwing down their bag of laundry with more force than was necessary. Now that it came to it, she wasn't at all sure she had the nerve for today's operations. Nipping in and out to the bathroom was one thing. Taking over Eric's kitchen seemed fraught with danger. "Not that I care what he was wearing," she added miserably, "and neither should you. We've got so much to do before he comes back. So if you check out that washing machine, I'll make a start on varnishing some twigs. Then we can both have a go at pp'ing the luggage tags. At least we can pick those up and run if Eric suddenly comes home."

"Dungarees." repeated Meryl. "Who on earth wears those these days?"

"Eric, apparently," snapped Beryl. "Let's just get *on* shall we?" Seizing the varnish, she began to shake the tin like a pioneer dairy farmer hoping for butter.

Meryl sauntered over to the washing machine and peered at the dial. "OK, OK. Keep your hair on. He'll be ages yet." She opened the machine, crammed their washing in, and slammed the door. "For one thing, he's only just left. For another, finding Pantybryn's tricky enough, isn't it, even for normal people? It could take Eric the rest of the summer."

***

He'd be there in no time, thought Eric, delighted with Arnold's detailed directions, guiding every step of his journey. And what a journey it was proving to be. Cresting the brow of yet another hill, he felt his spirits soaring skyward along with the van. Perhaps this was what people meant by being "on top of the world". Certainly it summed up his own feelings as he crossed the vast, upland bog separating Landoobrey from the secluded valley in which the Pugh Sisters lived. Why, he wondered, had Arnold failed to mention how beautiful it was up here? Then he remembered it probably wasn't on a trike.

Making a left turn at a remote crossroads, Eric felt the van tilt abruptly downhill. Signifying, he hoped, that he was about to enter a secluded valley. His hopes were confirmed as the rolling mountain scenery gave way to small, green fields divided by straggling hedges bursting with leaf and may blossom.

So far, so good, thought Eric, starting to look out as Arnold had instructed for a farm gate bearing the name "Pantybryn". Moments later he was upon it, scrambling to make the turn and accelerating away up the bumpy track.

Something was wrong, he thought, eyeing the piles of junk and scrap metal littering the fields alongside the drive. Surely Arnold would have mentioned these hideous landmarks? Putting the van into reverse he consulted the sign on the gate again. "Pantygwyn", it said. Heart thudding, Eric flung the van back onto the road. Drawn like a vertigo sufferer to a cliff, he'd been about to visit the Williams Twins.

Somewhat chastened, he drove on to the next gateway where he read and reread the handwritten sign. Satisfied it said "Pantybryn", he nosed the van onto the track, trundling ever upwards to a walled and gated farmyard. Here he parked behind the Pugh Sisters' bright-green 2CV; capable, according to Arnold, of carrying four farmers and a pig across a ploughed field. And looking as if it had recently done so.

Shielding his eyes from the sun, Eric peered across the sloping cobbles of the yard towards an old stone farmhouse and a cluster of barns arranged in a U shape. The layout made sense, with the bulk of the outbuildings sheltering the house from the worst of the weather.

Less easily explained was a woman, standing at the top of the yard with what looked like four sets of bathroom scales, arranged one at each corner of a large, dark-brown horse.

Don't ask, Eric told himself. Just don't ask.

He knocked politely on the gate. The woman looked up, dropped the horse's rope and hurried over.

"You must be young Eric," she called, deftly hurdling an excitable collie who'd beaten her to the gate by a short head. "Frank the Mail *said* you'd be coming … About the pony and trap, isn't it, for the Summer Spectacular and Carnival? … How truly *marvellous* to meet you. Have an acid drop?"

The non sequitur was accompanied by a small paper bag, whipped from the pocket of her boiler suit and thrust under Eric's nose.

Up close, Eric could see how very pretty the woman was. A couple of years younger than himself, he judged, lithe as a willow, and possessed of an extraordinary shininess, from the dark, glossy cap of her bobbed hair, via sparkling, violet eyes, to the subtle wet-rose sheen of her lips.

"The postman, eh?" he said, dragging his gaze from her face as he helped himself from the bag.

The woman nodded. "He calls here for his elevenses and brings us *all* the news. How our cousins are keeping out at Cwmfedwyn. Where people have been on their holidays and whether they had a nice time. Who's married, pregnant, divorced or dead. In fact," she added thoughtfully, "about the only thing he *doesn't* very often bring us is any post."

"No?" said Eric. "Well, with a postman like that, who needs letters, eh?"

They shared a smile. "Anyway, he's a great friend of Arnold's at the shop where you went this morning for some ... " She stopped.

"Milk?" suggested Eric.

She shook her head, staring at the floor.

"Jeans? Polo shirts?"

"No." Blushing, she whispered, "*Tweed knickers.*" Before Eric could put her right, she rushed on. "Naturally, Arnold told him all that you bought, how much you paid and that he'd given you directions for coming up this afternoon about the trap."

"Naturally," sighed Eric, "but I feel I ought to point out there's been a slight misunderstanding about that underwear ..."

"Mmm. Well, each to his own, I say. I'm Min, by the way." She thought for a moment then added, "By which I don't mean I'm at home, although of course I *am*. It's my name, do you see?"

With that she extended a small, grubby hand. Eric shook it carefully, only to find that, despite her lissom physique, she had a grip like a pair of pliers.

"I do indeed," he said, retrieving his hand as soon as was decent.

Min beamed. "Good." She opened the gate with a sweeping gesture of welcome. "Come in, come in. Meet the menagerie."

Eric rounded the gate and Min began her introductions, pointing out little groups of animals and birds that Eric had only dimly registered up till now. "Over there by the duck pond," she said, "we have our hens, Itsy and Mitsy, and our cockerel, Bertie."

Min looked expectantly at Eric who felt obliged to raise a hand in salute.

"Hello," he said, pitching his voice across the cobbles to the chickens.

"That's the way," said Min. "Now, *on* the pond we have Gertrude coming towards us, Mabel swimming away … or … wait a minute, *is* that Mabel? Yes, I believe it is. Mabel then, swimming away, Gertrude coming towards us, Clara, Petunia, Cynthia and Pearl to the left and George to the right."

Again, she waited.

"Hi," said Eric, getting the hang of it and sketching another wave.

"And here, of course," went on Min, "we have Timmy the dog. Say hello, Tim."

To Eric's amazement, the dog grinned all over its face.

"Hey, Timmy," said Eric, grinning back.

"And over there by the wall," said Min, "are our cats. The black one's called Blackie, the white one Whitey and the ginger one …"

"Don't tell me," said Eric. "Ginger?"

"*Yes*," said Min. "Well *done*."

"Yo, cats," yelled Eric, by now thoroughly enjoying himself. The feeling of well-being he'd experienced on the mountain seemed amplified in this isolated farmyard. In fact, he was beginning to feel like a character in a Disney film. Expecting at any moment to be surrounded by twittering bluebirds and perhaps a chipmunk or two.

"Up at the top of the yard," Min was saying, "beyond the duck pond, is Desmond the horse."

"Dessie, my man," shouted Eric, disappointed when the horse raised neither head nor hoof but merely turned away.

"That's the lot for now," said Min. "Everyone else is either in the barns or out on the pasture." She glanced towards Eric's feet. "Apart from Mickey and Minnie, of course."

Eric followed her glance in time to see two mice scuttling away from the toes of his shoes. Watching them go, he shook his head in wonder.

"You really know that these particular mice are called Mickey and Minnie?"

Min giggled. "Well, I know that they *might* be."

Eric blushed. "Nice acid drops," he said, changing the subject.

"*Aren't* they?" Min offered the bag again. "We buy them from a young man in the market. Mo and I can't get enough of 'em ... Oh, talking of Mo, we ought to go and find her, didn't we, to ask about you borrowing the trap?"

Eric, who'd completely forgotten there was a reason for his visit, forced himself to concentrate. "Do you think there'll be any problem?"

"No fear," said Min. "We'd be pleased to lend it. The Summer Spectacular and Carnival is *such* a good idea …" She broke off and looked warily in the direction of the Williams' farm, "… even if not everyone thinks so." Before Eric could comment on this she added, "I'm sure Mo'll tell you the same. Come along."

Feeling another rush of happiness and resisting the urge to kick both feet out to the side, Eric fell into step beside Min. "As a matter of interest," he said, "are yours and your sister's names short for something?"

"Oh, no" said Min. "We both got our names because of the midwife. Mo's a few years older than me and when she was born, Mam said, 'What is it?' meaning was it a boy or a girl. The midwife, who was lighting a ciggie at the time, said 'Just a mo', while she went to have a look, and the name stuck. Then, when I was born, the same thing happened, only guess what she said that time?"

"Just a min?" hazarded Eric.

"How *clever* of you. Yes. That's exactly right." She beamed at Eric, who couldn't help thinking it was a good thing the midwife hadn't plumped, on that occasion, for just a tick, or half a jiffy.

Together, Eric and Min skirted the duck pond, scattered the chickens, waved at the horse and hurdled the dog all the way to a rusty lean-to slumped against the rear of one of the barns.

"Our glory-hole, explained Min, bustling up to a cracked, grimy window in the nearest end of the shed. "Oh *good*, she's still in there."

"That you, Min?" came a disembodied voice.

Min moved to the other end of the lean-to and called in through the low, narrow entrance. "Yes, Mo," she said, "it's me and I've got young Eric with me. What do you think of that?"

"Marvellous," came the voice. "What's he like?"

Min flushed, glancing up at Eric from under her eyelashes. "He's lovely," she said quietly.

"He's what?"

Obligingly, Eric turned away.

"Lovely," hissed Min, then, more loudly, "but never mind that now, Mo. Did you find what you were looking for?"

"Yep."

There was a commotion then in the little doorway as Mo backed out, her chocolate-brown corduroys straining across her large, round, jiggling posterior. Like a bumblebee, Eric decided, coming out of a flower. Even down to the glowing proboscis of her ciggy sticking out the front.

"Buzz buzz," he said without meaning to, and Min smiled.

Clear of the doorway, the woman turned and Eric saw her to be well the other side of fifty, with salt and pepper hair, weather-beaten features and copious chins, beginning to lose the battle with gravity. Her smile, though, like Min's, illuminated her entire face and a good portion of the surrounding landscape.

The woman dropped what she was carrying, stepped over it and strode across to pump Eric's hand. "I'm Mo," she said. "Super to meet you." For the second time that day, Eric found himself retrieving a set of bruised and battered knuckles. Mo eyed him mischievously. "Postman's told us all about *you*."

"Yes," said Eric, "so Min was saying." He was about to add something further, on the subject of his underwear, when he realised neither woman was listening. Both were far more interested in inspecting Mo's hard-won piece of salvage.

"Will it be OK?" asked Min.

"What's to go wrong," Mo demanded, "with an ironing board? Especially this one. They made 'em to last in Mam's day."

As if to prove her point, she set about trying to put it up, swearing as it collapsed for the umpteenth time across her sturdily booted feet.

"She had the same trouble with a deck chair once at Rhyl," confided Min to an amused Eric.

Taking the ancient wooden ironing board from her sister, she put it up in one swift movement and gave it an experimental wobble with the flat of her hand.

"Will it do you, ma'am?" asked Mo with a grin.

"Ooh, yes," breathed Min. "It'll do just fine."

"My sister Min," said Mo, turning to Eric, "is worried about our being able to press our good clothes in time for the Summer Spectacular."

Eric stared. "But that's weeks away."

"Yes," piped up Min, "but we've got to find the *iron* yet, haven't we? Remind me, Mo," she added excitedly, "is it a steam iron?"

"Good grief it's not that old," said Mo. "Pretty sure it works off the electric."

***

"We clean up for visitors," warned Mo, her clumping footsteps following Eric down the path towards the back door of the cottage. "And we don't get many."

"Apart from you," added Min, "but we didn't know in time that you were coming."

"I'm sure it's fine," said Eric, chuckling. This false modesty was typical in his experience of women the world over. Protesting about the state of their homes when clearly they'd been polishing anything that couldn't run away since dawn.

He was looking forward to seeing the inside of a real farmhouse as depicted in all those glossy, Lifestyle magazines Imogen had been so fond of. Closing his eyes, he could already smell the musty tang of dried herbs and a lingering aroma of baking. There would be a long, scrubbed oak table too, he decided, a gleaming Aga and a stone floor you could see your face in … Mindful of the latter, he paused at a cast iron boot-puller and removed his shoes.

"I'd leave them on if I were you," said Mo. "Your socks'll get filthy."

Chuckling again, Eric pushed open the door and stepped down onto a flagstone floor bearing a layer of mud, grit and straw not unlike the farmyard itself.

"We did warn you," said Min cheerfully, as she and Mo put the ironing board in pride of place on top of a sack of cow food, which, in turn, stood between a bucket of bolts and a pile of machinery parts.

"Shall we have some cake?" Mo slapped her hands down her cords and sent up a cloud of dust which, Eric felt, would ground aircraft if word got out. Coughing, he watched the dust spiralling upwards to land softly on the cobwebs, festooning the smoke-blackened beams.

"That would be lovely," he said, unwittingly triggering a fingertip search of the kitchen for the cake tin.

It looked like taking a while so Eric tottered to the least rickety chair at the table. So much, he thought, for the rustic charms of a country kitchen. Yet, for all its ramshackle untidiness, there was a warmth and welcome about this cluttered, comfy room, the like of which Eric had never before experienced.

And, he mused, who really needed an oak table requiring hours of scrubbing when the wipe-down properties of yellow Formica spoke for themselves? Particularly if you wanted to use the table, as the sisters apparently did, to house a chunk of chain undergoing some sort of repair?

"That chain in your way?" called Min, lifting a horse rug from a window seat and peering underneath.

Eric smiled and rested his folded hands on the grimy links. "Not at all."

"Good," said Min. "We should have it back on the muck spreader by tomorrow."

Eric put his hands in his lap.

Finally the cake tin was unearthed and opened to reveal a couple of nub ends of cake, still wearing their High Street Bakery wrappers.

"Min and I are rubbish at baking," explained Mo.

And bang, thought Eric, goes another rural myth.

As the three of them chomped on the cake, the conversation turned to the subject of the pony and trap, with Mo fully endorsing the sisters' willingness to lend it. What was more, she added, the entire kit, including the harness currently piled on top of the fridge, would be decked out in garlands of flowers in honour of the occasion.

"The only problem might be," said Min rather fearfully, "the business of getting it up the road without the Williams Twins seeing it. They're dead against the Summer Spectacular and we'd rather not attract too much attention to our own involvement. We have to live next door to them, you see?"

Eric nodded, recognising that, in this context, half a mile's distance probably did constitute "next door".

"You're right to tread carefully," he agreed, "especially as, thanks to that listening device planted in Ms Harris's chest, we're pretty sure they now know all our plans for the big day, including using your pony and trap for the Carnival Queen." He thought for a moment then asked, "Not especially early risers are they, the Twins?"

Mo and Min shook their heads. "Definitely not," said Mo.

"So how about you bring the pony and trap over to my place as early as you can on the day? We could decorate it there."

Min beamed. "That would work," she said. "Thanks, Eric."

"By the way," said Eric tentatively, "I went up the Williams' drive a little way by accident on the way here. What a mess! Scrap metal and piles of rubbish everywhere. It must be pretty unpleasant living near that little lot."

The sisters exchanged glances. "Unpleasant and a bit scary," admitted Min. "We get lorries up and down all the time bringing scrap and other rubbish.

Then there are the boy racers going to buy bits off the cars."

"Makes you wonder," said Eric, "how the Twins ever get any farming done?"

Mo snorted. "They don't farm. At least not in the conventional sense." She glanced at Min as if seeking permission to continue. Min nodded and Mo went on, "Although we think they might have started growing some sort of cash crop in their big barn."

"That's right," Min put in. "They've blacked out the windows so we can't look in, but there seems to be some sort of harvest every now and again, resulting in dozens of courier vans going up there. Not *delivering*, according to one driver I spoke to, but *collecting* things, bound for all over the country – like a mail-order business being run from the farm."

"Wow," said Eric. Then a thought struck him. "Do you suppose that's why they're so against the Summer Spectacular, in case it brings a lot of strangers to the area? People who might report them for running an illegal scrap yard or even work out what they're producing in the barn?"

"I'd like to work that out, myself," said Mo grimly. "One of these days I'm going to sneak up there for a peek in that shed. I've a pretty good idea what I might find, too."

"Drugs, you mean?" whispered Eric.

Mo shrugged. "Make sense, wouldn't it?"

"Perhaps," giggled Min nervously, "that's why they've bought that old hotel on the back road out of town? Plenty of outbuildings there, and much easier access for the vans ..." She broke off as an indignant whinny sounded in the distance. "Heavens, I forgot Desmond."

"You go and see to him," said Mo, as Min flew out of the door. "I'll make us all a nice drop of squash."

***

Carrying a tray with a large jug of orange squash and some glasses, Eric and Mo followed Min up to the top of the yard.

Settling themselves on a plank, supported by two piles of breeze-blocks, they watched as Min attempted to get the horse to put one hairy foot on each of the four pairs of scales.

"Tut," said Mo. "I've *told* her that won't work."

Eric was forced to agree. Apart from the business of working out the weight distribution between the four points, he doubted the scales were up to it. Not that this was likely to matter because no sooner did Min get one foot on than Desmond took it off again. Preferring it seemed to stand on the feet of his handler.

"Leave that for now," called Mo. "Come and have a drink."

Min helped herself to a glass from the tray. "Do you think he's fat?" she asked, directing Eric's gaze towards the horse.

Eric pursed his lips. It must be hard, he thought, to be solely responsible for the nutritional needs of such a beast.

"Absolutely," he said. "Nice and fat."

"Hear that, Mo?" wailed Min. "Eric thinks he's fat. What shall we do?"

"Cut the bugger's rations again, that's what," said Mo.

109

There was a scuffle within the square of scales as the horse turned to glare at Eric through its fringe.

"Well," said Eric quickly. "When I say 'fat' I suppose what I really mean is 'thin'."

Desmond shook his head, still glaring. "Too little," he seemed to be saying, "and far, far too late."

"How's the squash?" asked Mo.

"Lovely." Eric tilted his glass to his lips again.

"Ooh, do look at Timmy," said Min as the dog waded into the duck pond, his tongue slapping the murky, green water. "Funny how he always wants to drink water from the pond rather than the tap, given it's exactly the same stuff."

Eric paused mid-slurp.

"Not quite the same," argued Mo. "The tap water's filtered."

Eric slurped on.

"Yes," said Min, "but only through one of your old vests."

Eric slid his glass back onto the tray.

"Well, ladies," he said, "delightful though it's been, I must love you and leave you. Thank you so much again for saying we can use the pony and trap."

Min blushed. "You're welcome, and you must come again … any time you like."

"I'll look forward to that," said Eric, meaning it.

***

Intent on finding his way to Pantybryn and back, Eric had quite forgotten his quest for a chunk of wood with which to make his new piece. Until he saw it.

Half hidden by undergrowth it was what other people might describe as a log. To Eric, though, it was the severed head of a goddess, weeping into the dried, dead tendrils of her hair.

Kneeling, he eased a waxy knot of ivy from her forehead and ran his fingers down her face. Barnacled with bark, her beauty had yet to be revealed. Except in the bare planes of her cheekbones, weathered by time to smooth, grey marble.

"Take me," she whispered, her words no more than a passing breeze. "Take me with you."

Eric scooped up his new piece, *A Goddess Weeping*, and ran for the van.

A nearby stand of trees swayed and moaned, calling their goodbyes in the fierce howl of loss. It was to be expected, Eric told himself. They were her parents, grandparents and perhaps her children. They would miss her.

CHAPTER TEN

"Here he comes, everyone," cried Hetty, as the bar door opened to reveal Eric, silhouetted against the evening sun, "the hero of the hour."

Not wishing to impede the progress of an advancing hero, Eric stepped aside.

"I meant you," chuckled Hetty.

"Me?"

Eric made his way to the bar, amid a barrage of back-slapping. He hadn't expected such a welcome merely for securing the loan of a pony and trap. Especially as, surely, no one could yet be aware he'd done so?

"Just a half for me," he said hastily as Hetty flipped a pint glass and aimed it at the tap.

"Half be damned." Hetty handed him the pint, waving aside his offer of payment. "Have that one on the Summer Spectacular. In fact, have half a dozen if you like. If anyone deserves it, you do, eh?"

"Do I?"

"Tsk," said Hetty. "Don't be modest, young Eric. Your next-door neighbour, Posh Godfrey, heard you giving the Twins what for the other evening."

"Did he?"

"Yep. Your first night in town, wasn't it? Seems the old boy was woken by Dilys Daydream come to make sure she'd turned his gas off, shortly before he heard you, plain as day yelling at the Twins somewhere outside."

"Was I?"

"According to Posh Godfrey, yes," said Hetty firmly. "And your bravery, Eric, has finally given this town enough backbone to come out in support of the Summer Spectacular!" She looked happily around the crowded bar. "Bet you never thought we'd get this sort of turnout, did you, for the band auditions?"

"No," admitted Eric. "But how come they've only just heard about my, er, bravery if it happened my first night in town?"

"Ah, well," said Hetty, "it's taken till now to get a new District Nurse following the departure of that treacherous Dilys Daydream who's taken a new post, by the way, in the Scottish Highlands. Called on Posh Godfrey today, she did, the new one, and he told her everything. Must have been bursting with the news, poor old sod. And not only with news, what with waiting this long for someone to help him to the commode."

"Right," said Eric, beginning to suffer from information overload, and still unable to recall the details of any act of of bravery on his part.

"Mind you," went on Hetty. "He was lucky to still have a commode, given the entire downstairs of his cottage had been mysteriously emptied, according to the new nurse, of everything from his Whatnot to his Welsh dresser."

Eric stared. The words Welsh dresser had started a sequence of images in his head, beginning with a darkened garden full of incongruous pieces of furniture and ending with his ill-advised run in with the Williams Twins.

"Of *course*," he said, snapping his fingers. "That was the night I got a little bit … er, a little bit p…"

"Plastered?" prompted one eavesdropper.

"Paralytic?" suggested another.

"Pissed?" offered Hetty.

"Well, all of the above, I suppose," said Eric. "But I was going to say *puzzled* by a Welsh dresser, in the doorway of what I initially took to be my cottage, but was, in fact, the cottage next door."

"Posh Godfrey's cottage, in other words?" suggested Hetty. "From which a quantity of furniture was later discovered to be missing? And where, presumably, you also encountered the Twins, probably in the very act of stealing it?"

"Must have been," mumbled Eric. "Now that I come to think of it ..."

"So," said Hetty, slowly, "all this time you've had first-hand evidence of criminal activity on the part of the Twins and you decided to sit on it?"

"I don't think I sat on the dresser," mumbled Eric as further details of the night in question drifted out of his subconscious, "but I might have sat on something else. An oak settle maybe?"

"Right, well, I'll run this by PC George. Ask him to investigate the matter based on your eye-witness account. Or," added Hetty, slyly, "perhaps I should say *pie-eyed* witness account?"

She had a point, thought Eric, his cheeks burning at the memory, if you could call it that, of his drunken escapade. He was sure it hadn't been his finest hour in spite of Posh Godfrey's claim to the contrary.

At that moment, Hetty's voice cut across his thoughts. "I hear you've successfully secured the loan of the pony and trap, eh, young Eric?"

"Ah, yes," said Eric, glad to be on safer ground. Then a thought struck him. "But how did you know?"

"Frank the Mail told me," said Hetty, rather to Eric's annoyance. Was the postman to beat him to everything? "He popped in teatime and said the sisters were more than willing to lend it. Still, well done you for making it official."

"Yes, well, I think it was the right thing to do," said Eric, slightly mollified, "because I was able to fix up some details the postman missed. Like the sisters bringing the trap over early on the morning of the event to be decorated at my place. They were anxious, you see, not to be spotted by the Williams Twins."

"Good point," said Hetty. "Great gals aren't they?" she added, with a twinkle. "Especially little Min?"

"They certainly are," agreed Eric, recalling what a good time he'd had at Pantybryn and realising how keen he was to have another. "I might have to go again, before the big day, just to finalise things."

"You'd be daft not to," agreed Hetty, "now that you know the way. I assume you did get there all right?"

"More or less," said Eric, squirming at the memory of his mix up with the farm names. He took another swig of slurry to steady his nerves. "And," he lowered his voice, "the Pugh Sisters have got some interesting observations, I can tell you, about various other things the Twins might be up to."

Hetty leant forwards, along with half a dozen other people scattered along the bar. "Yes?"

Eric eyed the eavesdroppers. Perhaps it wouldn't do, he thought, to go repeating the Pugh Sisters' suspicions in public.

He tapped the side of his nose. "Too many walls in here," he said quietly, "and even the people have ears." Frowning at his pint he put it down, just out of reach of his hand. "So, tell me about this grand turnout here this evening."

Hetty glanced around the bar. "Well, this lot are the overspill, not to say rejects, from Mel's auditions and band practice currently in progress in the upstairs long room."

"Ah," said Eric. "I suppose that explains the noise?"

Hetty nodded and they both paused to absorb the low hum, which had been bothering Eric all the way from the cottage, where he'd called to drop off the van and his new sculpture.

"Seems we're a tad oversubscribed," Hetty explained, "with didgeridoos."

Eric stared. "How are people going to march with those?"

"Your guess is as good as mine, young Eric, but Mel's keen to keep them in so I dare say they'll find a way."

"He certainly got his band project off the ground pretty quickly," said Eric, impressed.

"He did indeed. Assisted, I should add, by Mrs Jenks who despatched Arnold with his trike and a megaphone the minute Mel told her about the auditions."

Eric nodded. "Seems to have worked."

"Yes," said Hetty. "Everyone wants to be in a marching band."

"Regardless of ability, eh?" smiled Eric.

"You said it. We had some who could play but not march, and some who could march but not play."

"And those," said Eric, "are the rejects now overflowing your bar?"

"Bless you, no. Those were the successful applicants. This lot," Hetty waved a hand around the crowded room, "couldn't do either but I've given them a couple of beers on the house for showing willing."

"Smart thinking," said Eric.

"Yes, well, I wanted to keep people on side. There are a load more that failed to make the grade next door, too, in the snug. Wanted to know, they did, what else they could do towards the event. I suggested they start planning some games and stalls for the big day, being as you've got the vintage parade well in hand."

"Well, I wouldn't go so far ..." Eric stopped because Hetty wasn't listening, having disappeared below bar level, apparently searching for something on a shelf.

"Ah, here it is," she said, coming up for air and blowing dust off a clipboard. "Perhaps you'd like to do me a little favour, young Eric?"

"I'd be pleased to," said Eric, which wasn't strictly true. He'd promised himself an early night gazing at his *A Goddess Weeping*, whose half-formed face was haunting him even now.

"Great. Just pop next door, would you, and make a note of what everyone would like to do, what space they'll need and any special equipment we might have to get hold of."

Glad of an excuse to leave his practically untouched slurry on the bar, Eric went through to the snug where several little groups of people were engaged in drawing up plans and drafting signage for various activities. Eric smiled. Reluctant as he might have been to get involved in the Summer Spectacular it was heart-warming to see the little community pulling together in the pursuit of harmless fun.

Starting at the first table on the left Eric peered over the burly shoulder of the farmer who'd recently had a run in with his VAT return. Catching sight of a piece of paper lying in the centre of the table Eric blinked and blinked again. "Wring the duck's neck," he read aloud, "and win a prize."

" 'S'right," said the farmer.

Eric picked up the paper and tapped it. "We can't have this, can we?"

"Why not?" grunted the farmer. "Games of skill or chance, Hetty said. Lot of skill, wringing a duck's neck."

"But you can't be going to use live ducks?"

"Not for long," the farmer pointed out.

"Not at *all*," said Eric, emboldened by his sip of slurry. "I'm afraid we'll have to rethink this game."

"But we've made the poster now," said a small woman to the farmer's right, flapping a large sheet of paper and twiddling a magic marker.

Eric thought for a moment. "Tell you what," he said, "why don't you scrub out the 'W' at the front, turn the small 'r' into a capital and make it into a game of hoopla? *Ring* the duck's neck and win a prize? Preferably using ornamental ducks."

"Good idea," enthused the woman, air tracing with her tongue as she made the redundant "W" into a butterfly.

"Says you," muttered the farmer. "I'll have to kill the buggers meself, now."

Entering "VAT farmer – Hoopla" on his clipboard, Eric set off for the next table where plans were afoot for a game of Whack-a-mole. Bearing the ducks in mind, Eric feared the worst. With good reason as it turned out.

"They aren't supposed to be real moles," he explained to the evident disappointment of two strapping young labourers engaged in drawing complicated underground maps of where to put their traps. "We'll get you a Whack-a-mole device from … er … well, from a reputable Whack-a-mole device supplier, and it'll be just as much fun I assure you."

Eric then proceeded to a table in the corner where a couple were sitting so far apart they could only be married.

"And what's your game?" asked Eric, clearly startling the man of the partnership.

"How do you mean?" he asked with a guilty glance at his wife.

"I mean what game or stall did you have in mind for the Summer Spectacular?"

"We're going to do pin the tail on the donkey," said the woman, tight-lipped and gripping her handbag in her lap.

"Great," enthused Eric. Then a thought occurred to him. "Just as long as you're not intending to use a real donkey, eh?"

"'Course not," said the woman.

"Good," said Eric.

"Because we haven't got one." She jerked her head in the direction of her spouse. "We've got him, though, and a couple of old grey blankets I can stitch into an outfit."

Not sure if she was joking, and somehow doubting it, Eric entered their names on his clipboard. Then he tottered off to where a Church of Wales parson was being measured for a dunk–the–vicar contraption.

Here at least, thought Eric, looking at a set of blueprints lying on a table, was the promise of some good, old-fashioned fun. Perhaps they were unaware, though, that the dunking equipment could be hired?

"No need," he said, "to make your own machine. The Summer Spectacular can supply one."

"We'd prefer to make our own," said a dour-faced man, "with modifications."

"Such as?" asked Eric, intrigued.

"*Much* deeper water," chortled a small woman in a hat, "with an ice-making facility built in. Queuing up, they'll be, in the chapel to help build that."

Deciding that the most vital piece of kit the Summer Spectacular would need was a fleet of ambulances, Eric made a note to this effect on his clipboard.

He was about to head back to the bar when he caught a piquant aroma of lavender and mothballs rising above the general air of smoke and slurry.

Tracking the scent to two ladies sitting side by side sharing an orange juice, he plumped himself down at their table.

"Hello ladies," he said, embarrassed by a sudden stomach rumble reminding him that he'd had nothing to eat since his cake at Pantybryn.

"Young Eric sounds hungry," observed the thinner of the two ladies. "Have we anything we could give him, Ethel?"

The plumper lady dug in a copious holdall. "Only an acid drop, Ivy," she said coming up with a small brown paper bag. "That any good?"

She waved the bag at Eric who helped himself gratefully. Popping the acid drop into his mouth he found the taste instantly familiar. As was the warm, fuzzy glow that always seemed to accompany these particular sweets.

"Did these come from the market?" he asked, crunching.

Ethel looked at the unmarked bag. "How clever of you. Yes, we got them from the Williams boy, Darrell."

"The Williams boy?"

"Well, his surname isn't actually Williams," Ivy put in. "He's one of the Williams's right enough, but his surname's George, owing to a distant cousin of the Williams Twins having married a George. A Mr George that is, not a man called George. Do you see?"

"I think so," said Eric, who didn't really. "So his name's Darrell George?"

"Well, no," admitted Ethel, "because his first name isn't actually Darrell. Or at least, it is, but that isn't the name he uses. Like lots of people in Wales he uses his second name, which in his case is his *middle* name, and it's Sidney."

"Right," said Eric, groping for the light. "So he's known as Sidney George?"

"No. He's known as Sid the Sweets."

Eric clutched the table, unsure whether it was the logic or the acid drop making his head spin. Something, though, was troubling him from way back at the start of the conversation.

"Does everyone know who Sid the Sweets really is?" he asked, thinking of Min and her repeated expeditions to the market for acid drops. Unaware perhaps exactly who she was dealing with. "That he's a close relation of the Williams Twins?"

"I shouldn't think so," said Ethel, "because the Williams family tree is even more of a monkey puzzle than most. Took us ages to work it out, didn't it Ivy?"

Ivy nodded. "It's a hobby of ours," she explained, "tracing who's really who around here."

"Keeps you busy I should think?" suggested Eric. Then, realising he was still clutching his clipboard, he dragged his thoughts back to the matter at hand. "So, what would you like to do at the Summer Spectacular?"

"We'd like to have a stall, please, for our crafts," said Ivy.

"Lovely," beamed Eric. "And what crafts in particular?"

"We're hand-knitters," said Ethel. "Would you like to see some of our things?"

With that, she dug once again in the holdall and produced a selection of multicoloured items.

Eric stared at the woollies. "I see now," he said, "why you're called hand-knitters. You actually knit *hands*. Lots of little matching pairs of them …"

"No, young Eric," said Ivy gently, "we knit gloves." Turning aside, she made round-the-twist signs at her companion.

And who could blame her, thought Eric, excusing himself and stepping to the street door where he took a few lungfuls of pure, clean air in an effort to clear his increasingly muddled head. Perhaps some food would help, he thought. A nice warm salad, maybe, with croutons.

Upon enquiring, he was informed that salad, to Hetty, was a dish best served cold and over her dead body in a pub. She did, however, deign to sell him a pie. He'd barely finished this when a commotion on the staircase signified the arrival of Mel's band.

First to pop through the door was Ms Harris wearing a skin-tight tunic and a tuba. Spotting Eric, she hastened to explain that she'd only been trying the tunic on for size and had been unable to get it off again. The same, it seemed, went for the tuba. No expert in the deployment of brass instruments about the person, Eric was nonetheless convinced it shouldn't really be pinning both her arms to her sides. Fascinated, he asked how she planned to remove the tunic, or the tuba, for bed.

Ms Harris turned wistful eyes towards Mel, bobbing in the throng behind her. "I have hopes," she murmured, "of being relieved of both before the night's out."

After helping Ms Harris to a seat and a drink with a very long straw, Eric sought out the actor.

"Hello," he said and grinned, noticing for the first time that Mel was wearing a pair of dungarees, identical to his own. "What's with the strides?"

"Great, aren't they? I was in Mrs Jenks' shop earlier, publicising my band auditions, and Arnold told me how keen you'd been to buy some. If they're good enough for Eric, I thought, they're good enough for me. And they're super comfy, aren't they?"

As he said this, Mel put both hands in his pockets, apparently making some adjustments in his undergarments.

"The dungarees are, yes," admitted Eric. Eyeing the fidgeting Mel, he added, "Arnold didn't by chance persuade you into anything else, did he, while you were there? Some other garments I'm supposed to have shown an interest in?"

Mel took a step towards Eric and lowered his voice. "As a matter of fact he did," he said, giving things another tweak. "These tweed knickers. Don't know how you put up with them, though. Itch like anything, don't they? Any tips, old man?"

"Stick with it," Eric advised. "You'll get used to them."

***

"Like to come up," asked Mel, "for the second half of band practice?"

Eric hesitated, then caught the look of pleading in his friend's eyes. "OK," he said, "but I can only stay for a little while. I've got … er, something I ought to be doing at home."

"Great." Mel pulled a referee's whistle from the bib of his dungarees and blew it. "Back to work, boys and girls," he boomed.

Anything less like boys and girls, thought Eric, making his way up the stairs at a snail's pace to match his fellow climbers, he'd yet to see. Most of the band members appeared to be at least in their seventies. Even the didgeridoo players, although brightly dressed, were hardly in the first flush of youth

Eric couldn't help wondering whether Mel had done the right thing in rejecting some of the younger applicants. It could take a week to get these shuffling musicians even halfway round the town. And that was without some of them needing spare breath with which to blow their instruments.

Taking the actor aside, he outlined his concerns.

Mel nodded. "You're right but believe me the ones I turned down were beyond help. Candidates for rotten fruit all of them." He glanced around the room. "At least this lot can play a little. And if we still get the rotten fruit, well, that's another advantage, isn't it, of using the oldies? Some of them were in the war so they're used to marching under fire."

This seemed to Eric to be a rather defeatist attitude but he kept his thoughts to himself, merely murmuring that maybe they'd find an injection of new blood before Midsummer's Day.

As he said this, the door to the stairs opened to admit a bevy of beauties the sight of which rendered Eric speechless. Apparently the same went for Mel who was goggling unashamedly. Mentally reaching, Eric suspected, for his equity card and cigarette packet with which to impress the half-dozen or so teenage girls dressed like cheerleaders and clutching kazoos.

Even in the white heat of the moment the girls' choice of instrument struck an uneasy chord with Eric. "Damn," he said. "They've got kazoos. Hetty said we weren't to have those, didn't she?"

"Ye-es," replied Mel thoughtfully, "but that was in relation to the marching bands I wanted to get from the valleys. Don't see how she can object to home-grown kazoo players, do you?"

"But are they home-grown?"

"Oh, yes," said Mel. "At least I think so. I'm pretty sure two of them are Sally Stitch's girls, Eryl and Deryl. So it'll be OK won't it old man?"

Hearing the note of desperation in his friend's voice, Eric smiled. "'Course it will. I'd go for it if I were you."

"Welcome," said Mel, stepping into the path of the advancing beauties. "Welcome one and all to my happy band." He looked from Eryl to Deryl. "But where, I wonder, is Cheryl?"

The door opened again and Eric lost his heart, his soul and very nearly his bottom jaw. For there in the doorway, beautifully balanced on the stunning shoulders of Cheryl Stitch, was the missing face of his *A Goddess Weeping*.

***

"There go some more," giggled Terry as the group of teenagers entered the White Hart followed, at a distance, by Cheryl Stitch.

Alerted to the band auditions by Arnold's trike-mounted megaphone, the brothers were parked across the street from the pub washing down a twelve pack of lager with a few chips.

Tony burped loudly, tossed his empty wrapper aside and popped another can. "Silly arses," he remarked, laughing. "Little do they know, eh?"

Wiping his mouth with a stiff and slightly green tissue, Terry folded his own chip packet and stowed it neatly in the passenger foot well. "Little indeed," he agreed. Returning the tissue to the breast pocket of his jacket and tugging it into a greasy peak, he added, "'Spect they're wondering, mind, why we haven't gone steaming in there, yet, putting a stop to all their preparations, but …"

"Je-sus," interrupted Tony. "Have you got a point, Terry, or have you got a point?"

Multiple choice had never been Terry's long suit. "Er, how do you mean?" he hedged.

"Well, think about it. We *ought* to be making a song and dance about it, oughtn't we? Else they'll smell a rat for sure. I vote we get in there, right now, and do just that."

"Chuck some weight about?" asked Terry, meaning Tony's.

"Exactly."

"Great." Terry glanced down a neighbouring alleyway. "I need the loo first, though," he confided. "Funny taste there was on that fifth tin of lager."

***

In Eric's kitchen, unaware of the tidal wave their sisters had been causing at the pub, Beryl and Meryl were trying to stem two of their own.

Firstly, what appeared to be the entire contents of the local reservoir had burst out of Eric's washing machine. Secondly, an ever expanding pool of varnish was oozing all over his stripped pine tabletop.

Unfortunately the girls had been locked, for some time now, in the business of apportioning blame at the expense of the salvage operation.

"Washing machines," said Beryl, belatedly wading to the scullery for the mop, "don't just flood of their own accord."

"Are you saying it's my fault?" demanded a red-faced Meryl, pulling a length of kitchen towel from Eric's roll and dabbing at the varnish.

"Well you loaded it, didn't you?"

Meryl tapped her foot then stopped as a soapy swell threatened to capsize Beryl. "Yes, but you could have checked it, couldn't you, if you were so worried?"

"I wasn't worried, not to start with, but any fool could have seen that overloading it wasn't going to help, especially when it came to having to get all that wet stuff out and haul it down the garden."

"But I didn't *know* when I loaded it that the water wasn't going to drain away. And it seemed fine to start with, after I twiddled the knob and got it going."

"Exactly," said Beryl quietly, "after *you* twiddled the knob."

The sisters faced one another across the churning foam.

"Well," said Meryl, rallying, "one thing I'm definitely not to blame for is this blasted varnish going everywhere. Who was doing a victory dash round the table when we finished the last of the luggage tags?"

"We both were." Beryl's voice cracked as she said this, remembering how well things had been going at that point. All the varnishing done and the miniatures outside drying. All the tags finished and stashed in the biscuit tin back at the tent…

"Er, right," said Meryl, "so we were." Then a thought struck her. "But who left the lid off the varnish tin, eh?"

There was no answer to that, thought Beryl, squeezing the mop into the sink. Changing tack, she said, "At least I'm cleaning things up over here. Not like some people just shoving varnish round and round a tabletop."

"Feel free to try it yourself if you're so clever. This stuff's like a mixture of engine oil and golden syrup, with a dash of Super Glue for good measure."

"I don't know why you don't just paint it in," said Beryl as if she'd been harbouring this brilliant idea all along, "if it's *so* hard cleaning it up?"

"Genius!" Meryl abandoned the kitchen roll and grabbed the varnish brush. Two minutes later she stood back to admire her handiwork.

"There" said Beryl, paddling over to join her. "You'd never know we'd done it, would you?"

"*We* didn't do it," said Meryl under her breath.

***

Arriving home, Eric collected his *A Goddess Weeping* from the back of the van and let himself into the cottage. As soon as he set foot in his kitchen he realised something was wrong. Flying like a feather in a force-ten gale, he didn't stop till he hit the sink. Ricocheting off that he then back-pedalled furiously before crashing to the floor. Worse, he'd no choice but to let go of his *A Goddess Weeping* who turned two backward somersaults and a half twist before slamming down on his head.

Coming round a few moments later Eric surveyed the slick, soapy surface of the lino inches from his face. He was never going to be able to stand up on that. Swivelling onto his knees he crawled up a chair, sat on it and laid his throbbing head on the kitchen table.

***

"Damn," said Meryl, watching with Beryl from the darkness beyond the kitchen window "Another ten minutes, that floor would have been dry."

"Not to mention the varnish on the tabletop," said Beryl.

CHAPTER ELEVEN

At midnight that night, the town clock struck thirteen, in spite of Arnold's best efforts earlier in the day with a spanner and an oil can. The old man counted the bongs and hoped no one else was awake to hear them.

It was such a shame, he thought, gazing bleakly around his attic bedroom high above the shop. "Keeper Of The Clock" ought to be a grand and revered position but the cantankerous old timepiece was making him an object of ridicule. He'd said as much to Mrs Jenks, who'd volunteered him for the job some weeks back. Predictably, she'd told him to stop being a wimp and to get back up there and sort it out.

Arnold had obeyed but had been unable, so far, to solve any of the clock's eccentricities. Apart from the mysteries of the thirteen bongs, there was the business of it going slower on some of its four faces than on others. This was especially confusing for users of the White Hart who enjoyed two different views of the clock tower from the pub's front and rear entrances. Making it perfectly possible for a drinker to enter the Hart by the front door at twelve noon and eventually leave, via the back, a full two hours earlier.

A couple of streets away Eric slept on, seemingly oblivious to the wrong bongs of Arnold's clock. His face twitched, reflecting the bad dreams he was experiencing in the wake of his accident. From the teasel-headed troops of the tank regiment, to legless landladies; deviant devisers of macabre carnival games to avenging agents and sinister twins, everyone was after him. And he couldn't run away because he was stuck firmly in a set of stocks. Trapped and at the mercy of his pursuers.

All this, however, was merely the harmless stuff of Eric's imagination.

***

In London, Miranda had just received some excellent news. "That would be wonnerful," she said as the electronic clock on the wall of the wine bar clicked over to midnight. "Simply wonnerful."

Raising her glass, she waved it in the blurred faces of her companions, whilst vaguely wondering why there appeared to be two of them. Her Saturday night appointment for dinner and drinks, which had turned out not to include dinner, had been with one journalist only: Steve Martin from *Hi There!* magazine who, joy of joys, wanted to do an interview with Eric. Closing one eye she finally achieved single vision. "Eric will be thrilled."

"So he should be," said Steve. "It isn't everyone we invite to take part in our Chez Yeux series."

"Says you," chortled Miranda, burying her nose once again in the wild flower bouquet of her Gewürztraminer. This unpronounceable plonk had been Steve's recommendation for her third bottle and so far she couldn't fault it.

"Chez Yeux," corrected Steve. "And you'll tell Eric, won't you, that we'll need the biggest reception room he's got because we'll be bringing the full lighting rig? Plus we'll want space for the make-up teams to work, rest areas for the photographers, as well as a quiet space for myself and a couple of PAs?"

"Well, I'll tell him, but at this rate he may need a bigger house. From what I gather he's basically got an up one two, down one two. Er, I should say an up up, two two, down …" She gave it up. "A very small cottage."

Steve frowned. "I'd prefer the location to be authentic, of course. Give our readers an insight into Eric's home life and surroundings. The little things that make him tick as an artist and as a man." He brightened. "But then again, what they don't know won't hurt them, eh? Recce it, Miranda, and let me know if we need to hire somewhere larger."

"Righty-ho ho ho," said Miranda happily.

"Oh, and we'll need Eric's address ASAP to diarise transport. Plus the crew will need overnight accommodation, meals, drinks, use of a local gym if poss. All of which I guess I can leave my people to talk to your people about?"

Miranda nodded like a dog on a parcel shelf but she failed, for two reasons, to meet the journalist's eyes. One was that she still hadn't got an address for Eric because the name of his village didn't appear on any of her maps. The other was that, in spite of representing the hottest artistic property of the decade, she hadn't yet acquired any "people". Steve, however, didn't need to know either of these things.

"My people report to me," she said firmly. "So best your people talk to me and I talk to mine then back to yours."

"Er, OK," said Steve. "And you're sure Eric will be up for the interview? I mean, you and I both know it's what his career needs right now: a four-page spread in the most prestigious magazine on the planet, pandering to an art world desperate for anything Bagnall. But it'll be a big invasion of his privacy."

"Privacy schmivacy," said Miranda turning her empty wine bottle upside down and discovering it wasn't. Slapping Gewürztraminer from her lap she waved to the barman who waved back and winked.

Later, in the taxi, Miranda studied her companion. Was it the barman, she wondered, or the journalist? Taking a closer look she discovered it was neither, merely her own reflection in the window.

Good, she thought, relaxing back in her seat. She could do without any distractions tonight. She wanted to revel in the glory of her first ever *Hi There!* interview and go through her shoe collection. Already she suspected it contained nothing remotely suitable for Eric's big day, and that she'd need to buy some more. Not to mention a new two piece. Something in apple green, perhaps, to complement her russet curls.

But first of all, she told herself sternly as she clambered out of the taxi and made to pay the driver, who told her to get back in again because he'd only stopped at the lights, she had to find an address for Eric. It would be embarrassing to have to admit that her high-profile client was missing somewhere in West Wales. To say nothing of the fact that she could hardly recce his house for the interview without having the vaguest idea where it was.

At her apartment building, exhaustion struck along with the bullet-proof glass of the communal front door. One of these nights, she thought, she'd remember to open it before stepping through. She did so now and fell flat on her face in the foyer.

***

Unlike Miranda, Beryl knew perfectly well where Eric was and wished she didn't. She was desperate for sleep but every time she closed her eyes the entire Eric fiasco whirled in her mind like the spinning wheels of a fruit machine.

She shuddered now, as three more mismatched pictures clunked down in a row.

The first showed Eric, aquaplaning on his kitchen floor. The second, his bit of firewood hitting him squarely on the bonce. In the third, Eric was slumped in his chair with his head glued to his tabletop.

No one, she reasoned, could fail to suspect intruders after that little lot. And, daft as he was, surely even Eric wouldn't take falling over lying down?

"We've really come unstuck this time," she thought gloomily. Assuming Eric ever did it couldn't be long before he made a full-scale search of his house and grounds, desperate to find the mindless vandals responsible for washing his floor and re-varnishing his table. And when that happened, she realised with a jolt, she and Meryl would be sitting ducks. Unable to run away with all that wet washing to carry … unable to leave it behind because every last item had their name tags in …

Propping herself up on one elbow, she shook her sister, keen to share this latest anxiety. She shook, however, in vain.

At last, exhausted with worrying, Beryl's fair head hit her pillow and she too fell sound asleep. So much so that she was unaware when, a few hours later, the cool, bare feet of dawn crept into the tent to dance on her upturned cheek.

***

Someone else unaware of the dancing feet of dawn was Eric, who slept right though it, his nightmares worsening by the minute. He awoke, bathed in sweat, some time around ten. His initial relief at finding himself not in the stocks was replaced by one of horror, when he discovered that his kitchen table had turned overnight into a Venus fly trap with him, the hapless insect, caught in its sticky embrace. Attached to the table by his head, all he could do was wiggle his upper body until, with a hideous sucking noise, he broke free.

Breathing hard, he sat for a moment eyeing the imprint of his right ear on a background which gradually morphed from the tacky interior of a flesh-eating plant into the harmless surface of his stripped pine table.

His gaze travelled to his own limbs. Surprised to find that, far from the multi-jointed, exoskeletal structure he'd imagined, they were in fact the ordinary arms and legs of Eric Bagnall, severely concussed artist.

Something was different though, he thought, swaying on his chair and drifting in and out of an uneasy consciousness. Surely the table was shinier than he remembered it? As for the floor, he'd never seen it so clean. Befuddled as he was, Eric was certain he'd neither washed his floor nor shined his tabletop at any point since arriving in Landoobrey.

He glanced around, remembering all the other odd little things that had happened recently. His diminishing toiletries, for example, and his towel left damp and crumpled on the bathroom floor. The more he thought about it, the more convinced he became that he wasn't alone in his cottage. It was time, he decided, to make a phone call and rid himself of his troublesome intruders once and for all.

First, though, he had to rescue his *A Goddess Weeping,* who lay where she'd fallen, slumped against the skirting board at the far side of the room. Standing up, he slid one foot forwards like a doubtful skater on a thawing pond. Reassured by the judder of rubber on the now dry floor, he picked up his pace and his piece. Turning her over, he felt a frisson of excitement as the sublime features of Cheryl Stitch hovered on the gnarled wood like a hazy reflection on a choppy sea.

Clutching his sculpture Eric made a quick detour to the freezer before settling on his sofa to make his call.

***

" 'Lo?" said the voice at the other end of the line.

"That you, Hetty?" asked Eric, adjusting the bag of frozen peas he was wearing like a tam-o'-shanter on his throbbing head.

"Whose number did you ring?"

"Well, yours, of course."

"Oh. I expect it's me then."

Eric grinned, remembering the state he'd found Hetty in on his first morning in town. "Late night?"

"Not so much late as lively, young Eric, and not in a good way."

"Tell me about it," murmured Eric.

"Well," said Hetty. "Just after you'd gone we had a visit from the Williams Twins, tanked up, and seemingly determined to cause a humdinger of a fight."

"Oh dear," said Eric, his own troubles momentarily forgotten. "No damage I hope?"

Hetty sighed. "A few bruises and a bit of my best furniture, only fit for firewood. Just a normal Saturday night, of course, in that respect. Point was, the Twins came to deliver a warning: to forget about the Summer Spectacular or else. Spouting off again about how we don't welcome strangers here, which didn't go down too well with those two labourers working on the Whack-a-mole game. What with them being strangers themselves, I'm afraid they took it personal. All kicked off it did, big time."

"Sorry to hear that, Hetty," said Eric. Then being a stickler for accuracy, even in his present state, he added, "But when I said 'tell me about it' I didn't mean '*tell me about it*' as such."

"What did you mean then?"

"Just that my own night was quite lively as well. In fact, that's really why I've rung."

"Oh. Well, fire away, young Eric. How can I help?"

"I wondered if you could recommend a good vicar? There was one in the pub last night but I didn't get his name."

"Gosh, you're a fast worker," said Hetty, her broad grin evident in her voice. "Who's the lucky lady, I wonder?"

"What lucky lady?"

"Oh come on Eric, don't be coy. There are a couple of candidates to my knowledge. The question is, has this person got one sister or four?"

"Eh?" said Eric.

Hetty sighed. "You aren't planning on getting married, then?"

"Good grief, no."

"So what do you want a vicar for?"

"To exorcise my poltergeists," whispered Eric.

"Exercise your what?"

"Not ex*er*cise. God knows, the wretched things get enough of that. No, I need someone to ex*or*cise my poltergeists."

There was a pause. "Not up to your old tricks again last night, were you? Overindulging in the slurry?"

"You know perfectly well I barely touched a drop."

"Got a bang on the head then, did you, or some other cranial mishap?"

"As a matter of fact," said Eric with dignity, "I *did* get a bang on the head. Due, I suspect, to the poltergeists running amok in my house. *Using* things, Hetty, like my best soap and my towel. To say nothing of making my kitchen floor all wet and putting some sort of sticky, shiny substance all over my tabletop."

"And you think this is the work of poltergeists?"

"Well, what else can it be? I keep my doors locked, which rules out human intruders. And Mum always used to say the cottage had more spirits in it than your pub. Although, thinking about it, she might have meant the drinks cabinet …"

Just then an icy finger touched the nape of Eric's neck. He was about to share this with Hetty when another touched his forehead and he realised it was only his bag of peas melting. Other things, though, weren't so easily explained away… "Trust me, Hetty, all the evidence points to some mischievous little imps using my home as their own."

"You might be right there, young Eric," said Hetty, thoughtfully, "but I think, before we ask the vicar to go charging about with the holy water, a word with Mrs Jenks is called for."

"Mrs Jenks?" echoed Eric.

"Mm. I'm meeting her later, as it happens, at the Sunday Cinema Club in the village hall. Funnily enough, we're having *Poltergeist* followed by *The Exorcist*. How about you meet us there after the pictures, unless you fancy the films yourself?"

"Can't say I do, to be honest," replied Eric, for whom the programme was a sight too close to home.

"OK. Well if you pop over to the hall about nine o'clock, you can run us both back to your house and we can see what's what?"

"Right," said Eric wearily. "If you really think that'll help."

***

Eric put the phone down and regarded the comfy cushions of his sofa. He really ought to start work on his new piece, but concentration seemed impossible under the circumstances. Perhaps he could just curl up with a back copy of *Art Now* instead?

Digging in his box of magazines, almost the first thing Eric came across was a bundle of postcards sent home over the years by his globe-galloping parents. Their current 'retirement' with the Guardians of Eternal Peace had followed decades of live-in jobs, tenanting and managing pubs, clubs and hotels throughout the world. Always making sure, of course, that they returned to their beloved Landoobrey at least once a year to recharge their batteries. But, Eric reminded himself, the cottage was his now and no way was it big enough for the three of them. If mum and dad wanted to visit the area again, they'd need to find somewhere else to stay.

Putting the cards back in the box, he spotted his diary. So that's where it went, he thought, taking in back to the sofa with him and opening it at the ribboned page of his last entry. "Off to Landoobrey!" it said. There followed a detailed list of "Things To Do Before I Go". Eric smiled wryly. Was it only a mere five days ago that he'd abandoned the relative sanity of his old life for the sheer bedlam of his new one?

***

Towards evening, Eric awoke to find his diary on his chest and his bag of liquefied peas, sweating on his neck. What was it, he wondered, about Landoobrey that made every nap result in such discomfort? He'd little time, however, to dwell on the question because he needed to get to the village hall to pick up Hetty and Mrs Jenks.

He had no trouble spotting the pair emerging from the double doors. Hetty's Stetson was hard to miss, as was the white PVC cap which Mrs Jenks had donned for the occasion.

Half an hour later, he was back at the cottage, reeling from the theory put forward by his passengers, en route, that he'd almost certainly been harbouring two escaped schoolgirls in a tent in his garden. The theory was given weight, according to Hetty, by Mrs

Jenks having sold the girls a tin of varnish on the occasion of Eric's last visit to the shop. Varnish such as had subsequently turned up all over Eric's tabletop.

Reminded of that day in the shop, Eric was forced to agree that this was a valuable clue. Especially taken in conjunction with the scent of his very own brand of soap, borne on the breeze from the shop door.

He was also reeling from the journey itself. Or the "van drive from hell", as he was inclined to call it.

Neither woman had wanted to sit in the back, so Mrs Jenks had perched on Hetty's lap in the passenger seat, effectively blinding Eric to oncoming traffic. The pair of them had then proceeded to argue at every junction as to whether it was safe for him to pull out.

Lurching away from the final crossroads, Eric had stopped, halfway over the white line, confused by Hetty saying "Go!" and Mrs Jenks saying "Better not" due to the artic coming the other way. He'd resigned himself to the crash, when Mrs Jenks had identified the oncoming lorry as a bus stop, remarking that perhaps she ought to have worn her glasses.

Somehow they'd arrived in one piece and repaired to the veg patch, which both women favoured as being the most likely hideaway for Meryl and Beryl Stitch.

Eric looked around. "There's no one here," he said, "is there?"

"Not now," admitted Mrs Jenks, peering under the leaves of a gnarled old kohlrabi as if two girls might somehow have concealed themselves there, "but that's not to say they haven't been here. And if they have, they'll have left traces. Is there nothing different, young Eric, from how you remember it?"

"Well, I don't really remember it very well from when I was here as a boy," confessed Eric, "and I haven't set foot in the garden since I came back." He looked around the weed-infested, barren space, once the abundant domain of his parents, gardening erratically in between visits to the pub. "I suppose, though, that this patch of weeds looks a bit flat compared to the rest of it."

Hetty and Mrs Jenks followed his gaze. "I believe you're right," said Hetty. "And what's this?" She bent inelegantly at the waist, scrutinising a single, narrow indentation running from the flattened weeds to the overgrown garden path.

"Looks like a wheel track," said Mrs Jenks, angling her cap towards the ground.

Not to be outdone, Eric also stooped so that the three of them resembled a small flock of ostrich intent on a burrowing grub.

"Do you see it, young Eric?" asked Hetty, standing up and straightening her Stetson. "What do you think made that?"

"A unicycle?" Eric suggested, and instantly wished he hadn't.

Hetty clapped a hand to her forehead. "Why didn't we think of that, Mrs Jenks? A unicycle. Obvious mode of transport, isn't it, for two girls, a mountain of luggage and a tent?"

Mrs Jenks tittered. "And how lucky for them that Eric's mam and dad liked to keep a unicycle handy on the veg plot. But then again, what dedicated gardener doesn't?"

Eric ignored the sarcasm. "OK, it probably wasn't a unicycle." He thought for a moment. "But something they *did* like to keep handy was the wheelbarrow, bought from your shop, I believe, Mrs Jenks. And it isn't here now, is it?"

"Can't see one," agreed Hetty, prowling around. "But would a wheelbarrow have survived thirty-odd years outdoors?"

"Would've done if it was one of mine," said Mrs Jenks staunchly. "I remember that batch coming in. Best quality they were."

Eric gazed at Mrs Jenks. Did she remember every single item she'd ever sold? Then something in the corner of the plot caught his eye. He hurried towards it. "It wouldn't have been completely out of doors," he said, waving an ancient tarpaulin, which promptly came apart in his hands. "If I remember rightly, they used to keep it under this."

"That's not one of mine," put in Mrs Jenks. "Never had a tarpaulin go bad on me yet, I haven't."

"Well," said Hetty. "I think we've identified the getaway vehicle right enough. Fled those girls have, along with Eric's barrow. Er, I hope you're not going to think about pressing charges, young Eric, when we eventually catch up with them?"

"Good grief, no," said Eric. "What's a rotten old wheelbarrow?" Seeing Mrs Jenks's hurt expression, he added, "good quality though it undoubtedly was. As long as the girls are OK, eh?"

"Couple of survivors them two are," said Mrs Jenks. "Brought up the hard way on left-over chips and run-over meat. I dare say they'll manage, wherever they've gone."

CHAPTER TWELVE

Blinkered as he'd been on his "van drive from hell", Eric had failed to spot Beryl, standing at the gate to the chip shop yard. Beryl, however, hadn't failed to spot him.

"Guess what I've just seen," she called, making her way back to the tent and crawling inside.

Meryl tied the last of the luggage tags to its corresponding miniature and sat back on her heels. "Give up. What?"

"Eric, speeding off up the road with Hetty the Hart and Mrs Jenks stacked on the passenger seat of his van. What d'you suppose they're up to?"

"Looking for Eric's intruders, perhaps? Even he must have sussed that someone had been in his cottage yesterday. It'd be typical of Hetty and Mrs Jenks to offer to help him hunt down the culprits."

"Come to think of it," said Beryl, squatting alongside her sister, "they did look a bit like a posse. Good job we moved when we did, I suppose?" She ducked as a bowlful of peelings splattered on the roof of the tent, "even if it does mean living in a compost heap."

"You got that right, pardner," drawled Meryl, spinning and firing an imaginary pair of pistols, determined, it seemed, to pursue the posse theme. "Reckon we broke camp and circled the wagons just in time."

Beryl sighed. "It's a shame, though, because in spite of everything, it was lovely living at the cottage, wasn't it? All mod cons and no slops?"

"Yes it was," agreed Meryl, holstering the pistols. "But we're stuck here I'm afraid until the money comes through." She began to wrap each labelled miniature in a square of toilet paper before placing it in a cardboard box. "And that's always assuming we can beat Eric to it when the cash arrives in his postbox."

Beryl froze. "We will, won't we? It'd be dreadful if the money fell into the wrong hands after all our hard work."

"As long as we get up early and check his postbox *every* day before school, we'll be fine."

"Good." Beryl ducked again as another bowlful hit. "That cash can't come soon enough if you ask me."

"It won't come *at all* unless we get this lot posted off. So, if you've nothing better to do, you might see about writing the covering letter whilst I finish packing?"

Seizing a biro and her school exercise book, Beryl said thoughtfully, "I don't know why we can't just ask for the money to be sent here, to the flat, instead of to Eric's place?"

Meryl paused in the act of adding another layer of sculptures to the box. "You really haven't thought that one through, have you Beryl?"

"Haven't I?"

"Clearly not. In case you've forgotten, the flat doesn't have an outside postbox like Eric's. It has a letterbox in the door, which Mam checks every morning. And Mam getting her hands on all that money doesn't bear thinking about. Besides, how suspicious is it going to look to Eric's agent, finding a different address on his letter to the one she's bound to have on his file?"

Beryl blushed. "Sorry, Meryl. I wasn't thinking straight. You still reckon, do you," she added, nervously, "that I should be the one to write the letter?"

"Yep. Your handwriting's much more grown-up than mine. I should have a practice first, though, at making it look as neat as you can."

"OK." Beryl turned her attention once more to her exercise book, and noticed her geography homework, which had yet to be copied out in best and handed in.

She sighed. It was so hard keeping up with everything in the tent. Perhaps they could go up to the flat later and she could do it there? It might be quite nice, mightn't it, to see Mam again?

Turning the page, she penned a few experimental words until she felt comfortable to begin. "Do I put 'Dear Ms Barton', do you think," she asked, "or 'Dear Miranda'?"

***

Having despatched their precious parcel, first thing Monday morning, with its covering letter, ostensibly from Eric, asking for the cash by return of post, Meryl and Beryl spent the next few days in a state of happy anticipation.

They'd only been able to afford a second-class stamp but the postmistress seemed confident the parcel *could* reach London within a day or two given fair weather and a following wind. And, as Beryl kept reminding herself, the weather *had* continued fair, even a little breezy at times, which seemed an excellent omen. Having calculated that a forty-eight-hour turnaround was therefore possible, if highly unlikely, she and Meryl had begun checking Eric's postbox every morning.

Creeping away empty-handed again on the Thursday, Beryl found the strain of rifling through someone else's postbox beginning to tell on her. In fact, she almost envied Eric, tucked up in his little bed without a care in the world.

***

Far from not having a care in the world, Eric felt his world crumbling around him as he wrestled to begin his new piece. He'd lost count of the times he'd sharpened his chisels and arranged them in ascending order of size on the parlour sideboard, only to feel compelled to put them in descending order instead.

In the end, he'd decided to stand them all up in the rack designed for the purpose, which he'd finally run to earth in a box labelled "Light Bulbs". But he still couldn't bring himself to make that vital first cut.

Repeated visits to the sitting room to gaze at his photo of *A Deep Depression in Driftwood* hadn't helped. Neither, he had to admit, had the frequent breaks he'd taken, driving out into the countryside viewing items of interest for his parade.

Now it was Thursday, and he was no nearer starting his piece than he had been first thing Monday morning. Not only that, but the next Summer Spectacular meeting was scheduled for this evening. And, while he now had an impressive list of ancient farm machinery pledged for the big day, he still hadn't visited Moggs Morgan about the all-important steamroller. Lately the property of the Tarmac and now the pride and joy of Moggs, it was to be the centrepiece of Eric's parade.

Flinging down his tools, he grabbed his jacket and headed for the hills.

***

"Moggs Morgan: Sheepdog Puppies and Driveways Tarmacced" said the hand-painted sign on top of the mountain.

Eric slammed on his brakes. He'd been driving along with his head in the clouds, he realised. Well, not just his head. All of him, including the van, due to the sheer altitude of the single-track road leading to Moggs Morgan's farm.

Following the large arrow on the sign, Eric turned off onto a predictably well-made drive with the suggestion of a hard shoulder on its left-hand side. It made a welcome change, he thought, cruising the smooth tarmac, for his battered sump and a suspension weakened by all the other farm tracks he'd tackled this week.

Arriving in a similarly well-surfaced yard, Eric parked beneath another sign saying "Visitors' Parking. Please Report to Reception".

This, to judge by the logo, had started out life as the property of the local council. It had also, Eric concluded, been erected as a joke. There was nothing remotely resembling a reception area among the dilapidated buildings surrounding the farmyard.

In fact, he was hard put to identify anything that might even constitute human habitation. The only structure that wasn't evidently animal housing was a small, two-storey building, semi-detached with a cowshed. But the cowshed part was in far better

149

condition, thought Eric, getting out of the van and going over for a closer look. It at least had four standing walls; a luxury not enjoyed by the house itself, the front elevation of which had fallen outwards, to land in a sprawling heap at the edge of the yard. The resulting hole meant a large portion of the house was open to the elements, in spite of someone's best efforts with some plastic fertiliser bags, tacked over the gaps.

The front door, however, remained in splendid isolation. Balanced in its rotting frame, it looked incapable of withstanding such a thing as a knock, so Eric coughed politely. When that failed to attract the householder's attention, he scaled the pile of stones and poked his head between two fertiliser bags.

It was the wrong thing to do, he realised, as the man sitting at a table in front of a smoke-blackened range leapt backwards, knocked his chair into the ashy grate and rocketed forwards again.

"Sorry," said Eric, unsure whether to retreat or advance, and deciding to do neither until the man had recovered. "Er, anyone home?"

It was a lame question but it got a response. "Anyone home, boy?" shouted the man, making big tufts of cotton wool bounce in both his ears. "Anyone home? Where do you think I am, down the bleeding pub?"

"No," said Eric, balancing precariously on the stones and feeling at a distinct disadvantage in the presence of this enormous man. Although in his fifties, at least, he had not only height and weight on his side but the level ground of his earthen floor.

Conscious that his visit had got off to a bad start and that poking your head, willy nilly, though someone's front wall was hardly the way to go about asking a favour, Eric tried a placating smile. "Would you be Mr Moggs Morgan?" he enquired, pitching his voice against the wads of cotton wool still quivering in the man's ears.

The man shook his head. "No. I'm Rameses the Great hiding out on a Welsh mountain in case the Hittites get me. 'Course I'm Moggs Morgan. Who do you think I am, boy?"

"Oh, right. Well, that's good because you're the man I've come to see. Perhaps I might just step inside for a minute?"

"Aye," shouted the man, grudgingly. "Reckon you might."

Eric made to step through the wall but this only served to further excite Moggs Morgan.

"I have a door," he roared, pointing.

"So you do," said Eric slithering backwards into the yard and approaching the rotting timber edifice only to find it padlocked. Popping back through the fertiliser bags he advised his host of this latest difficulty.

"I must a come in through the back last time," muttered Moggs. "You'll want the key. Gi's yer 'and."

Eric did so and felt the unexpected weight of a screwdriver, slapped into his palm. The padlock key having been lost, Moggs informed him, some decades before, access was to be achieved by unscrewing the hasp and staple attaching the door to its crumbling frame. As a responsible householder, Eric couldn't help but deplore this casual approach to security. But then again, he reminded himself, based on his brief glimpse through the fertiliser bags, the lack of anything worth stealing was probably deterrent enough.

At last, and in response to a vague gesture of welcome, Eric stepped into the mountain abode of Moggs Morgan. Dimly he made out the man's thatch of iron-grey hair interspersed with the off-white of his cotton wool, sticking out from beneath a black beret. Immediately south of the hair and beret was the bristly collar of a shirt, which Eric had no trouble identifying as a Jenks special, almost certainly made of tweed. Topping off the ensemble was a battle dress tunic of uncertain vintage.

Eric handed back the cumbersome "key", which Moggs slipped into the pocket of his threadbare trousers. Then he closed the door behind Eric, reducing the room to the brightness of a submarine in a power cut.

As his eyes adjusted to the gloom, Eric saw that he was in the main living area of the house where a solitary window, in the back wall, failed to let in any light. This was due not only to the grime of decades but to dozens of empty yoghurt pots, stacked one inside the other and rising in tall, wavering columns on the windowsill.

Also rising in a tall, wavering column was some form of home-made Acrow prop holding up the ceiling in the vicinity of the missing front wall.

Seeing Eric's concerned glance, Moggs boomed, "Safe as houses, boy. Don't you fret. Keeping my bedroom floor level, that is, not for me to fetch up in the yard again. Happened, that did, night the wall fell out. Dreaming, I was, about angels, kissing my face. Turned out be snowflakes blowing in on me. Made for a softer landing, mind …"

Moggs laughed uproariously and Eric did his best to join in. Wondering as he did so how anyone could survive the challenges of such a home.

His laughter subsiding to a chuckle, Moggs heaved a stack of yellowing *Farmers Weekly*'s from a somewhat incongruous chaise longue and waved Eric to it.

"You'd be little Eric, I presume?" he yelled.

"Young Eric," corrected Eric, perching on the extreme edge of the once elegant piece of furniture to avoid what he strongly suspected was a mouse's nest, deep in the brocade. Then, remembering that young Eric wasn't actually his name either, he added. "Well, just Eric will do."

"Eric it is then," said Moggs, busying himself at the fireplace where he piled up part-burnt logs before sprinkling them liberally with paraffin and tossing in a lighted match. Then, running a dampened forefinger over his eyebrows, he turned to Eric.

"You OK, lad?"

Eric could only nod. He'd yet to get over the controlled explosion and was privately fearing for a row of what looked like tweed socks, smouldering on a length of baler twine before the inferno.

"Tea?" asked Moggs, shaking a soot-encrusted kettle, finding it empty and crossing to a brass tap over a galvanised bucket in what remained of the front corner of the room.

"Yes, please," whispered Eric wishing, possibly for the first time in his life, that he might be offered something stronger.

"Speak up, lad," instructed Moggs, hovering with the kettle

Eric took a deep breath. "Yes, please," he bellowed.

Moggs flung the kettle into the flames. "It'll take a while," he observed. "Best get on with what you've come for, eh? Summat you want to ask me, ain't there? Summat to do with my steamroller?"

Eric sighed. "Frank the Mail told you, didn't he?"

"Aye, boy," roared Moggs. "How did you know?"

"Put it down to a lucky guess. But yes, I have come about the steamroller: to ask if you'd very kindly be prepared to lend it to us as the main feature of our parade in the Summer Spectacular?"

"Well, I would," said Moggs to Eric's delight. "And then again, I wouldn't."

"Ah," said Eric. "Hetty said you might have reservations about taking it out on the road. But it's unlikely isn't it that anyone from the Tarmac would see you? And even if they did, surely one steamroller looks very much like another?"

"Best you come out and take a look, lad, whilst that there kettle gets aboiling."

Moggs strode across the bare three yards of his living room, to a narrow door in the opposite corner to the range. Flinging it wide, he stepped straight into a field and a herd of jostling, inquisitive cows. Eyeing them sternly, Moggs led Eric along the back of the cowshed and took a left turn between two ancient stone barns.

"There she is," said Moggs, his craggy face softening in the subdued light of a huge lean-to supported on its open side by tall, steel poles.

For a moment, Eric said nothing because the steamroller, while sufficient in itself to arrest speech, was the least surprising item in a fleet of vehicles, lined up beneath the corrugated canopy of the roof.

Feeling Moggs's expectant eyes on him, he said loudly, "She's lovely, but a bit conspicuous, I agree."

Moggs nodded. "Big on livery the Tarmac were. Bright yellow with black writing. They had it on everything from a dumper truck to a donkey jacket. So it's hard to see, lad, isn't it, how I wouldn't get noticed if I took her out?"

Eric was forced to agree but the answer seemed obvious. "You could paint her up?" he suggested. "Cover the trademark at least? Be all right then, wouldn't it?"

Moggs grinned. "Well, damn. You might be right. And she'd welcome a bit of a spruce up. Part of my retirement fund, she is, but a bit special if I says it meself. First big vehicle I ever drove she was, back when I was a lad and she a museum piece even then. I'll give it some thought, lad."

"Thanks," said Eric. "We'd certainly appreciate it." His gaze travelled further along the row. "Er, are the other vehicles part of your retirement fund, too?"

"Certainly are, lad. Never seemed to have a job that carried a pension scheme. But I reckon these'll fetch a pretty penny if ever I find meself short."

"Mm," said Eric, eyeing the second vehicle along. "So you were a bus driver were you at some point?"

" 'S'right, lad. Easiest one to get away with, that was, for all it's pretty big. Just went off on me route one day and never went back."

"Right," said Eric. "And the little tank?"

"National Service. Figured they owed me big time after what they put me through there."

Lowering his voice as much as was feasible, allowing for the cotton wool, Eric said, "You know, do you, that there's a tank regiment operating in these parts?"

"Is there by damn? Best not take her out for a bit, eh?"

"*Do* you take her out?"

"Not if I can help it," admitted Moggs, "but she's useful if the Landy ever lets me down and I need to get round the stock."

"The Landy?" queried Eric.

"Aye," Moggs gestured to a four-by-four parked at the end of the line. "The Land Rover. See it?"

Eric nodded. He did indeed see it. And he could clearly make out the familiar pine tree of the Forestry Commission logo on the driver's door.

***

"So you'll have a think about that respray will you?" asked Eric, reclining on the chaise longue and accepting his third cup of tea. This beverage, he'd quickly discovered, being merely a medium for suspending something far more potent in. Which was fine by him, he thought, feeling the stresses and strains of his futile artistic endeavours easing with every swallow.

"Will do, lad," boomed Moggs, sloshing more brandy.

Eric winced. His hearing seemed to have become more acute in line with the volume of alcohol he'd consumed. This reminded him of something he'd been meaning to ask Moggs. "Any idea when your ears will be better?" he enquired as politely as was possible at top volume.

"Better?" echoed Moggs mournfully. "Doubt they'll get better, boy, at my time of life. Been struggling to hear anything, I have, these last few days."

"Don't suppose the cotton wool helps, does it?"

Moggs's hands flew to his ears like a go-go dancer concerned for her clip-ons. "Cotton wool!" he shouted. "Well, damn, boy, you've hit on something there. Put it in Tuesday, I did, starting up that rackety old JCB of mine." Tugging the cotton wool free he added, "Musta forgot to take it out. Go on, lad, say something. Anything, just to prove I'm cured."

Eric thought for a moment, trying not to dwell on a growing conviction that Moggs couldn't have bathed, shaved or taken his hat off for at least three days.

"Mud in your eye," he said at last. Then, seeing Moggs knuckling his eye sockets, he added, "Not literally, of course."

"Shame," grinned Moggs blinking hard. "For a minute there I thought you'd cured me short-sightedness 'n' all."

They laughed longer and louder than was strictly necessary at this and it was the start of a highly convivial afternoon. Unhampered by his makeshift ear defenders, Moggs was a good listener and Eric found himself sharing the ups and downs of life in his new home. Culminating in his unlooked for secondment to the Summer Spectacular committee and his growing unease over what the Williams Twins might do to ensure the event didn't come off.

"Wouldn't put anything past them two," agreed Moggs. "Just like their dad, they are." He peered at Eric over the rim of his teacup. "He'd have had no truck with *you*, lad," he said with a sad waggle of his large, grey head. "Didn't hold with outsiders, he didn't. And he'd have been doubly narked about an incomer getting involved with this here Summer Spectacular, calculated to bring even more strangers to the town."

"Why?" Eric asked. "What's wrong with outsiders?"

"Nothing in my book, boy, but the way old man Williams looked at it, you get a lot of people coming into the area and they start fancying a hobby farm or a second home here. And what happens then? Property prices go up, that's what. Which would've been dead against the old man's interests being as he was intent on buying up every farm and smallholding he could get his hands on to leave to those Twins."

Eric nodded thoughtfully. "So he drove out the competition, eh? Makes sense, I suppose. What doesn't make sense, though, is why he went to all that effort for the Twins' sake. Nasty piece of work they are. Both of them."

"Family ain't it, boy?" asked Moggs, his voice softening. "You got to do right by your family whatever it takes."

"Mmm," said Eric. He was reminded of the lift he'd given Sally Stitch, struggling home with her ill-gotten supper and so many mouths to feed. He said as much to Moggs, who leaned forwards in his chair.

"How is old Sal," he asked, "and her brood? All well are they?"

"I think so," said Eric.

"And how's that youngest girl? Beryl, isn't it?"

"Er, fine, I think. Why?"

"No reason, boy, except I had an auntie called Beryl once. And, coincidentally, a wife."

CHAPTER THIRTEEN

Gazing at the plug in the bottom of the basin, Eric felt another burst of song coming on. He flung his arms wide. "On a cleeear day,' he gurgled, then came up spluttering. Perhaps there were better places for a singsong.

He reached for his towel, delighted to find it exactly where it should be: neatly folded on the bathroom radiator. In fact, he reminded himself, everything in the cottage was exactly as it should be these days.

Perching on the edge of the bath, Eric draped his towel over his head and began vigorously rubbing his wet hair. "Silly me," he said as he tumbled off the edge of the bath, "thinking I'd got poltergeists." Weaving his way to the bedroom to get dressed, he took some comfort from the fact that only Hetty and Mrs Jenks knew of his foolish fears. And they were surely the souls of discretion?

***

It was touch and go, Eric decided ten minutes later, whether he would make it to the Summer Spectacular meeting. For some reason he appeared to have parked the van on the hedge in front of the cottage. He could only assume, from a flattened shrub directly below the open driver's door, that gravity had assisted him in getting out. Getting back in again wasn't going to be so easy.

Finally he fetched a chair, climbed into the van, started her up and drove off the hedge, crash landing into the path of a passing tractor. The driver avoided him by inches, waved his pipe in a casual manner and drove on. That was the beauty of Landoobrey, Eric told himself, setting off in the opposite direction to the village hall. No one made a fuss.

Realising his mistake, Eric executed a multipoint turn, opened his window and breathed deeply. He really ought to sober up a bit before the meeting.

***

"Aha," said Mel as Eric tottered into the village hall just after seven. "Here's Eric. How are the poltergeists, old boy? Not still giving trouble, I hope?"

The committee, which had now expanded to also include Arnold and Mrs Jenks, erupted into laughter in between making spooky whooing noises.

Eric looked reproachfully at Hetty, who had the grace to blush.

"Sorry, young Eric," mumbled Hetty. "It just sort of slipped out, but we've only told the committee."

"Right," said Eric, knowing as well as she did that telling the committee was tantamount to telling the entire town. Especially Arnold, who had the ear of the postman. Throw him in, thought Eric, and it wouldn't be long before the details of his ghost-busting phone call to Hetty were known throughout the county.

"Rather a peculiar night that was in more ways than one," he said, changing the subject. "Why, at one point I even thought I heard the town clock strike *thirteen*."

All eyes turned to Arnold who whoo-whoo-ed again, but half-heartedly.

"OK, everyone. Settle down," said Hetty. "Happily, I can now report Eric's poltergeists well and truly laid to rest." She winked at Eric before resuming what appeared to be an ongoing conversation with Mrs Jenks.

Eric took his seat, next to Ms Harris, who proceeded to tell him how disappointed she was not to have been frisked, upon arrival, for electronic devices. "I'm clean, of course," she added, patting her bosom, "but I was hoping for a once-over from Mel. Been keeping himself to himself, though, he has this evening. Wouldn't even take a glass of my home-made ginger beer."

With a sad glance at the actor who seemed, Eric had to agree, unnaturally quiet, she picked up the bottle in front of her and poured a glass each for Eric and Arnold.

The ginger beer looked good and Eric drank deeply, only to find his upper lip welded to his gum by the soft drink equivalent of a scorpion sting.

Taking his stricken expression for a smile, Ms Harris grinned back. "Good stuff, eh? The young man who unblocks my gutters swears by it. Asks for a bottle, he does, every time he pops round."

Eric could well believe it.

Fellow victim, Arnold, then asked for the recipe, causing Ms Harris to twitter delightedly and Eric to look at him aghast.

"What on earth do you want that for?" he hissed.

"Thought I might make some as a treat for Mrs Jenks," said Arnold.

Eric sighed. No one seemed remotely ready to start the meeting, so he fell to massaging his temples, hoping to ward off a threatening hangover. As he did so he caught sight of Mel, gazing into space and humming softly to himself.

"You OK, Mel?" asked Eric,

The actor turned his dreamy eyes to him. "Have you ever made a daisy chain, Eric?"

"Maybe," said Eric cautiously. "Many years ago, perhaps. When I was a child."

"Ever made one and danced barefoot in the dewy dawn, wearing it like a crown?"

"Definitely not."

"Well, I have, dear boy. This very morning in fact, and all because of my beautiful Musa."

"Ah," said Eric, who'd felt all along there'd be a woman behind Mel's pole-axed demeanour. "Known her long, have you?"

Mel laughed. "You could say that. She's been away for a while but she's back now, lovelier than ever. She's not a person, though. More an irresistible, creative force. My Muse, in fact."

Eric sat up and took notice. "How did you get her back?"

"Well," Mel settled himself more comfortably in his chair, "I don't know if I've mentioned my forthcoming one-man show, *Ben Hur*? I'll happily recap if …"

"No," said Eric hastily. "I know all about *Ben Hur*. No need for a recap."

"Oh. Well, the good news is it's no longer a one-man show. There was so much interest among the band members when I happened to mention it at practice the other night that I'm rewriting the whole thing, potentially for a cast of nearly half-a-dozen, and all because I told them my rehearsals would be on the same basis as the band practice."

"But," said Eric, spotting the obvious flaw, "Hetty supplies free drinks for everyone at band practice, even those who didn't actually make it into the band."

"I know. Ingenious isn't it? Don't know why I didn't think of it myself."

"Possibly because of the cost?" suggested Eric.

"Yes, well. There's that of course but I've a nice little cheque coming soon. My repeat fees, you know, for a bit of telly I did a while back. Can't think of a better way to spend 'em. Got me so fired up it has, my rewrite, I managed to dash off a dozen or more pages after the pub last night."

"Any of them remotely legible this morning?" asked Eric, shrewdly.

"No," admitted Mel, "but the point is, I'm raring to go again." He paused, then added, "It's hard to explain to a non-artist such as yourself, Eric, but when creative inspiration strikes there truly is nothing like it."

Eric gazed enviously at his friend. This was precisely the feeling he'd hoped for from his *A Goddess Weeping* but so far it hadn't happened. Perhaps what he needed was to spend more time with Cheryl Stitch to relight his creative fire? But how? Visiting her at the chip shop flat would be impossible without a very good excuse. After all, while he would know his motives in wishing to visit a stunning, teenage girl were purely artistic, he could hardly tell anyone else that, could he?

"Mind you," went on Mel, unaware of Eric's inner anguish, "I'm pretty sure the buzz I get from my little bit of play-writing is nothing to the euphoria experienced by a true artist. Like that chap, I forget his name, who did that sculpture, *A Deep Depression in Driftwood*. There was a pic of it in a Sunday sup last weekend. So *moving* … Ever seen it, dear boy?"

Eric avoided the actor's eyes, relieved beyond measure when Hetty's voice boomed across the table.

"Right, everyone. Can I have your attention? Mrs Jenks has just been telling me a bit of news concerning a conversation she happened to overhear in the shop today between Tony and Terry Williams."

The shopkeeper smiled and studied her fingernails. "Well, the glass was to hand in "Household Goods"," she explained, "where I went to fetch them a bit of carbolic. And that wall's only thin …"

"Quite," interrupted Hetty, glossing over Mrs Jenks's precise method of overhearing. "Anyway, it seems they were having a bit of a laugh at Mrs Jenks' attempt at a Summer Spectacular poster, which she'd left on the counter…"

"Oh, dear," put in Eric. "Not going too well, eh, Mrs Jenks?"

"Actually, it was going very well indeed, young Eric," said Mrs Jenks with some heat. "What caused them to laugh was the fact that, as they intend to pull the venue at the very last minute, there isn't going to *be* a Summer Spectacular."

"Pull it," frowned Eric. "How, if the old Earl gifted the field to the town?"

"That's just the point," said Hetty, "isn't it Mrs Jenks? Seems the Twins intend to challenge our right to use the field because the old Earl's gift was never written down."

"'Tis written down …" said Arnold, who'd been cleaning his teeth with the end of his pen. Popping them back in his mouth, he went on, "for everyone to see, if they use their eyes. Well," he corrected himself, "everyone as happens to be looking when Idris the Market Tavern lifts his bar hatch to come out and clean the tables."

"Which he doesn't," Hetty pointed out, "ever."

"No," agreed Arnold, "and neither did his father before him, or his father before that, which is lucky for us."

"Why is that lucky?" asked Ms Harris.

Arnold carefully folded a piece of paper to a point, and began to clean his ears. "Means the old Earl's pledge has barely seen the light of day in all these years," he said wincing. "Carved it with a dagger, he did, on the underside of the hatch. And his words and signature are still there to this day, fresh as paint."

"Well," breathed Hetty, "good old Idris, eh? Means we can proceed, safe in the knowledge that, if push comes to shove, we can prove beyond a shadow of a doubt that the field belongs to the town?"

"Hear, hear!" shouted Mel.

"Glad that's settled," beamed Mrs Jenks. She glanced at Hetty. "Can we tell 'em the good bit now?"

"Don't see why not," said Hetty, smothering a laugh. Turning to the group she added, "Mrs Jenks also happened to overhear the Twins discussing the sort of guests they intend to cater for at the hotel. Perhaps you can guess what they are, if I tell you they won't be needing much in the way of suitcases?

"Nudists?" said Eric, his eyes widening.

Hetty slapped the table. "Got it in one, young Eric. Seems they've spotted a gap in the market for a secluded little haven where bashful naturists can take their holidays."

"Prudie nudies, in effect?" suggested Ms Harris with a little giggle.

"Exactly," said Mrs Jenks. "So it's easy to see why, isn't it, our plans for a full-blown parade, passing within a stone's throw of the place, to say nothing of hopefully hundreds of people, gathering on the field next door, hasn't gone down too well?"

"And if the Summer Spectacular succeeds as we hope it will," added Mel, a slow smile spreading over his features, "that road could be crawling with traffic every day for the rest of the summer, whether the Twins like it or not."

"I can see now why they're so determined to put the boot in," said Eric.

"In more ways than one," agreed Hetty with feeling. "Told you, didn't I, Eric, about the fight in the pub the other night?"

"You certainly did. Humdinger of a punch-up I believe you said."

"I'll say," put in Ms Harris, her eyes shining, "and Mel was magnificent, wasn't he, Hetty?"

"Was he?" Hetty looked doubtfully at the actor, who flushed and studied the tabletop.

"Oh, *yes*," breathed Ms Harris. "He never moved a muscle. Just stood there behind that crowd of girls in those impossibly short skirts looking utterly *superior* …"

Mel squirmed under Eric's enquiring glance then raised an elegant hand to his profile. "The face, dear boy," he mouthed. "Never risk the face."

"Anyway," said Hetty, "at least we can get on now with planning the event, safe in the knowledge that there's not a damn thing the Twins can do about it."

***

Hetty then handed round lists of suppliers, sparking some animated discussion on the relative merits of frame tents over canvas pole, and brass versus glass for the trophies.

Eric tuned out somewhat but perked up again when the discussion reverted to their plans for the day itself. Proudly, he confirmed that he'd now secured the loan of many classic pieces of farming history for the parade, including the steamroller.

"Great," said Hetty. "Well, the parade, it seems, is coming along nicely." She produced Eric's clipboard from the previous Saturday and showed it round. "So I vote we have a quick review of the games and attractions people've so far volunteered to host down on the field."

Everyone pored over Eric's scribbled notes and agreed that, given the woman out to stick pins in her husband and the surprises in store for the vicar, the ambulances were a must. There was then some unbridled hilarity over the partially crossed out note Eric had made on the subject of hand-knitting.

"Right," said Hetty, wiping her eyes. "So, any more for any more?"

Mrs Jenks elbowed Arnold, who'd also tuned out to the point of falling asleep. Waking, noisily, he admitted to having the wherewithal, inherited from an uncle in the fairground business, to provide a rifle range.

"Duck Shoot game it is," he explained. "Get a lot of ducks you do, going round on a belt. Folks take pot shots at 'em."

"Best not have ducks, eh?" suggested Eric, fearing the VAT farmer sneaking some extra targets into the tent. "How about using tin cans instead?"

Everyone nodded their approval and Hetty volunteered to supply some from the pub. "And the beauty of that," she added, "is we've a practically limitless supply of targets. So as soon as some get shot up we can put out some more."

"Won't need 'em," said Arnold.

"Oh, I don't know," said Hetty, "we might. There are some good shots around here, especially when they've got their eyes on a prize."

"Won't need prizes neither," whispered Arnold, who'd spent hours as a boy watching his uncle bending the barrels on his guns. His uncle never having lost so much as a goldfish in thirty-odd years in the game.

Mrs Jenks raised her hand. "Me and the lads thought about running a little poker school. Purely for fun of course."

"OK." Hetty made a tentative note, evidently fearing hustling on a grand scale. "So you'll need a tent, I guess, with some proper lighting in case it's a dull day."

"We'll want the tent," agreed Mrs Jenks, "but the dimmer we can keep the lighting the better."

Ms Harris then remembered that she'd brought along a written request from the WI, who wanted to host a coconut shy.

This was initially greeted with enthusiasm, until the plans for the sideshow were examined in detail and found to include a life-size cut-out of a Williams twin with a coconut balanced on each hand, one on his head and one barely covering his modesty. Worse, the draughtswoman responsible for the sketch had pencilled in a pile of missiles looking suspiciously like cricket balls with spikes in.

Objections were raised and, with a sigh, Ms Harris produced a second drawing. "Is this one any better?"

It depicted the other Williams twin with playing cards rather than coconuts arranged around his person and a pile of well-sharpened darts.

"I can see the thinking behind it," said Hetty, shuffling the two drawings, clearly unable to decide which was worse, "but please tell the WI that, whilst we'd be delighted for them to run the coconut shy and the darts game if they wish, they'd better lose the Williams Twins. Now, any more ideas anyone?"

Arnold cleared his throat. "Sal Stitch asked me to run something by the committee. Might take a bit of setting up but she reckons it'd be a real crowd puller."

Hetty's pen hovered over her pad. "Let's have it then."

"Well," enthused Arnold, "it seems she wants to hold a cookery demonstration with blind taster sessions whereby people can win a cash prize for correctly identifying the animal species the meat came from …"

"Whoa!" Hetty flung down her pen. "I'm afraid we really can't have that. We could end up with half the attendance going down bad. Tell her she can do a cookery demonstration if she wants, but using only proper meat."

"She'll be put out," said Arnold nervously, "and I don't know as I want to be the one to tell her."

"I'll do it," said Eric to everyone's surprise, including his own. "Well," he added, thinking on his feet, "it'll be better coming from a committee member that *hasn't* already given her the go-ahead, won't it?"

Hetty made a note on her pad. "That's settled then. I just hope, Eric, that you don't live to regret it."

Eric hoped so too. But what, he asked himself, was a nasty ten minutes with Sal if it gained him just a fleeting glimpse of his very own Musa?

***

"Same again?" asked the starry-eyed new landlady of the Black Lion, a recently renovated pub just across the street from the village hall.

Tony Williams barely heard her, intent as he was on watching Terry, bent double at the inner door to the hall, eavesdropping on the meeting. There being so little space in the foyer, Tony was obliged to wait for his brother in the pub, where the stench of furniture polish and fresh flowers was beginning to turn his stomach.

He turned from the window to find the landlady's expectant eyes on him.

"Same again?" she repeated, waving his glass.

Tony scowled. There was something about her bright, friendly tone that set his teeth on edge. As did her repeated requests that he should call her Trisha.

Having no intention of calling her anything that wasn't rude, Tony merely nodded and peeled another note from the greasy wad in his pocket.

"Get you a clean one this time, shall I?" Trisha offered, turning his murky glass to the pink-shaded light behind the bar.

Tony shook his head, glaring. The layers of spit and dried froth were the only things giving his so-called "real ale" any taste at all.

"Just as you like." The landlady turned her attention to pouring the pint, carefully, and adding a little logo in the deep, creamy head. "Bernard and I swear by our finishing touches," she simpered, handing Tony his glass and pointing to the logo. "Saw it done once, in our old local, back in Kent. Decided we had to learn the knack for when we got a pub of our own. It's all about brand reinforcement, isn't it?"

Tony, for whom it was all about being stuck here till Terry came back, said nothing, merely opening his throat and chucking the pint down, the rampant lion standing no chance against the ebbing tide.

"Er, same again, again?" asked Trisha, her pert bottom having barely brushed the pink brocade of her comfy stool behind the bar.

Tony nodded.

"'Course, we never thought we'd be able to afford our very own dream pub," she went on, pouring more quickly this time, skimping a little on the logo and releasing the glass a split second before it was jerked out of her hand. "But when we saw the Black Lion advertised, for a fraction of the price of a pub back home, we just knew we could make it a proper little palace and … *More*?" she asked as the empty glass hit the bar top, with a thud.

"Of course more," said Tony, peeling off another note. "Don't they drink in these pubs of yours 'back home'?"

Trisha worked the pump like a Gamblers Anonymous failure on a one-armed bandit and did away with the logo altogether. "Well, they *do*," she said panting, "but I suppose the difference is, people tend to sip things."

"Humph." Tony swallowed his pint, slammed it down ready for another and ambled back to the gleaming window.

Blinking a little, he found himself longing for the good old days, when the outside of the pub window had been caked with the bird shit of a hundred summers, the inside sepia with smoke. The days of old Dan Dribbles, pouring pints of beer and saliva, well into his eighties, before collapsing and dying behind the bar one night. And it was nobody's fault, Tony reminded himself, turning back towards the bar, that his nightly tendency to collapse there, and not die, had meant it was some time before his death was noticed.

The subsequent auction of the Black Lion had resulted in this characterless, pseudo-pub, full of exposed beams, inglenook fireplaces and horse brasses, with a carpet, of all things, on the floor. How was a man expected to stay upright, with nothing to stick his feet to?

Traipsing cautiously back across the room, he cringed, in passing, at the ambient racket issuing from a pair of pink, faux-fur-clad speakers.

He'd just fetched up at the bar, telling himself he wasn't, repeat, wasn't getting the taste for the crystal clear, hoppy beer, with a subtle hint of herbs, when the street door crashed open.

Gazing down the barrel-like bulge of his fresh pint, Tony nodded at his brother. "All right, Terry?"

"No," said Terry, making pint signs at the hovering landlady. "In fact, I'd go as far as to say its all an absolute bloody disaster. What's more, I very nearly got caught. Came out they did, all of a sudden. Luckily I had the presence of mind to turn away, pretending to tie my laces. They didn't suspect a thing."

Tony eyed his brother's footwear. Only Terry, he thought, could pretend to tie the laces of his gumboots. He let it go. "Out with it then," he said. "What happened?"

Five minutes later, Terry's account of the meeting drew to a close. "So you see," he said, "they're still full steam ahead for this blasted event. And what's more, thanks to you talking so loudly in Mrs Jenks' shop earlier, they now know all about our plans for the hotel. Had a good laugh they did, I can tell you."

Tony frowned. "As I recall it was *you* talking loudly … but aren't you forgetting that, no matter how much they go full steam ahead with the Summer Spectacular, it isn't going to happen is it – not when we pull the plug on the venue?"

Terry's face took on the wary expression of a messenger, wishing he'd worn his bulletproof vest. "Yes, well, that was the other thing I meant to tell you," he muttered. "Seems that actually the old Earl *did* put it in writing, about his gifting the field to the town. Carved it with a dagger, he did, on the underside of the bar hatch in the Market Tavern. Part of the fabric of the building, that is, Tony, screwed to the wall for eternity. So, all in all, I'm afraid we haven't a leg to stand on."

Tony smiled grimly. "Maybe not, but what we *have* got is a screwdriver, isn't it, and a box of matches?"

CHAPTER FOURTEEN

The morning after the meeting, Eric knocked on the street door of the chip shop flat.

The sound he made, midway between a scratch and a tap, was indicative, he thought, of the mixed feelings he had about his visit. Part of him hoped not to get an answer so as to avoid his nasty ten minutes with Sally Stitch whose tiger-yellow eyes were not, he suspected, the only cat-like thing about her. The other part of him, the artist part, hoped he *did* get an answer. Preferably from his Muse and preferably minus her mother.

There was a patter of bare feet on bare stairs followed by the doorknob twisting, slowly. For a fleeting moment, Eric's thoughts turned once again to the supernatural as he stared into the empty hallway. Then a sniffle from knee level prompted him to look downwards. There, he discovered a small boy wearing an oversized shirt on his undersized person and very little else as far as Eric could see.

Eric smiled. "Hello, little chap. Is your mum in please?"

The boy removed his dummy with an audible plop and stared at Eric. "Gone to shag a peasant," he replied.

"Eh?" said Eric. The child made to repeat himself but was interrupted by a rich chuckle from further up the stairs.

"He means," said the girl, skipping lightly down the last few steps and scooping the boy up, "she's gone to the Stag and Pheasant. She cleans there Mondays and Fridays."

"Ah," said Eric. "And you would be Eryl, perhaps, or is it Deryl? Or maybe Cheryl?" he added craftily, knowing full well that this young lady wasn't the object of his visit.

"I'm Eryl," smiled the girl. "Sally's eldest. You're young Eric, aren't you? Come to see Mam about her not cooking iffy meat for the Summer Spectacular?"

Eric sighed. "Do I take it Frank the Mail's been?"

"Well, yes, as it happens."

"That figures," said Eric.

"But as I say, Mam isn't here at the moment. There's only me and the little 'uns. Talking of which, do you want to come up? I've left the baby on his own."

"Thanks."

Reeling from the mixed aroma of chips and who knew what delicacy Sal had served up for last night's dinner, Eric followed Eryl up the narrow, wooden staircase. It was a blow about Cheryl but good news about Sal. Perhaps he could just leave her a note?

"Park yourself," invited Eryl, "and hold him for a minute would you?"

"Right." Eric perched on the edge of the sofa as Eryl handed him the toddler, and, to his great concern, disappeared through a heavy brocade curtain slung across the cramped living room.

"You won't be long, will you?" he called, trying to get a grip on his wriggling charge and avoid a dummy up the left nostril.

"No." Eryl popped back through the curtain with a baby balanced on her hip. "Here I am. You OK?"

"Fine," lied Eric, finally distracting the child with a Lego brick.

Plucking a bottle from the mantelpiece over the gas fire, Eryl touched it to her cheek, threw some laundry off a chair and began feeding the baby. She looked thoughtfully at Eric.

"You were in the pub last Saturday night weren't you, doing the band practice?"

"I was there," admitted Eric, "but not strictly speaking for the band practice. That's more Mel's bag."

Eryl grinned. "That's the actor isn't it? He looked pleased to see us lot arrive."

"That's because he was," said Eric. "More so than you can ever know."

They sat for a while in a silence broken only by the toddler, banging his brick on Eric's head.

"Pack it in," said Eryl, and was instantly obeyed.

"You're marvellous with the children," said Eric, feeling doubly inadequate, "yet you can't be very old yourself?"

"Nice of you to say so but I'm seventeen. Mam had me and Cheryl by the time she was my age. Closely followed by Deryl, Meryl, Beryl, Harry, Barry and Garry. That's Barry," she added with a nod of her curly brown hair towards the toddler.

"Wow!" said Eric. "Quite a houseful?"

"Mm," agreed Eryl, "but we're two down at the moment, what with Meryl and Beryl having gone to live in a tent in the yard. Just for the summertime, of course."

"Well they *were* living there," muttered Eric.

"No," said Eryl glancing towards the window of the flat. "They're living there now. You can see their tent quite plainly if you look. They did disappear for a while but they're back now." She giggled. "Complete with a wheelbarrow, of all things, and a pile of wet washing. Can you believe that?"

"Wet *washing?*" queried Eric as light began to dawn on the slippery subject of his kitchen floor.

"Yes. Why?"

"Oh, nothing."

"Funny thing is," went on Eryl, "I don't think any of us realised how much extra space we'd had until Beryl and Meryl popped in last night to do their homework. Bursting at the seams we were again then, but generally speaking the flat's only really full in the evenings and in the school holidays. The rest of the time everyone usually seems to be out somewhere."

"Leaving you," said Eric, "holding the baby?"

Eryl looked fondly down at the infant dozing in her arms. "I don't mind. I love children. Hope to have as many as I can of my own one day. Not like Cheryl and Deryl. They both want careers."

"Careers?" prompted Eric, wondering what future life his Muse had set her sights on.

"Mm. Deryl wants to be an engineer. Bright, too, she is. In fact she looks like being the only one of us older girls to stick school after the age of sixteen. Cheryl, on the other hand, quit last year to become a model."

Eric's heart soared. If that wasn't serendipity he didn't know what was.

"A model, eh?"

"Yeah." Eryl nodded her head towards a small table, where several black and white photos lay alongside a school exercise book. "Any spare money she has, she's always getting those silly little passport photos done. Sends the best of them off to agents in the hope of getting discovered."

"And what does she do in the meantime?" asked Eric, gazing hungrily at the pictures. Here was his chance, he thought, of obtaining a permanent likeness of his Muse. Something he could consult in the dark days ahead, grappling with his new piece.

"In the meantime," said Eryl dryly, "she's a cleaner like Mam."

Eric smiled. Then, easing out from under the now drowsing toddler, he crossed to the table. "Perhaps I could leave a note for your mum?" he said, picking up the exercise book and palming a photo in the process. "OK if I use a piece of this?"

"I think it's a school book but take a piece by all means."

Turning the pages of the book, looking for a clean sheet, certain random words caught Eric's eye. "Dear Miranda" he read, perplexed to see this phrase repeated to halfway down the page followed by several lines of "Dear Ms Barton". How odd, he thought, that someone here should know two people each with part of his agent's name. Which reminded him, he still hadn't called Miranda back about those wretched replicas …

"Do you need a pen?" asked Eryl.

Eric patted the front pocket of his dungarees. "Got one here," he said.

A moment later he signed his note with a flourish. "There. That should do it. Well, I'd best be off now. You'll be OK will you, on your own?"

Eryl smiled. "I won't be on my own for long. Cheryl's latest job is up at the old folks' flats. She starts even earlier than Mam so she's usually back by eleven."

Eric eyed a clock on the wall. Another hour, he felt, was pushing it if he didn't want to arouse Eryl's suspicions, to say nothing of the danger of running into Sal.

"Right, well, as I say, I'd best be off." He made for the door, catching a whiff, from the little galley kitchen in passing. Curious to know what might have been on yesterday's menu, he paused, sniffing. "What's that meat I can smell?" he asked.

Eryl sniffed, too. "Pork?" she suggested.

"Oh, good," said Eric.

"At least, everyone always says hedgehog smells a bit like pork when you cook it."

***

Closing the street door softly behind him, Eric ran to his van and drove along the street of Victorian terraced houses until he was out of sight of the flat.

He stopped and pulled out his photo of Cheryl, his breath catching in his throat, not so much because of her undeniable beauty but because of the way her face fitted seamlessly with his vision of his *A Goddess Weeping*. Showing him exactly where and how he should wield his chisels. Delighted, he held the photo to his lips and kissed it. Then he put the van into gear and drove off towards home.

As it happened, his route took him within a stone's throw of the old folks' flats. The flats and, to a certain extent the occupants, had been new, he remembered, when he'd stayed here in his youth. Against his better judgement he turned the wheel in that direction.

Purely, he told himself, to see how things might have changed in the intervening years.

Pulling into the long, narrow cul-de-sac, he felt for a moment as though he'd wandered onto the set of the film *Oliver!* In particular, the scene with all the little maids, dressed in mob caps and frilly aprons, singing and dancing, waving feather dusters and beating mats on the balcony rails, all along the curved Georgian crescent.

As he watched, however, subtle differences became apparent. Like the fact that this wasn't a Georgian crescent so much as a rather dreary maisonette complex, and the little maids, merely a handful of teenage cleaners, dressed in grubby nylon overalls. Plus they were yelling rather than singing; hanging out of the flat windows, keeping up a lively dialogue, the crux of which appeared to be who was dating who and how drunk they'd all managed to get the previous night.

To Eric's dismay the chief culprit was Cheryl Stitch. Appearing at an upstairs window, her face puffy, eyes pink and squinting, thin lips gripping a cigarette.

"Utterly rat-arsed, I was," she growled, hurling the decaying contents of a flower vase into the street below. "Up-chucking all bleeding night."

Disappointment hit Eric along with the soggy brown contents of the vase. Finding their way like a guided missile through the open driver's window of the van.

***

Crashed and burned, thought Eric, later that day, running trembling fingers through his still damp hair and staring at the metaphorical wreckage of his new piece. Or the rotten old log, as he was now inclined to call it.

Tempting as it was to blame Cheryl Stitch for tearing his vision of her as a goddess to shreds, he was aware that the real fault lay with himself. Believing he could actually carve a masterpiece when his only demonstrable talent, to date, lay in adapting what nature herself had provided for him.

All of which meant that, at some point, he'd have to tell Miranda that his second piece wouldn't be forthcoming. And that there was no way he was doing those blasted replicas, either.

**

In far away London, Miranda's first reaction upon seeing fifty varnished twigs wrapped in loo roll was to throw up her hands in horror. Her second, prompted by the intrigued demeanour of the Tate's merchandising manager, who happened to be present when Miranda opened the box, was to make jazz hands instead and waggle them delightedly.

"Aren't they super?" she asked, eyeing Delecta, hoping she'd made the right call.

"Absolutely marvellous," breathed Delecta. "So real ... so *raw* ... so *Bagnall* ... We can certainly shift these. Well done, Miranda."

Miranda blushed. "To be honest, I didn't even know Eric was doing them till they turned up this morning. Still, as long as you think they're OK?"

"OK? They're perfect. Lucky you, having *such* an obliging client."

Miranda nodded doubtfully. Recalling that Eric wasn't obliging at all, what with his running off to Wales leaving no forwarding address.

"Well, I wouldn't go that far," she said, "but it's one less thing to get after him about."

"*Do* you have to get after him?" asked Delecta, dripping sympathy.

"*All* the time, I'm afraid," said Miranda, settling down for a moan. "He's my worst client in that respect. I've been trying to reach him all week about these replicas and the small matter of a progress report on his new piece. Plus, I need to speak to him about an interview I've lined up for him with *Hi There!* magazine …"

"Not *Hi There!*?" interrupted Delecta, clearly impressed.

"Yes." Miranda permitted herself a smug smile. "It's a bit of a coup for me, provided Eric will agree to it."

"He's bound to isn't he?"

"Not necessarily. The whole point of his dropping out down in Wales was to get away from the press. I think that's partly why he never answers his wretched phone."

"Tut," said Delecta. "Sounds like a trip to Wales is in order?"

"Well, that's another thing," Miranda reached for the rather grubby envelope, which had been tucked in the cardboard box, alongside the miniatures. "I don't know exactly where … Eureka!"

"Come again?" said Delecta.

Miranda said nothing, being too busy staring at Eric's address at the top left-hand corner of the letter.

It wasn't at all what she'd expected to see and it went some way towards explaining why she hadn't been able to locate his village on the map. Still, assuming it was correct, she now knew precisely where her client was, right down to his postcode.

"You're right," she said, opening her desk diary. "A trip to Wales *is* in order. I've got to secure his agreement to the interview for one thing, and recce his cottage. To say nothing of taking a dekko at his new piece. Now, when can I diarise it?"

Miranda turned pages full of her large, round writing, dismayed to see that preparations for an exhibition by her graffiti artists would take up at least the next few weeks. The third week in June, however, looked clear.

"Worst case, I'll go then," she said, seizing a pen and marking off several days, "if I still haven't managed to reach him by phone."

"That's the way," said Delecta, unwrapping more of the twigs and arranging them on Miranda's desk, the better to gaze at them.

Idly, Miranda scanned the rest of the missive, making a note of her client's request to be paid in cash ASAP to the address shown.

As she dropped the letter into her in tray, she noticed a second page containing a few paragraphs of writing and a carefully drawn map. "That would be too easy," thought Miranda, scanning the map for Welsh place names and finding none. This was explained to a certain extent by the text, which began, "The Shinanogawa is the longest river in Japan …"

Miranda was still trying to work out the significance of this when her phone rang. "Miranda

Barton," she said, plucking up the receiver and recognising a familiar mumble at the other end of the line. Frantically she waved at Delecta. "It's Eric," she mouthed, flicking the phone onto speaker.

"Well, hello stranger," she said. "Were your ears burning?"

"No," Eric's voice came tinnily from the speaker. "At least, I expect I'd have noticed … Oh, I see. Figure of speech. Well, no, they weren't. Why?"

Miranda glanced at Delecta who was holding her own ears, carefully, as if they might be hot. Smothering a giggle, Miranda went on, "We were just talking about you."

"We?"

"Myself and Delecta, the merchandising manager from the Tate. You remember Delecta don't you?"

"One of the ravers you were telling me about?"

"Well, I wouldn't put it quite like that," said Miranda, beginning to regret the speaker-phone, "but she's certainly been known to rave about your piece. She was getting quite excited just now on the subject of your miniatures, too."

"Ah," said Eric. "Well, if you remember, I never actually said I'd do those replicas. Only that I'd think about it. And I can only say I'm sorry it's taken me so long to get back to you with my decision."

Miranda shared a wink with Delecta.

"Not to worry, Eric," she said, reaching out to cradle one of the twigs in her large hand. "We can see how busy you must've been. And actions speak louder than words, don't they?"

"Ye-es," said Eric. "Well, you're right about my being busy. You wouldn't believe what's happened to me since I moved here. First of all I got roped into organising this Carnival and Summer Spectacular thing. Then it turns out I've been harbouring two escaped schoolgirls in my garden who accidentally flooded my kitchen floor, resulting in my getting severe concussion ..."

"Beastly for you," murmured Miranda, stifling a yawn.

"Yes, well, it was rather. So I'm sorry not to have been able to let you know before but what with one thing and another I can't do those replicas and that's that."

Miranda and Delecta looked at one another, then at the miniatures scattered all over the desk.

"You can't do them?" repeated Miranda.

"That's right. I can't."

"Let's get this straight, Eric. Are you saying you *didn't* already send me a batch of fifty replicas of *A Deep Depression in Driftwood* with a covering letter asking for your payment in cash and enclosing a map of Japan?"

"Certainly not." Eric's bewilderment was evident in his voice. "I think I'd remember if I had, don't you?"

Miranda looked helplessly at Delecta. It was a fair point.

"He did say he'd been concussed," whispered Delecta. "Perhaps he still is?"

Miranda nodded, her mind racing. A concussed Eric, she thought, might be a very useful thing at this juncture.

She leant towards the phone. "I think you'd better pop along to the doctor, Eric, soon as you can, because next thing you'll be telling me you don't remember agreeing to that *Hi There!* interview we discussed the other day, and to my coming down in a couple of weeks time to recce your house for the photo shoot?"

"But I don't …"

"Tsk," interrupted Miranda. "As I say, it's the doc's for you, I reckon. Get that concussion of yours checked out, eh? Well, must dash. Speak soon."

"Smart work, Miranda," murmured Delecta as the line went dead.

CHAPTER FIFTEEN

Fanny By Gaslight, Eric thought. That was what Miranda's tactics reminded him of. A dastardly plot to make him out to be mentally unhinged for her own ends.

Admittedly, there'd been times since arriving in Landoobrey when he hadn't been in full possession of his faculties. Quite a lot of them if he was honest. He'd been concussed once, drunk several times, had a strange reaction to some harmless acid drops and been constantly confused pretty much from day one. But he was certain that at no point had he agreed to be interviewed by *Hi There!* magazine. Any more than he'd sent Miranda fifty replicas of his first piece. Or a map of Japan.

Enough was enough, he decided, dialling his agent back. But he was too late. Miranda had gone, leaving Eric to fume as the answer phone cut in, advising him that the offices of Miranda Barton were now closed for the weekend.

He dropped the handset. Let her have her little games. Because, thinking about it, there was no way, was there, that she could really visit him to recce the cottage? Not when she only had the name of his village to go on? A village, which he knew from personal experience, to have been missed off every map of Wales ever printed. And if Miranda couldn't visit, neither could *Hi There!*

It was some comfort but the whole affair had made Eric feel restless and vulnerable. A change of scene was called for, he decided, remembering that Mrs Jenks was rumoured to have recently expanded her

"Gents Outfitting" to include some relatively normal clothes. Cocking a wary eye at the darkening sky, he collected his anorak, locked the cottage and set off. If he was lucky he might beat the impending rain.

It was strange, he thought, walking briskly, that the extraordinary spell of fine weather should look like coming to an end on this of all days. As if the clouds massing on the distant horizon were a portent of the outside world nudging at the door of his hideaway.

***

Stepping into Mrs Jenks's shop he found comfort in the dingy interior. The everyday items haphazardly arranged and the shopkeeper herself, draped over the counter, absorbed in perusing several scraps of paper. As he approached he saw that these were the labels from a dozen or so tins stacked at the end of the counter, naked and shiny, bearing the names of their contents in scrawly red felt tip.

"Young Eric," said Mrs Jenks, whipping her glasses off. "Heard the news have you?"

"What news?" asked Eric politely. He'd been in town long enough now to know that what constituted "news" in Mrs Jenks' book wasn't necessarily anything of the sort.

"Someone's lifted the bar hatch at the Market Tavern."

Eric sighed. It was as he'd feared. "Isn't that rather what it's meant for, Mrs Jenks?"

Mrs Jenks stared. "What it's meant for? Oh, I see. Well, yes, but when I say lifted, young Eric, what I really mean is pinched."

"No one would pinch a bar hatch," objected Eric.

"They would from the Market Tavern. The *Market Tavern*, young Eric," repeated Mrs Jenks meaningfully

Suddenly Eric got it. "You mean the bar hatch with the old Earl's pledge carved on the underside?"

"Yep. Just unscrewed it they did and had it away. Second prize they'll have, those Twins, if I ever catch up with them. Put Hetty in a right tizz, it has, too, being worried all over again about the venue. She's put up a reward for information, just in case anyone saw or heard anything the night of the theft."

"Good old Hetty, eh?" said Eric.

"Mm," agreed Mrs Jenks. "Have to get up pretty early, you would, to catch her out. Talking of which," went on the shopkeeper, smoothly changing the subject, "I heard *you* was about pretty early yourself, today. Been to the chip shop flat, I gather? And for a squint round the old folks' complex? Not thinking of moving in just yet are we?" She went into peals of laughter. Eric could do nothing but grin awkwardly.

"No," he assured her, "not me." Then, remembering the excuse he'd given himself for visiting there, he added, "I just went by to see how they might have changed. They were newly built, you see, when I was last here."

Mrs Jenks nodded. "I remember them going up. Arnold had a fancy for putting his name down but I soon put a stop to that."

Putting her glasses back on and taking up a pen, she said, "Now then, young Eric, being as you're here you can give me a hand with this competition. I've got to state in less than a dozen words why this tinned veg beats all others."

"And does it?" asked Eric.

"Does it what?"

"Beat all others?"

Mrs Jenks stared. "How should I know? Never touch the stuff. That won't stop me winning a holiday to Rhyl, though, not when I'm giving myself a few goes to cover all the phrases I can think of." She gestured at the pile of labels. "So, thinking cap on, young Eric, and if you happens to be the one as comes up with the goods you can come with me."

Before Eric could answer she shot a glance at the front window of the shop, where the threatened rain made sagging puddles on the dark-brown awnings. "Damn," she muttered. "There's the rain on, and me with washing out, too. Just a tick." Reaching under the counter she came up with a walkie-talkie. "Arnold's idea," she explained to Eric. "To help us keep tabs on one another, now that we've expanded the shop." The radio crackled and spluttered into life as she squeezed the button. "Mrs Jenks to Arnold," she said rather self-consciously. "Are you reading me?"

There was a corresponding crackle from the other end accompanied by a high-pitched whistle, which would, Eric felt, drive any neighbouring sheepdogs into a state of utter frenzy.

"Arnold here," said a disembodied voice. "Over."

"Over where?" queried Mrs Jenks.

"What do you mean 'over where'? Over," said the voice.

"You said 'over' then you got cut off. Twice."

"No," said the voice. "I said 'over' because we're supposed to if you remember, so the other person knows they can speak. Over."

"Are we? Er … over."

"Yes. Over."

"Oh. Well, if you say so. Please state your position. Over."

"I'm in "Gents Outfitting" stacking pullovers. Over."

"Ah, good. Just nip out the back, would you, and fetch the washing in?"

There was silence. Tapping her foot, Mrs Jenks added through clenched teeth. "*Over.*"

"Done it," said the voice, with a triumphant giggle. "Ages ago, afore the rain came. Over and out."

"Slippery as a peach in syrup, he is," muttered Mrs Jenks, replacing the walkie-talkie beneath the counter. "Now then, where were we?"

"Trying to do your competition," said Eric. Then, desperate not to win a holiday with Mrs Jenks, he added, "But I'm afraid I can't help right now. I really only came in to take a look at your new menswear stock?"

The notion of a significant sale was sufficient to divert Mrs Jenks from pretty much anything else. "Well, why didn't you say so? If you was going out the back you could have saved me all that trouble over 'over' and asked Arnold about the washing when you got there."

"So I could," smiled Eric. "Just pop along there now shall I?"

"Aye, lad, off you go. I dare say I'll work this here slogan out for myself."

Eric left the shop, thrilled to have found a supply of jeans, cords and tops with which to restock his wardrobe.

Hurrying through the now torrential rain, he was startled by a car horn nearby. He raised the edge of his hood and peered at a lime-green Citroen parked at the kerb.

"You'll get soaked," yelled Min from the depths of the driver's seat, where her bright yellow oilskins clashed horribly with the car. "Hop in."

"Are you sure?"

"'Course."

Min swept the passenger seat clean of pastie wrappers, banana skins, a copy of the local paper, and a ripped and faded seed packet, the contents of which had begun to sprout in the mossy depths of the passenger foot well. "But I'd leave your hood up if I were you."

Sound advice, thought Eric, climbing into the car, where the rain still pattered on his head.

"That's the drawback of having a soft top," said Min, nodding towards the remnants of a fabric roof, flapping in the squally wind.

"Do you mean me or the car?"

"The car," giggled Min, her eyes shining. "Best belt up," she added.

"Of course," said Eric, aware that some people liked to drive without distractions.

They sat for a few moments in companionable silence.

"I meant the seatbelt," said Min eventually.

"Of course," said Eric again.

Feeling slightly foolish, he reached for the seatbelt and found only a fringe of frayed webbing where the metal clasp ought to have been. He offered this for Min's inspection.

"Ah, yes. Goat ate it, now I come to think about it. You'll have to hold it."

"What if we have to stop suddenly?"

"Hold it tighter," advised Min.

With some misgivings, Eric clamped the end of the seatbelt to his hip. It quickly became apparent, however, that he was unlikely to need it.

Releasing the brake, Min gunned the accelerator until finally they were neck and neck with a woman on the pavement, carrying a shopping basket and walking a Yorkie. Embarrassed, Eric avoided the woman's eyes.

Fortunately, a parked car then forced Min to jerk the 2CV out into the road, where she proceeded to go even more slowly, hugging the opposite kerb. "Is there room your side, Eric?" she called anxiously.

Eric eyed the distance. "Room for another car actually, Min," he called back, alarmed to then find himself face to face with the driver's door of a big white van, cruising through the gap. It was a bit like bumper cars, he thought, in slow motion.

"Can I go back in now?"

The tail lights of the van were ahead of them so Eric gave the thumbs-up. Veering back to the kerb, Min mounted it and bumped back down again, testing the legendary Citroen suspension to its limit. Worse, she almost ran over the same woman, walking the dog. Beginning to feel like a chauffeur-driven kerb-crawler, Eric buried his face in his hood.

Conversation was clearly the last thing on Min's mind as they continued by degrees up the high street. Nonetheless, she had a brave stab at it. "So, how've you been, young Eric?" she called, "It seems ages since we've seen you."

"I've been meaning to come up again," said Eric, willing Min to look at the road, "but I don't seem to have had a minute. I'd like to, though, some time."

"Actually, I need to talk to you about that," said Min. "Maybe we could have a few words when we get to your house?"

"By all means," muttered Eric, who was just hoping they would.

"Great." Clearing the high street, Min pushed her foot down a little harder on the throttle. "Hold tight, Eric. I'm changing up."

Min stirred the gearbox, finally finding second and sending the car forwards at a fractionally higher speed.

As she did so, a strange noise started somewhere in the front of the vehicle, causing her to brake with little regard for the lorry on her tail pipe. "There it is again," she squealed. "That noise. Do you hear it?"

Eric nodded, as Min steered the car into the side of the road, attracting a loud honk from the lorry and giving a cheery wave in return.

They sat for a moment and Eric twisted his head, this way and that, the better to hear past his hood. "It's stopped," he said at last.

"Mmm," agreed Min. "Weird isn't it? Should I drive on again, do you think?"

"Better had," said Eric. He was grateful for the lift and it was lovely to see Min again, but there was no denying he'd have got home quicker and stayed drier if he'd walked. "We'll listen out for it, shall we?"

Min ambled back out into the road and gradually increased her speed until the noise started again. Seeing her about to take her foot off, Eric said, "Keep going, Min."

"Are you sure it's safe?"

Eric said nothing. Safe didn't really come into it.

Tipping his head to one side, he eyed the glove compartment thoughtfully. Then leaning forwards he unclipped it and peered inside. There, a dozen or so acid-drop bags blew around like feathers in a wind tunnel. Laughing, he reached in and rustled some in his hand. "Here are your culprits," he announced.

"That'll be me," confessed Min. Then, with a longing glance at the passenger seat, she added, "that's where I sit, as a rule."

"You don't usually do the driving then?" asked Eric, fastening the glove compartment.

Min shook her head then ducked well below the level of the steering wheel as a cattle lorry overtook them. "Not if I can help it. I'm far happier in the pony and trap – no complicated buttons and levers to worry about and no funny noises."

Eric smiled. "Well, I think we've explained the noises now. At a certain speed you get the wind up and it sets all these bags in motion."

Min nodded ruefully. " 'T'isn't only at a certain speed that I get the wind up. It happens to me as soon as I get in the car."

***

Arriving at last at the cottage, Eric hung their outdoor clothes to drip in the hallway.

Min, he realised, was his first proper visitor. Not counting Beryl and Meryl, of course, who'd only ever dropped in when he was out. And what a delightful visitor she was turning out to be; exclaiming in rapture over the cottage, its fixtures and fittings and, above all, its cleanliness. The only drawback to her enthusiasm was her minnow-like tendency to dart off in all directions when he wasn't looking.

She'd disappeared now into the sitting room where, Eric belatedly remembered, his pile of souvenir postcards sat for all to see. Fortunately Min hadn't noticed them, being too busy gazing up at the framed photo of his masterpiece.

"What a beautiful, beautiful picture," she breathed. "It's of that famous sculpture, isn't it? *A Deep Depression in Driftwood*? Where on earth did you get it?"

Eric shuffled awkwardly. "Er, … someone gave it to me," he said, which was true enough.

"You *are* lucky," sighed Min. "Mo and I reckon the only thing that'd persuade us to go to London would be seeing that for real." She turned to Eric. "Oh, I *wish* I had my glasses with me. Perhaps next time I'll bring them for a proper look?"

No fear, thought Eric, aware that she would then be able to read the small print below the photo. Then the penny dropped.

"You wear glasses?"

"For some things, yes."

"Driving?" hazarded Eric.

"Technically, yes."

It explained a lot. Gently, Eric steered Min towards the kitchen. "How about a cup of tea?" he offered. "Warm us up a bit after our journey."

Installing his guest at the kitchen table, Eric then wished he hadn't. Glasses or no glasses, Min had spotted the outline of his right ear in the varnish.

"This looks like someone's *ear*, here," she said, tracing the shape with a curious forefinger. "How do you suppose that happened?"

"Who knows?" Eric put her cup and saucer over the mark and changed the subject. "Er, you said you had something to ask me?"

Min looked up. "That's right, so I did. Well, the thing is …"

"Yes?" said Eric encouragingly.

"You know when you came up to the farm and Mo and I were telling you about the blacked-out windows of the Williams Twins' barn?"

"Gosh, yes," said Eric. In point of fact, what with one thing and another, he'd forgotten all about it. "Did you ever get to the bottom of all that?"

Min shook her head. "No, but just lately there's been lots of white vans on the road again, evidently collecting stuff from their place. Mo says we should sneak over there one night to see what the Twins are up to and … um, I wondered whether you would come too? As a witness."

Eric paused in the act of pouring milk. "A witness to what?"

"That's just it. We don't know. It might be nothing, of course … but why would they black out the barn windows unless they had something to hide?

And what are all those vans doing, going up there at all hours?"

"Both very fair questions," said Eric, "but what if we get caught?"

"The Twins go off clubbing once a month and they're always out till dawn so it ought to be quite safe if we go then."

The words "ought to be" weren't lost on Eric, but something about Min's imploring expression made him throw caution to the wind.

"Count me in," he said cheerfully.

"Do you mean it?" Min blew delicately on her tea and beamed at him. "It would be wonderful if you did?"

"Of course," replied Eric.

"Great. Well, tomorrow night, being Saturday, should be the Twins' night out. Is that too short notice for you?"

"Not at all," lied Eric. Then, seeing Min's anxious expression, he added, "It's a date."

Smiling, Min settled down and began to sip her tea as Eric told her all about the theft of the bar hatch from the Market Tavern, delighted to have beaten the postman to this particular piece of news.

Much later, having seen Min to her car, Eric returned to the cottage, unlocked his parlour door and found himself looking at his *A Goddess Weeping* in an altogether new light. Tentatively, he picked up a chisel.

***

"It's a date," repeated Min to herself as she crept home, adding the words to her secret stash of possible compliments from Eric.

This small depository already contained, "I must love you and leave you," which Eric had said the day he'd visited her home, and "I look forward to it", in response to her suggestion that he might visit again. It wasn't much, she thought, but it gave her hope …

CHAPTER SIXTEEN

Eric's first thought upon arriving at the Pugh Sisters' yard the following evening was that he'd missed the boat. Or, to be more accurate, the 2CV, which was nowhere to be seen. Much as he'd been looking forward to seeing Min again, the idea of not visiting the Twins' barn was a big relief.

Gleefully he threw the van into reverse ready for the off. At that moment, however, he heard a distant shout as Min careered out of the house.

"Thank goodness I heard the van," she said, fetching up at the driver's door. "I was afraid you'd think we'd gone without you and be heading off home."

"Not at all," said Eric, slipping the van back into neutral and turning off the engine.

"The reason our car's not here," added Min, glancing at the empty parking space, "is that Mo's had to go and visit a cousin who's unwell according to the Frank the Mail. You and I can still go, though," she said, looking hopefully at Eric.

"Great," said Eric. "What shall we do? Take the van instead?"

Min shook her head. "Heavens, no. It's not exactly suitable for off-road driving, is it? No, I thought we could take the horses."

"Take the horses?" echoed Eric. "Won't they be in the way?"

Min giggled. "Not take them just for the sake of it. I mean we can ride them. Horses are quieter than cars and much better at going across country. Plus, if it turns out the Twins haven't gone clubbing after all, we can just turn round, can't we, and gallop off into the night?"

"Mm," said Eric, who couldn't help feeling that walking off into the day would be hard enough, given his lack of experience at riding. He put this to Min.

"Oh, you'll be fine," she said airily. "Come on, let's go and get a cup of tea and maybe an acid drop or two for sustenance, until it's dark enough to leave."

Eric barely heard her, so preoccupied was he with the business of having to ride a horse. To make matters worse, they passed the field on the way to the house, where the two animals selected for the journey were grazing.

Or rather, one of them was grazing. The other, Desmond, was penned in a little space with virtually no grass at all. "You'll be riding him," said Min, oblivious it seemed to the murderous glint in the horse's eye.

**

"Right," said Min as they downed the last of their tea, "I reckon it's as dark as it's going to get this time of the year and with such a big moon. Best go and saddle up."

Eric then found himself piled high with Desmond's tack for the walk to the paddocks. Fortunately he wasn't required to dress his mount, merely to assist Min as she set about the job, quickly and efficiently. Leading the horses out, Eric made to shut Desmond's gate behind him.

"It's OK," said Min, "you can leave it open. Airs the field."

Eric looked doubtfully at her. "Really?" he asked.

"'Course not," said Min, giggling. "Now, let's get you aboard."

A bruising couple of minutes followed, during which Eric made only fleeting contact with his saddle due to the overzealous efforts of Min in giving him a leg up. Finally he landed, quite by chance, astride the large, flat back. As he took up the reins he felt Desmond shift beneath him like the scariest roller-coaster at the fair.

"He's off, Min," yelled Eric, clutching his saddle.

Min looked up from mounting her own pony. "He isn't," she said smiling. "He's just getting comfy, resting his back foot."

"You mean I haven't gone anywhere?"

"Not yet." Min gathered her reins. "We'll go now, shall we?"

Desmond then went into what felt like perpetual motion, rolling and plunging first this way, then the other. "He's bucking, Min," called Eric, glad to have remembered the technical term for it.

Min turned in her saddle and ran a professional eye over things. "No he's not."

"What's he doing then?"

"He's walking, very slowly. You need to gee him up a bit, Eric."

"Is that wise?"

"Of course."

"What if he won't stop?"

"Oh, you needn't worry on that score," replied Min. "Stopping's what Desmond does best."

***

For the next twenty minutes, Eric was to discover that Min never spoke a truer word. Under instruction from her to "urge him on", Eric always seemed to be mid-urge when Desmond put in a crafty stop, sending Eric skidding down his neck.

"It's like riding a nodding donkey on an oil field," he grumbled, scrambling out of the clinging, black bog for the umpteenth time. It didn't help that he was blinded by Mo's crash helmet, which was several sizes too large for him and mainly held up by his nose. In spite of everything, though, he was enjoying his ride.

There was something about Min's company, he thought, riding blindly alongside her and taking her word for it about the scenery, subdued to sepia, apparently, by the moonlight, that made him happy. It also made him think, rather unaccountably, of his new piece and how well it was coming on.

Finally, Min called a halt and Eric removed his hat, to discover they had arrived at a large clearing, midway along a sunken lane leading to the large, grey outline of Pantygwyn in the distance.

"This is the other way into the Twins' farm," explained Min, "from the top road. Gets so overgrown, they have to be really drunk to drive it. We'll be fine though, on foot."

Eric grinned, before applying himself to his first intentional dismount of the evening. Back on terra firma, he tied Desmond to a tree, which the horse proceeded to devour, twig by twig.

After a quick breather, Eric and Min set off, following the sunken lane through woodland until they came to a steep bank separating the Williams' farmyard from the trees. Dropping onto their fronts, they elbowed their way up the slope, to arrive commando-style in the yard. The farmhouse was in darkness with no sign of the Twins' Land Rover, which was all to the good.

The barn lay opposite the house. Springing into a crouch, Min gestured Eric to follow her as she sprinted for the double doors at the far end of the building.

"This is it," she grinned, sliding the bolt.

The doors creaked outwards to meet them, the sound echoing like the long, low moan of a sleeping beast.

Taking a deep breath, they stepped into the gloomy interior and drew the doors to behind them. Next minute, Eric flung himself to the ground as a hideous whirring noise came from nowhere and an eerie, white light flickered in the cavernous space.

"It's only my torch," hissed Min. "You have to wind it up to make it work."

Eric eyed the little torch, the output of which was roughly equivalent to a birthday cake candle in a draught. He said nothing, however, having neglected to bring a torch of any kind himself.

Winding like someone trying to land a blue whale, Min played the light around the barn. "Hello," she muttered, tip-toeing towards the shifting shape of some sort of equipment tucked against the apex wall. "What's this?"

Eric joined her and together they peered at what seemed to be an industrial food mixer, its paddles suspended over a large, stainless-steel bowl.

"Someone's been making something," said Eric.

"Acid drops," whispered Min. "Can't you smell them?"

Before he could stop her, Min reached into the bowl and picked off a piece of the hard, shiny residue sticking to the sides. She nibbled the mixture from her finger, crunching happily.

"Definitely acid drops," she confirmed, picking off another piece for Eric. "This must be where they're made, by that young chap from the market, I expect. But why do you suppose he wants to set up in business here with the Twins?"

"He's related to them," said Eric, sucking his sweet and remembering his conversation with Ethel and Ivy in the pub.

Min sniffed. "Not his fault, I suppose. But sweet-making can't be all that's going on here, can it? Else why black out the windows?"

"Good point," said Eric. "Let's see what else we can find, eh?"

They passed deeper into the barn where the air was thick with a smell that was at once peculiar and very familiar. Taking a closer look at the shelves lining the walls and the centre section, Eric and Min clutched one another, giggling.

"All utterly innocent after all," gasped Min, writhing against Eric's chest.

"Utterly," howled Eric, wondering what on earth could have come over the pair of them, but deciding to make the most of it.

***

Still laughing, they made their way back towards the horses. As they left the yard, Eric turned and took a last look at the vast bulk of the barn, etched against the moonlit sky. Surely it hadn't seemed quite that big on the inside?

The next minute, the barn was forgotten as little Min caught her foot on the steep bank and stumbled into his arms.

Eric made to release her, then thought better of it.

"A puddle can hold the moon," he told himself, "if only for a little while."

"Am I the moon?" Min breathed.

Eric blushed. Surely he hadn't said that out loud? "Yes," he said, "I'm beginning to think you are."

"Big and round?" she asked, her eyes sparkling in her small, slim face.

Eric shook his head. "Pale and beautiful."

Min smiled. "Makes you the puddle, then?"

"Mm," agreed Eric. "Wet."

"I was thinking more of deep and mysterious," Min assured him, pressing further into his arms.

How long they might have remained like that was hard to say. Eric hoped it might be days or even weeks. At that moment, however, a shrill whinny shattered the mood.

"Oh," said Min, drawing away, "that's Desmond."

"Probably finished his tree," murmured Eric.

"No, that wasn't his hungry whinny. It was more like something scared him."

Eric glanced along the lane, hearing another, smaller whinny as he did so.

"And that's Petal," wailed Min, beginning to run, fleet as a deer, towards the sound.

Floundering in her wake, Eric's own progress was best described as now-you-see-him-now-you-don't as he battled to stay upright on the bramble-strewn path. Min's eyesight, he thought, must be far better than his in the dark.

Scrambling to his feet again, Eric almost ran up the back of Min, frozen into stillness a little way short of the clearing where they'd left the horses. Following her agonised gaze, he saw them now, whirling and pulling at their tethers as a figure, ghost-grey in the moonlight, danced beside them.

***

Finding the horses had been such a surprise it had almost caused lifelong non-driver, Terry Williams, to crash the Land Rover.

The wretched thing had been out of control, if he was honest, ever since he'd turned off the top road. Seeing the animals, tethered in the clearing, he'd jumped on the middle pedal, it being the only one he hadn't tried, up till now. The vehicle had obligingly lurched to a halt, with no need even to cut the engine.

Seizing a torch, Terry had tumbled from the driver's seat, and crawled towards the horses, finding himself distracted by a riding hat, lying near to the larger of the two animals. Grinning, he tried the hat on for size, and stood up, feeling a familiar compulsion to dance.

And why not, he thought, flicking the switch on his powerful torch and strobing the beam across himself. There was no one to see him, out here in the middle of nowhere …

***

There was no mistaking that skinny, gyrating body, thought Eric, watching in horror with Min. Or that oversized flat cap, squashed, now, under the weight of Mo's large, round riding hat.

Oblivious to his audience, Terry proceeded to cavort ever more wildly, gurning and crossing his eyes in his own personal spotlight.

This game seemed likely to amuse him for a while, making it impossible, Eric realised, to get to the horses without being seen. And, already, Desmond had become aware of their presence and was whickering in Min's direction, threatening to give the game away.

There was nothing for it, Eric decided, but to front it out, get rid of Terry and be on their way.

"Hey," he called, "that you Terry?"

The leaping figure juddered to a halt and peered through the beam of the torch.

"Who's that?" he asked, stepping backwards and tripping into a clump of briar.

"It's me, Eric Bagnall. I've got Min Pugh with me."

Terry spun the torch in their direction. "Ha," he said, struggling like a rabbit in a net. "Caught you."

"Caught us doing what?" enquired Eric calmly. "Taking an equine excursion on a lovely evening, and breaking our journey with a brief perambulation to stretch our legs?"

There was a baffled silence.

"Eh?" said Terry at last.

"Never mind," said Eric. Then, looking around he asked, as casually as he could, "Where's Tony tonight?"

"Everyone always wants to know where Tony is," grumbled Terry peevishly, finally ripping clear of the undergrowth and regaining his feet. "Everywhere we go, everything we do, it's Tony this, Tony that. Don't ask me why."

"Perhaps because he's bigger than you?" suggested Eric.

"Big as he is," shouted Terry, his face taking on a maniacal glow in the beam of his torch, "I've knackered him tonight. Serves him right, too. Sneaking off for a knee trembler with Last Chance Trudy, who'd already promised one to me for a fiver, although I don't really like cocktails. Filched the Land Rover keys, didn't I? Drove off and left him there."

Terry went into paroxysms of giggles at this and Eric began to wonder whether everyone was right to fear Tony the most.

"Which is not to say," warned Terry, his laughter stopping as suddenly as it had begun, "as I won't tell him all about you two being up here, looking all starry eyed like you're off your heads on something. Warned him, I did, as you were trouble, soon as I set eyes on you." He thought for a moment. "Or at least, he warned me. But I agreed."

"And what trouble am I causing now?" asked Eric, realising that he did feel a little light-headed in spite of a day with no slurry whatsoever.

"Exactly," piped up Min. "As Eric says, we were simply out for a ride and decided to take a stroll."

"Attagirl," thought Eric proudly.

"I mean," went on Min, "it's not as if we went to your yard, or anything, knowing full well you'd be out, or looked in the big barn with the double doors."

Eric held his breath.

"You didn't?" asked Terry at last.

"Certainly not," said Min smoothly.

"We-ell … that's good 'cos I'd have had something to say about that, I can tell you."

"Of course you would," cut in Eric, "and rightly so. But as Min says, we've done nothing wrong."

Terry removed Mo's riding hat and twirled it on his skinny forefinger.

"*She* hasn't," he agreed, "but *you* have. Getting involved with that bloody event Hetty's been planning. Not that there's going to *be* an event now," he added triumphantly, "thanks to me and Tony."

"Oh, yes," said Eric. "How's that then?"

Terry sniggered. "Summat missing, ain't there, from the Market Tavern? Summat vital to you lot and your stupid plans?"

"And what would that be, Terry?" asked Eric.

Terry opened his mouth to reply, then clearly thought better of it. "Hey, trying to trap me are you?" he shouted. "Typical smart arse Londoner, that's what Tony would say. Baffling us locals with long words and crafty questions … not to mention … ". His eyes alighted on Min. "… pinching our women. Make a regular habit of that, don't you?"

"I haven't pinched her," said Eric truthfully, raising his voice to cover a little giggle from Min.

"That's right," she agreed, adding in a whispered aside to Eric, "Bit of cuddling maybe, and rather a nice hug, but definitely no pinching."

Eric grinned in spite of himself and instantly wished he hadn't

"Funny, is it?" yelled Terry. "Well laugh at this, then." Hurling the riding hat into a distant bush, he began fumbling with the knots in the horses' tethers.

"If you two are so bloody fond of walking," he screeched, "you can do some more of it, can't you? Right up your street that ought to be, legging it home. And don't let me catch you strolling around in the moonlight and not looking in our barn again."

Whooping and dancing, he jumped into the Land Rover, started the engine and drove the vehicle back and forth on the narrow track, gunning the accelerator and keeping one hand on the horn. Loosed from their tethers, the horses backed away, spun on their hind legs and took off.

Terry, who happened to have been going forwards at the time, fishtailed the back end of the Land Rover as he, too, sped away.

Min looked helplessly after the galloping horses and surrendered a shaking hand to Eric. He took it gratefully, allowing her to steer him through the treacherous undergrowth and across a wide, open field in pursuit of the ponies. Not that there was any real hope of catching them, he thought … unless …

"Giddyup, Desmond!" he shouted, aware of Min's appalled eyes on him.

Eric crossed his fingers, delighted when the larger of the two rapidly vanishing shadows pulled up short and thrust his massive head towards the ground.

"Oh, well done, Eric," panted Min, as Petal also slithered to a halt.

Eric resisted the urge to huff on his fingernails but, in truth, he was pretty pleased with himself.

"Just a little something I taught him on the way," he explained.

Smiling, he led the way to where the horses had stopped, alongside what looked like the makings of a big bonfire. Wandering over for a closer look, he stubbed his toe against something low and hard.

Stooping, he ran his hands over a large, flat piece of wood, finding it smooth and square, with a slightly bevelled edge. It occurred to him that it would make a wonderful plinth for his new piece.

At that moment, there was the whoosh of tyres on tarmac and the glare of lights beyond a nearby gate.

Eric snapped upright. "What's that?"

"Only a car," said Min, "on the public road, which is actually closer to us now than the Twins' place. We could even ride back that way."

As Min began a detailed inspection of the horses, Eric tiptoed to the gate with his piece of wood. He could pick it up later, he thought, with the van.

***

Waking the next morning, Eric had trouble separating fact from fantasy regarding his nocturnal adventures with Min.

The ride on Desmond had been real enough, he decided, wincing. The innocent discoveries in the barn were also clear in his mind, as was the encounter with Terry on the sunken lane. But had he really dared to cuddle such a divine creature as little Min? And been cuddled back?

Eric made his way to the bathroom, happening as he did so to catch sight of his scantily clad reflection in the landing mirror. Cursing his unwariness, he backtracked a couple of steps, sucked in his stomach, corrected his tendency to walk with his toes turned up and made the pass again. That was better, he thought, filing the pose away for future reference. Blushing as he realised why.

CHAPTER SEVENTEEN

"It's a mystery," said Beryl, as she and Meryl made their way to school via Eric's postbox first thing Tuesday morning, "because when I went to copy it out in best it wasn't there. Yet I did it, I know I did."

"Did what?" muttered Meryl, head down against another of the showers, which had persisted in the wake of Friday's heavy rain.

"My geography homework. I traced a map of Japan and everything but it's gone. I can always do it again, of course. In fact, I'll have to because it's so late now, Rabbitty Rees is getting tetchy. But it's still a mystery. Right there it was in my rough book and now it isn't."

Meryl stepped into a doorway and turned to face her sister. "Are you saying something's missing from your exercise book?"

"Well, yes. I thought I'd made that plain. But why have we stopped? We'll be late for school at this rate, to say nothing of Eric, maybe getting up early and checking his mail before we do."

"Eric won't be getting up early," said Meryl, briskly. "He was on the raz again last night with Mel Meredith, so he may not get up at all. Now, about this missing homework of yours: when and where did you last see it?"

"Just after I'd done it, I suppose. In my rough book, as I told you."

"And this would be the same book, would it, in which you wrote our covering letter about Eric's replicas?"

Beryl beamed. "That's the one. I wrote the letter on a spare page, just before my rough homework, then I tore it out and … Oh, dear."

"Exactly," said Meryl. "*Oh, dear*. You know what you've done, don't you? You've posted your homework to London, along with the letter."

"Surely not," whispered Beryl.

"Surely *so*, Beryl. And I wouldn't mind betting that's why there's been no sign of the money. How suspicious must Miranda Thingy have been, finding a chunk of your homework in with Eric's letter, not to mention a map of Japan?"

Her sister hung her head, hot tears mingling with the rain dripping from her hood. "Gosh, Meryl, I'm sorry. How could I have been so stupid?"

"Years of practice?" suggested Meryl.

Beryl took this on her wobbling chin. "I suppose there's no point," she asked, in a small voice, "in checking the postbox now, just in case?"

"None whatever," replied Meryl, adding, "But we might as well, being as it's on our way."

A few minutes later the entire homework incident was forgotten in the giddy whirl of finding a large, padded envelope in Eric's postbox.

"It's definitely from her, isn't it?" asked Beryl.

Meryl turned the envelope over and whooped to see a glossy return-address label stuck to the flap. "Definitely. Look, this is her logo interwoven with a montage of her clients' names – with 'Sculptor, Eric Bagnall', right at the top."

"Wow," said Beryl. "So it'll be the money, won't it?"

Meryl squeezed the soft, plump parcel. "There's only one way to find out."

Seizing the flap, she tore the envelope open, allowing a thick wad of cash to tumble free. There was also a handwritten note, scrawled on Miranda's headed paper.

Beryl leaned closer.

"Eric," she read aloud. "Thanks so much for the miniature replicas of your piece. They're wonderful – Delecta-ble even! Hope you've diarised my visit to your cottage. Speak soon, Miranda."

Beryl looked up guiltily. "I suppose we oughtn't to have read that?"

Meryl shrugged. "It's not as if it made any sense, is it? What was all that 'Delecta-ble' stuff? And 'diarised'? Sounds to me like a problem in the loo department. Still, she said the miniatures were wonderful, which is great ..." A loud bong interrupted Meryl's flow, as the town clock began to strike three. She glanced at her watch. "Wow – nine o'clock already. We'd best make tracks for school."

"Just a minute," said Beryl, running her hand around the inside of the postbox and extracting a thin, plain, white card. "Ah, I thought there was something else in here. Better not leave this here, eh?"

"Why not?" asked Meryl.

Seeing her chance to redeem herself, Beryl explained, "Because it'd be awful, wouldn't it, if Eric happened to mention this postcard to Frank the Mail, and Frank asked him if he got the parcel, delivered on the same day?"

"Gosh, yes," agreed Meryl. "What does it say, anyway?"

Beryl turned the card over. "Nothing much. Seems to be from his mam and dad, going on about being pee'ed off with the Guardians of Eternal Peace … thinking of applying for a new job ... blah, blah, blah ... oh, and that they might be seeing him very soon."

"Hardly life and death stuff then?" suggested Meryl. "I should bung it in your satchel for now. We can always bin it somewhere, later."

In belated deference to Eric's probable hangover, they tiptoed away.

***

As it happened, Meryl and Beryl needn't have worried about Eric's hangover. To his amazement, he didn't have one. He'd woken with a clear head and a growing conviction that, like a man sufficiently exposed to a particular virus, he had become immune to slurry.

It helped, of course, that he was in such a positive frame of mind these days. His new piece had taken on a life of its own, oddly enough since his adventure with Min on Saturday night. Beckoning him from his bed shortly after dawn every morning, regardless of the lateness of his night before.

Brushing wood shavings from his sweater, he made his way from the parlour to the kitchen. A spot of breakfast, he thought, and a couple more hours on his piece, then he ought to be on his way. He'd heard a whisper in the pub last night about an elderly Fordson tractor, tucked away on a smallholding belonging to a Mrs Mann. If she was willing to exhibit it, this would make nearly two dozen implements and pieces of machinery, lined up for

Eric's parade. More than enough, he decided, for a decent show of Landoobrey's rich agricultural heritage.

Passing the front door he realised that, for the first time since arriving in his new home, he'd forgotten to lock up. Still, where was the harm in that, he asked himself. He was among friends. Friends with whom he'd spent a wonderful, if somewhat riotous, weekend. A weekend, which even the memory of his telephone conversation with Miranda couldn't spoil. Because the more he thought about that, the more certain he was that his threatened interview with *Hi There!* magazine could never come off.

***

A few hours later, Eric drove back down the mountain, trying to shift a lingering smell of mud and teenage feet from his nostrils. What a way to live, he thought, recalling the leaky touring caravan occupied by the widow, Mrs Mann, and her three sons.

To add to the family's discomfort, the caravan sat facing the bones of their dream home, an ancient farmhouse standing roofless and partially gutted on the opposite side of the yard.

According to Mrs Mann, her late husband, Jeff, had started the project with enthusiasm, a self-help book on building, and no prior knowledge of a lurking aneurysm. Exhausted by his day job, working a fifty-hour week driving lorries, he'd barely got as far as rendering the farmhouse uninhabitable before dropping dead. The boys, each of whom appeared to have modelled himself in his father's image, complete with bobble hats, oversized boots and boiler suits, had all since taken a turn with the book. But so far they'd lacked the nerve to carry on the good work.

Eric sighed. Burdened by debt, their only hope of solvency appeared to rest with two hundred turkey chicks, pre-ordered by Jeff, to be fattened as a cash crop for Christmas. It was hard to see, though, how the little family might survive until December. Or the turkeys, come to that.

And in the meantime, thought Eric, changing down to negotiate a tricky bend, Mrs Mann had still seen fit to smile a lot and press food upon him during his visit. Rather odd food, he had to admit because, while he'd grown used to being offered cake at practically every farm he'd been to, Mrs Mann's had been the first fishcake he'd encountered.

Even then, he reminded himself, this had been something of a misnomer given the lack of fish in it. A shortcoming easily explained by the presence in a galvanised bucket by the sink of one very small, economy brand tin, previously housing a pilchard. The widow having evidently been mashing spuds and crumbing stale bread since daybreak to make it into a meal.

"Hope I'm not taking anyone's second helping?" Eric had said, chewing gamely under the watchful eyes of the Mann boys.

"No." The breaking voice of the youngest lad belied his efforts to be just like his dad. "You're taking Mum's first."

It had been then that Eric had conceived his fabrication of a special Summer Spectacular fee, payable to the exhibitors of particularly rare pieces of machinery. The family had argued, probably with good reason, that their elderly Fordson Major hardly qualified as "rare". Eric, however, had stuck to his guns and left a fat cheque in his wake, hoping it would make some difference to life in the flimsy caravan, barely one step up from a tent.

And talking of tents, he thought, climbing out of the van and sprinting through the rain for his cottage, he could only hope his erstwhile lodgers were managing OK, now that the wet season had arrived.

***

Meryl and Beryl were managing very well and paying noisy homage to the man unwittingly responsible.

"Good old Eric," cried Beryl for the umpteenth time as she and Meryl counted the cash yet again. The money had burned several holes in Meryl's pocket over the past few hours and the girls had raced home with it directly after school.

"Good old us, too," she reminded Beryl. "After all, we did all the hard work, didn't we?"

"We certainly did," agreed Beryl. "The whole process, from finding out that Eric is really a famous, reclusive artist, right through to making a set of replicas of his masterpiece and getting paid for them. I never thought we would, did you?"

"Of course!" Meryl looked genuinely surprised at the question.

"What, right from the start, when we first saw his photo of *A Deep Depression in Driftwood* in his sitting room and I said it looked like a bit of wood with a hole in it? Which I still do, by the way."

"Right from then," said Meryl, planting a smacking kiss on the crisp, new notes. "And this,

Beryl, is our ticket out of this grotty old chip shop yard and into a smart, up-to-the-minute camp site. We've earned it, too, when you think what we went through to finally get those replicas off to London."

"With my covering letter," Beryl put in, "which did the trick, didn't it? Even allowing for my little homework blunder."

Meryl smiled. "Yes, Beryl, it did the trick. And the money's ours now to do as we wish with."

"Mmm." Beryl eyed the notes. "I reckon we'd have a job to spend it all on a camp site, though, even if we paid in advance right through the summer."

"Well, we've got our expenses to cover, don't forget. To say nothing of our time, and wear and tear on our nerves, especially when it all went pear-shaped that night in Eric's cottage."

"Even so," persisted Beryl, "I still think there'll be plenty of cash left over. What do you think we should do with it if there is?"

Meryl thought for a moment. "We could give it to charity, I suppose?"

"Or to the Summer Spectacular?" suggested Beryl. "That way it would benefit the whole town, wouldn't it? It'd be quite fitting, too, the world-renowned sculptor, Eric Bagnall, making an anonymous donation to the town that's given him sanctuary." She frowned briefly. "Amongst other things, of course, like severe concussion, probably, and a night with his head stuck to his kitchen table ... Still, he'd approve of his gift, wouldn't he, if he knew he'd given it?"

"Which he won't, of course," Meryl reminded her. "But you're right. He'd love it. So we'll see ourselves sorted with our expenses and a decent pitch on a camp site, and we'll give the rest to the Summer Spectacular. Then, come the big day, we'll know, won't we, that we helped to make it what it was?"

"*Great,*" said Beryl, as a throat-clearing cough sounded over the patter of rain on the tent. "Choke up, chicken," she added, reaching over to pat her sister on the back.

"What?"

"I said choke up, chicken. You coughed, didn't you?"

"*Someone* coughed," admitted Meryl, "but it wasn't me …"

"No," said the unmistakeable voice of Hetty the Hart from just beyond the thin, fabric wall, "it was me."

***

Two pale faces appeared, by degrees, at the tent flap to gaze fearfully up at Hetty, standing with her arms folded across the chest of her mac, tapping one plimsolled foot on the damp yard.

"How long have you been there?" asked Meryl.

"Long enough, believe me. Thought I'd pop by to see what you're up to. Now I know."

"We can explain everything," said Beryl, hoping Meryl could.

"Come on then. I'm waiting."

Ten minutes later, Hetty's footsteps clumped away in the direction of Eric's cottage. Her mind boggling at the audacity of the schoolgirls, her pockets bulging with their hard-won cash.

"Oh, well," said Meryl. "I suppose we're not the first entrepreneurs to have made and lost a fortune in a single day."

"Maybe not," sobbed Beryl, "but it's a great, big bummer all the same."

***

Over at the cottage, Eric tore himself away from his sculpture and pottered down the hallway, delighted to find Hetty on his doorstep. His smile of welcome, however, was not immediately returned by his visitor, whose eyes were fixed on the chisel, balanced in the sticking-plastered fingers of his right hand.

Following her gaze, Eric cursed his absent-mindedness in bringing his tools along for the walk.

"Spot of maintenance," he mumbled. "Always something needs doing in the woodwork line …"

"It's no good, Eric," sighed Hetty, emptying the sodden crown of her Stetson and stepping past him into the hall. "I'm afraid the game's up."

"What game?"

"The one where you pretend to be a humble, retired woodwork teacher when really you're a world famous sculptor. Responsible, as I understand it, for the hottest artistic property of the decade."

"Ah," said Eric, "that game. How did you find out?"

"I didn't. It was all the work of your old friends, Beryl and Meryl. They've been invading your privacy yet again I'm afraid, but this time with rather more serious consequences."

Looking every one of her sixty-odd years, Hetty groped her way to the kitchen and sat down. "Mind if I park myself, young Eric? Between this and those blasted Twins having it away with the only proof of the town's ownership of the Bowen field, I'm fair done in."

"No joy, then, with the reward for the return of the bar hatch?"

Hetty shook her head. "Afraid not. And the printers, for once, were so quick off the mark, they'd done the print run before I could stop them. So, as of this moment, I've got several hundred leaflets and posters all showing the Summer Spectacular venue as the Bowen Field." She shook her head sadly. "It's going to look awful if we have to amend them all by hand, to say nothing of the time it's going to take. Time which, frankly, we haven't got."

"The bar hatch might still turn up, mightn't it?" said Eric encouragingly. "Provided it isn't burnt or buried, it's got to be somewhere, hasn't it?"

"Of course it has," agreed Hetty, "but given the hundreds of acres the Twins own, to say nothing of a multitude of outbuildings and the farmhouse itself, none of which we've any legal grounds for searching, I don't see how we're ever going to find it, do you?"

"I suppose not," said Eric.

"And as if all that wasn't bad enough, those wretched Stitch girls have to go causing trouble left, right and centre." Hetty thought for a moment, then said quietly, "I blame myself, really I do. Pleading their cause in your garden that evening, when all the time they were up to their freshly scrubbed necks in identity theft, art fraud and goodness knows what else."

Eric stared. He hadn't a clue what Hetty was talking about but it moved him to see her so down. "How about you start at the beginning?" he offered.

"OK. Well, pin back your lug-holes, young Eric, and prepare yourself for a shock."

Hetty's narrative finally drew to a close. "So there you have it, Eric. It all started with them eavesdropping on your phone call and snowballed from there. And this time you have my full blessing in bringing those two monkeys to justice."

Eric smiled. "Oh, I think that's a bit harsh, don't you? After all, there's a fine line I always think between crime and enterprise, and they've definitely been enterprising, haven't they?"

"But they've stolen your money," objected Hetty.

"Well, not really. There wouldn't have *been* any money if the girls hadn't made the replicas of my piece. A job which I'd no intention of doing myself. So perhaps there's no real harm done?"

Shrugging, Hetty reached into her coat pocket for the bulky wad of notes. "All the same, you'd better have this."

Eric made no move towards the money. "Why not let them keep it, eh, Hetty? Enough for them to go to a proper camp site at least, and to cover their time and expenses? Then, if they want to give the rest to the Summer Spectacular, as you say, that's fine, isn't it?"

"You sure, young Eric?"

Eric nodded. "I've been to that flat, don't forget, and I can practically smell the chip shop yard from here. I'd like to think the money will save them from both, for a little while at least."

"Fair enough," said Hetty, "only I think you should be the one to give it back to them. That way they'll have to face you and acknowledge what they've done."

Nodding, Eric took the money and followed Hetty to the door. "Thanks for coming, Hetty, and I'm sorry I've had to be less than honest with you. I didn't want it getting about the town who I really am."

Hetty smiled. "It was understandable, you keeping mum when you first arrived. Still, hopefully you know by now how discreet I can be?"

"Mm," said Eric. That was what worried him. "It's still raining," he said, opening the door and peering out. "That makes four days now without … Good grief, what's that?"

Joining him on the doorstep, Hetty followed his gaze to where a spindly figure appeared to cling to the north face of the town clock.

"Looks like a giant fly," she observed, "in a bright orange Pac-a-mac."

"Can't be though, can it?" asked Eric, doubtfully.

"Well, of course it can't. I only said it looked like it. It'll be Arnold washing the clock."

"In this weather?"

"Mrs Jenks reckons it's easier in the rain."

"Poor old Arnold," said Eric.

***

In point of fact, Arnold wasn't clinging to the clock face, as such, but to the top rung of his ladder. The precise length of time he'd been there was difficult to establish. Partly because of the fabled unreliability of the ancient timepiece but mainly because the big hand had just fallen off it. Closely followed by the contents of Arnold's bucket and very nearly Arnold himself. This near-miss had petrified the old man to the point where descent seemed impossible, even by the conventional route.

He glanced downwards, relieved to see that the large, ornate iron bar had missed the rapidly growing crowd bobbing beneath him. His relief, however, was short-lived, because the bar promptly bounced, coming up smartly to connect with the cauliflower ear of Paul Fall Down. An amateur boxer with numerous defeats under his belt, Paul had merely shaken his head and continued to play with a small piece of fluff on his sleeve.

The contents of the bucket were more widespread, depositing a foamy gunk on a multitude of heads, hats and brollies. Ms Harris, unaware of Arnold's sponge, perched and dripping on her dandelion hair, was heard to remark that this was the warmest rain she'd ever known.

Arnold resumed his contemplation of the clock face, finding himself touched, at first, by all the offers of help filtering up from below. Then he realised that everyone shouting, "Hey, Arnold, do you need a hand?" was probably meant to be funny.

Dismissing the antics of his audience, he turned his attention to the walkie-talkie, crackling in his top pocket. "'Lo?" he said.

"I'm getting the fire brigade," whistled Mrs Jenks.

"Right-ho."

Arnold risked another glance down to see Mrs Jenks running from door to door, urging the closest dwelling members of the volunteer force to "Jump to it, boys, for God's sake – that idiot Arnold's stuck up a ladder."

Arnold wasn't holding his breath. Not with the fire crew being made up largely of Hetty's darts team, whom he knew to have enjoyed a lengthy lunchtime in the Hart. Plus they lacked training. A shortcoming amply revealed when they'd all dashed to the scene of a recent fire, only to find that no one had thought to bring the engine.

Bearing this in mind, the one bright spot on Arnold's all too broad horizon was the presence of his pal, Frank the Mail, who'd had the sense to place one booted foot on the bottom rung of the ladder.

It wasn't much, but it made Arnold feel secure. As did the little bit of chat he was now carrying on with Frank, almost as if they were cosily ensconced in the back room of Mrs Jenks' shop.

"Who did you say it was from again?" Arnold called.

Frank addressed himself to the trembling rear view of his friend. "Some woman called Miranda Barton."

"And she's an agent you say?"

"*Artistic* agent, that's right. To 'Sculptor, Eric Bagnall', amongst others."

"And you reckon that's our Eric?"

"Must be. It was his house I took the parcel to."

"Didn't he do that *A Deep Depression in Driftwood*?" asked Arnold, surprising everyone, including himself.

"He certainly did," interjected Mel Meredith who, like a hundred others on the pavement, was following the earth-to-air conversation closely. "Fancy that, eh? Old Eric being a world-famous artist living right here in our humble midst."

CHAPTER EIGHTEEN

"Out of my way. This is for the artist."

There was no mistaking that voice, thought Eric, risking a peep through his parlour nets. Sure enough, there was the woman they called Chopsie manhandling yet another sapling towards him, its skinny limbs clawing at her legs and eyes.

"Well, so's this," replied Lucy Adams, doing the same with her eldest girl and having much the same trouble.

The two women, the tree and the teenager collided on the path to the cottage where the sapling embraced an elderly relative and refused to let go.

"The artist wants trees, not people," insisted Chopsie, tugging. "He's a sculpture."

Suiting his actions to her words, Eric stood rock still. With any luck they'd think he was out.

"He's definitely in," said Lucy, climbing over the sapling and Chopsie. "Mrs Jenks says he came straight home this morning after buying milk."

Eric sighed. He hadn't anticipated, when Hetty had rung to alert him to the revelations at the clock tower, that so many people would want to help with his next piece. Turning up at all hours with raw materials and reluctant models. The exception to the latter being Cheryl Stitch, who'd arrived eagerly and of her own accord, only to be turned away by a regretful Eric. And if that wasn't the ultimate irony, he thought, he'd like to know what was.

If he was honest, though, the phone call had taken a back seat at the time to the dreadful thought that had struck him in the wake of Hetty's visit.

Whichever way he looked at it, he couldn't ignore that fact that Meryl and Beryl must have sent Miranda his full address, in order for the cash to arrive in his postbox. So, in point of fact, his agent might be able to visit him after all …

***

Unlike Eric, Meryl and Beryl weren't expecting any visitors at all. Not stranded as they were on the aptly named Bryngwellys Campsite, just south of the town.

"Who but us would be daft enough to come here?" asked Beryl for the umpteenth time, gazing out over the boggy, midge-infested field divided by an upland stream.

"It's not as if we had much choice, is it?" Meryl shot back.

Beryl looked reproachfully at her sister. "We *did* have a choice. We could have gone home with Mam when she asked us to."

Beryl still hadn't got over meeting their mother a couple of days ago, when she and Meryl had been on the road to Bryngwellys. Head down, dragging a deer towards the town, Mam had looked up and given them that brilliant smile of hers. Saying how welcome they'd be if they felt like going back to the flat some time. Even hinting that she'd missed them …

"I meant we didn't have a choice of *camp sites,*" said Meryl.

"No," whispered Beryl, recalling how most of the local sites had turned out to be closed, due to lack of business. The exception being Bryngwellys, with its newly painted sign at the gate, boasting an impressive range of facilities.

They'd fallen for it, big time. Pushing Eric's wheel barrow, containing their belongings and two packs of freshly cooked chips up the long and winding track, telling each other that this was the life. A proper camp site with the prospect of a "luxury shower block, hot and cold running water, a club house and barbecue area", and money in their pockets for as many steaks and sausages as they could eat.

But the facilities had fallen a long way short of those promised by Mr Griffiths at the gate. A diversifying farmer, he'd only got as far as putting up the sign before realising the state of the holiday trade and going back to farming.

Hence the "hot and cold running water" was entirely cold, and running through the middle of the field. The "luxury shower block" and "club house" were as yet unbuilt, and the "barbecue area" merely a couple of breeze blocks and a wire rack. As for the toilets … Beryl shuddered, recalling the rough-hewn timber seat of the self-composting contraption, housed in a sheep shed and having scant regard for the application of scientific principles. Or sandpaper.

Beryl slapped another midge. "Can't we go back, Meryl?"

"Back to where? Eric's garden?" asked her sister with heavy sarcasm.

"No," said Beryl. "We both know that's not possible."

"Where then? The chip shop yard?"

Beryl shook her head. "Back to the flat, like Mam said. Back to our own beds and a bathroom indoors and maybe even a bit of cold venison for our tea tonight?"

"It'd mean losing all the money we paid in advance for this place," warned Meryl.

"Got to be better than losing our minds."

Meryl sighed. "OK, Beryl. You win. Let's start packing shall we?"

***

Having accepted the sapling and politely refused the daughter, Eric managed to put in a few more hours' work on his new piece before setting off to check out the route his grand parade would take come the big day. Time was speeding by and Eric wanted to be sure he'd covered everything with his exhaustive preparations.

Driving through the narrow streets, he was grateful for the protection of his van from his new-found celebrity status. Plenty of people waved, of course. Some even burst out of their houses clutching the odd log, but he simply waved back and sped on.

Driving out of the town on the B road, he spied a sorry little procession coming towards him. A procession immediately recognisable as his erstwhile squatters, pushing his parents' wheelbarrow.

"On the move again, girls?" he enquired, lowering his window as Meryl and Beryl drew level with him.

"Afraid so, Mr Bagnall," said Beryl in a small voice. "Our camp site wasn't what it was cracked up to be."

"That's a shame," said Eric, recalling how excited the girls had been the last time he'd seen them, and he'd said they could keep the money for their "new start". "Can I give you a lift somewhere?"

"We're off back to the chip shop yard," said Meryl quickly. Beryl frowned. She'd been under the impression they were going back to the flat. "If there's room for the tent," went on Meryl, "in between the piles of rotting potato peelings and reeking heaps of stale lard ..."

"Quite," said Eric awkwardly. "Well, let's get you loaded, eh?"

Half an hour later, Eric stopped the van at the yard gate, his ears ringing from the tales of woe imparted by his passengers on the subject of Bryngwellys.

"Well I guess this is us," whispered Meryl. "You sure we can't give you something for your petrol, Mr Bagnall? I'm afraid we're a bit short having lost our advance payment on the camp site, but you must take something?"

Hearing the jingle of a couple of coins in Meryl's pocket, Eric shook his head. "You keep whatever's left," he said. "You might need it."

"Thanks, Mr Bagnall," said Meryl, stepping to one side as the kitchen door of the chip shop flew open to emit a bucketful of reject batter. "At least there'll be no rent to pay here ... for obvious reasons."

Eric looked at the batter, oozing over the yard, and knew he was sunk. "Tell you what, girls, how about you come back to the cottage garden?"

"The cottage garden?" echoed Meryl, as if such a thought had never occurred to her. "*Really*?"

"Really," replied Eric. "You can be my watchdogs. So if I ever get any undesirable visitors – a woman in a suit, say, and very high heels – you can tell her I'm out, can't you?"

"Well, if you think we can be convincing?" demurred Meryl.

"Oh yes," said Eric. "I'm sure you can."

***

Back in the cottage, Eric headed straight for his studio, feeling a familiar rush of excitement as he did so. His new piece was all but finished. The trick now was to know when to stop.

Gently he removed the white muslin cover from his *A Goddess Weeping* and turned her to face the window. His heart thudded as her lips curved in the soft, June light. He nodded. She was ready, all bar her name, which he'd yet to carve into the bevelled edge of the plinth he'd rescued from the bonfire. The title of the piece would take some thinking about, however, for his goddess was no longer weeping but smiling, deep into his soul.

Turning to the plinth, which lay on the parlour floor, still wrapped in the sacking with which he'd covered it in the van, Eric was reminded once again of his moonlight adventures with Min. It was somehow fitting, he thought, that he'd stumbled across it in her company. That, feeling the aged wood beneath his fingers, he'd known, in his heart, he had to bring it home.

Even so, he lifted the bundle now with trepidation. What if it wasn't suitable after all? If his instincts had been wrong, and all he'd acquired was some grotty old remnant of a sideboard? There was, of course, only one way to find out …

Moments later, Eric stood stock still, the sacking dangling from his lifeless hand as his plinth was revealed in all its glory. Silently, he read the scratchy text again. There was no doubt about it, he thought.

Somehow he'd managed to steal back the Market Tavern bar hatch.

Hurrying to the telephone, Eric debated how much to reveal to Hetty of his nocturnal activities with Min, but the decision was made for him because he'd caught Hetty up to her neck in a brewery delivery. Keeping it brief, he delivered his news, then held the phone away from his ear as Hetty shouted a lot, apparently danced a bit, and finally instructed Eric to bring the bar hatch round ASAP.

Arriving at the White Hart, he found Hetty waiting outside, along with an excitable Mrs Jenks.

"You star, Eric," called the latter as he brought the van to a halt and opened the back doors.

Both women having agreed that this was, beyond a shadow of a doubt, the missing proof of the town's ownership of the Bowen Field, they fell to kissing Eric, before asking him to drop the bar hatch back to the Market Tavern, and the two of them down on the field.

"We can get the bus back," explained Hetty, "but a lift there would save time. There's so much to do, isn't there, Mrs Jenks, if we want to get this grand event of ours back on track?"

Mrs Jenks nodded joyfully. "Certainly is. Now that we can safely proceed, we've to get the field mown and plan the layout of the show ground; order up a couple of banners for the gateway and some signage for the road; organise the generators for the fast-food vans, the outside bar and the bouncy castle … The list is endless."

Hetty grinned at Eric's overwhelmed expression. "Don't worry, young Eric, you've more than done your bit. But time's marching on and, given the catching up we need to do, I suggest we plan one final meeting of the Summer Spectacular committee on Wednesday the eighteenth of June? That'll be four days ahead of Midsummer's Day and the event itself."

"I'll be there," smiled Eric.

***

Having seen Mrs Jenks and Hetty safely onto the field, Eric stood back to admire the flat, green pasture with its tall, sheltering hedges and easy access off the B road. It would make a fitting spot, he decided, for his vintage machinery to assemble after the parade. Especially as the field was set against the stunning backdrop of the prudie nudie hotel.

Covertly, Eric studied the house. Fronted by smooth lawns, a sweeping driveway and a shrubbery, it seemed to be turning its cold, stone shoulder to the neighbouring field. And, why not, thought Eric, given the pedigree of the place? According to local legend the grand Victorian pile, once the seat of the now defunct Bowen Family, had replaced an even earlier building on the same site. This had been a fortified farmhouse, which had burned to the ground centuries before the volunteer fire brigade had been formed to deal with just such an emergency. Although from what Eric could gather from a highly sceptical Arnold, it could just as easily have happened since.

Eric grinned, remembering how the old man had eventually been talked down from the clock tower by Mrs Jenks. Sitting in the White Hart with her walkie-talkie, a large brandy and the makings of a full house, occasionally murmuring, "That's the way, Arnold. Down you come. Over."

Before climbing back into the van, Eric took a last look at the mansion, with its rows of upper-storey windows gazing haughtily out over the high perimeter wall of the garden. At least, he realised with a start, the wall was high on the house side, but it came barely to his waist out here on the road. It was just as Hetty had said. There would be no privacy for any prudie nudies frisking in those grounds…

Grinning, Eric put the van into gear and drove away.

***

Some time later, the front door of the hotel crashed open to admit Tony Williams. Clutching a two-inch paint brush in one hand and a small tin of paint in the other, Terry slid down the long, curving banister to greet his brother.

"Hiya," he said, landing in a heap at the bottom and only just saving the paint. "You OK?"

Tony slipped off his Wellingtons and stumped across the black-and-white tiles of the hallway. "Not too bad. What you been up to?"

"Trying to paint the long gallery. It's hard going, though."

"Impossible, I should think, with a piddling little brush like that," observed Tony. "Why don't you get a bigger one?"

Terry regarded his brush, doubtfully. "What would be the point of that," he asked at last, "when it wouldn't go in the pot?"

Tony sighed. "Anything happened while I've been away?"

"Not really, except that Eric came along, dropped off Mrs Jenks and Hetty on the field, had a bit of a look at the house and drove away again."

Tony stared at his brother. "He dropped them on *our* field?"

Terry sniggered. "Yep. Spent an hour or so, they did, walking around, peering at the grass and stuff, then Mrs Jenks looked at her watch and the pair of them legged it for the bus stop."

"Well, I hope you told them where to get off," fumed Tony.

"Where to get off?" repeated Terry. "Well, no, because ..."

"Not where to get off the bus, Terry, where to get off strolling around on our field?"

"I didn't tell them anything. They didn't seem to be doing any harm and, in any case, I was on the loo when I saw them. Nicer, the loo is, here than the one at the farm. In fact, I think it's even nicer than Hetty's at the pub, which ..."

"Not doing any harm?" interrupted Tony. "So why were they here at all? They must know that, without the bar hatch as proof of ownership, we won't let them use the field?"

Terry thought for a moment. "Perhaps they think there's still a chance of them getting it back?" he suggested. "After all, they can't know, can they, that you burnt it?"

"You burnt it, you mean."

"Me?"

"I told you to burn it."

"No. You told me to build a bonfire, which I did," replied Terry sulkily. "You didn't say anything about lighting it."

"So where's the bar hatch now?"

"Still on the bonfire, I expect. Although I didn't see it there, last time I passed and ... Gosh, he wouldn't have, would he?"

"Who wouldn't have what?"

"That Eric. He was up our way, like I told you, with Min Pugh the other night ... He wouldn't have *taken* it would he, from the makings of the bonfire?"

"Ooh, let me see, now," said Tony with heavy sarcasm. "Which do you think's most likely? Eric and Min Pugh, stumbling on the only evidence of the town's ownership of the Bowen field and stealing it back again, or some kleptomaniac collector of pub paraphernalia, happening across a bar hatch in the middle of nowhere, and not being able to help himself?"

"*Not* being able to help himself?" echoed Terry. "Surely that's just what he would have done?"

"He would, Terry, if I hadn't just made him up as pretty much the most unlikely person to have found and taken the wretched thing."

"So are we saying it *was* Eric then, if it's really missing?"

"Doh ... of course it was."

Breathing hard, Tony stumped back across the hall to his wellies.

"Where are you going?" asked Terry.

"To the bonfire, of course, to see if that blasted bit of wood is still there. And you, boyo, had better start praying – very hard – that it *is*."

CHAPTER NINETEEN

By the time the day of the meeting came round, Eric was in a state of nervous collapse. Determined to prove himself worthy of being in sole charge of the parade, he'd dotted more I's and crossed more T's than a typewriter. This included compiling a set of notes covering everything from assembly points and emergency procedures to what to do in the event of a breakdown/seizure/hitch-hiker.

He'd then delivered copies to each and every one of his exhibitors, urging them to overhaul and fuel up their vehicles in plenty of time for the big day. Unfortunately, he'd run out of petrol on the last of these visits and been obliged to seek assistance from a chortling Moggs Morgan with a jerrycan.

No such embarrassment had occurred on the day of his visit to Pantybryn, to check on the arrangements for the pony and trap. The ongoing absence of Mo meant he'd been able to spend a wonderful couple of hours alone with Min. He smiled, now, recalling that she'd confirmed all that cuddling business as only too real. Even declared herself up for more …

Glancing at the clock, he slipped a copy of his notes into a carrier bag, eager to share them with the committee.

At the hall, the first person he saw was Arnold, enjoying a crafty cigarette just inside the double doors. "Town's come good," he yelled. "Once word got about that the old Earl's pledge had been found, and the venue safe as houses, there was no stopping 'em. Can't move in 'ere for bodies. Let's see the Twins put the blocks on this lot, eh?"

Eric peered through Arnold's smoke. The old man was right. The original committee of six had swollen to more like six hundred.

"Are they all here for the meeting?" he asked, shocked.

"Aye. And people have really come up trumps, I can tell you. WI, for instance, as well as running their games and sideshows, have managed to make our little event part of their area competition. Means we'll be getting women from all over South Wales showing off their 'andicrafts." Arnold paused, evidently savouring a moment's lecherous reflection. "Young Farmers have pulled out all the stops, too," he went on. "Organising a grand tug o' war for neighbouring clubs to come and try their luck. Foregone conclusion that is, though," he finished proudly. "Built like brick shit-houses our lot are."

Eric smiled.

"And them as you don't see here," added Arnold, "is off doing other things. Sorting out the field, some of 'em, whilst others'll be decorating floats and the like for the Carnival. Which reminds me, 'ow's your bit of that coming along, young Eric?"

"Great." Eric produced his sheaf of notes. "It's all here if you want to check it over? Routes, back-up routes, timetables, emergency procedures …"

Arnold eyed the reams of paper. "No ta, young Eric. Time for notes and talking's passed, I reckon. Time for action now."

Eric nodded. The old man was right. Besides, with so many people pitching in, he doubted there'd be much left for the original committee to do. He said as much to Arnold.

Arnold puffed contentedly on his cigarette. "Way I look at it, young Eric, we hatched the egg. Time now for this little bird to fly all on her own."

***

Pushing his way into the hall, Eric narrowly avoided being mown down by Mel's band marching doggedly round the perimeter.

Catching sight of Eric, Mel hurried over.

"This is dreadful," groaned the hapless bandleader. "I wanted this to be such a brilliant final rehearsal but Ms Harris has gone and muddled up all the music. Everyone's playing a different piece."

"I shouldn't worry about it," said Eric, covering his ears. "It sounds exactly the same as when they're all trying to play the same thing."

"Oh," said Mel. "That's a relief. At least, I suppose it is ..." Twirling his baton he rejoined the band just ahead of the didgeridoo players. These, for reasons of their comparative youth, formed the first ranks of the haphazard procession.

Today they were experimenting for the first time with the little sets of wheels made for them by the local blacksmith. Steering seemed to be something of a problem, but by and large the wheels were a success. And so, thought Eric, were the instruments themselves, adding a certain resonance to the proceedings. Not to mention some proper notes.

Nodding his approval, Eric made his way to where a plan of the field had been pinned up. This, it seemed, was in order that everyone would know exactly where to set up their stalls and sideshows, and any last-minute conflicts could be sorted out.

A particularly acrimonious example of this was a row currently in progress between the organisers of the ferret racing and the owner of the baby guinea pigs intended for the Kiddies Korner. "It'll be more like 'Kiddie's Karnage'," insisted the latter, "if you don't move your blasted ferrets to the other side of the field."

Leaving them to it, Eric pressed on in search of Hetty. His progress was slow, however, due to the need to stop and chat with a host of Landoobreyians he'd come to think of as old friends.

Ethel and Ivy were there, along with the woman trying her home-made donkey outfit on her husband.

The construction team from the chapel were also present, complete with photos of their pride and joy, an Olympic-sized Dunk The Vicar pool. This, it seemed, only wanted the finishing touches put to it before the big day. One of the finishing touches being the vicar himself, who stood a little apart from the group looking anxious. Eric regarded him thoughtfully. What had Hetty said, way back in his poltergeist days, about him wanting a vicar for a wedding?

Finally he ran Hetty to earth in the centre of the hall helping some children to try on a selection of somewhat cumbersome fancy dress costumes.

"Isn't this marvellous?" she called as Eric drew nearer. "We couldn't have hoped for a better turnout."

"Marvellous," agreed Eric, adding "Ouch" as he found himself impaled on the cardboard horn of a passing dragon.

"How about you cut some eye-holes in that thing?" suggested Hetty, addressing herself to the invisible owners of a dozen pairs of undersized legs, scuttling beneath the scarlet beast. Giggling, the children floundered away in search of scissors.

"Dear little mites," murmured Hetty.

"Mm," said Eric, surreptitiously massaging a region of his person already tenderised by Desmond. Catching Hetty's enquiring look, he put his hands in his pockets. "So, everything OK with the judges?" he asked.

Getting and keeping the judges for such events as the pony and pet shows had been, he knew, one of Hetty's biggest headaches. For a start, she'd had to promise absolute anonymity ahead of the event in order that bribery shouldn't be an issue. And safe conduct off the field, at the end of the day, to combat reprisals.

"Yep," said Hetty, proudly. "They've gone on the leaflets as 'to be announced', of course, but they've all cashed their cheques, which is good."

"Talking of leaflets," said Eric, "how's the publicity distribution been going?"

"Great. Postman's done a brilliant job, papering all the towns and villages from the Marches to the Gower.

"Good old Frank the Mail," said Eric, pleased the man's talent for spreading information had finally found a useful outlet. "I wouldn't mind a look at the posters, if there are any left?"

"Only a few," said Hetty. "Over there in the corner."

Eric fought his way to the corner of the room where just a few packs of posters and leaflets remained out of the hundreds originally ordered.

Not having been involved on the publicity side, this was Eric's first glimpse of the marketing material and he found himself approving of the bright blue, green and yellow designs and bold lettering. It wasn't difficult to imagine them catching the eye of jaded city dwellers, and tempting them to a day out in the countryside.

Idly, Eric picked up a handout for a proper read. A moment later his heart sank. There had been a misprint on a major scale.

Returning to the fancy dress area, he found Hetty extracting the head of an aspiring Tin Man from a rashly applied saucepan.

"Hetty," hissed Eric, tugging at her sleeve. "Something awful's happened." Waving a leaflet, he pointed to the third line down. "What does that mean?"

"Gosh," said Hetty, "you're asking something there. Now, let me see. Well, *Llan* means church and …"

"I didn't mean what does it mean, literally," interrupted Eric. "I meant, why is it there?"

"It's the name of the town, of course," said Hetty. "Got to put the name of the town on haven't you?"

"But I thought," whispered Eric, "the town was called Landoobrey?"

Hetty laughed heartily to the point where several children backed away in alarm. "Bless you, no, young Eric," she said, wiping her eyes, "although, now I come to think about it, your mam and dad used to call it Landoobrey in the old days, but only because they couldn't pronounce Llanrhystyddyralltarymynydd."

"Neither can I," said Eric, suddenly realising how often he'd seen that great, long word around the town and half-wondered what it meant.

"And why should you?" said Hetty cheerfully. "You just go right on calling it Landoobrey if it's easier. And before you ask, your secret is safe with me."

***

At about the time Eric had been worrying about the misprint on the posters, Miranda was having the same trouble with the fare display on the dashboard of her taxi.

"Are you sure there aren't too many noughts on that thing?" she grumbled, pulling out her chequebook.

Coming to Wales today had been a spur of the moment thing, prompted by several bottles of wine, shared with Delecta at lunchtime.

The black cab driver, who'd also been surprised at the amount of the fare, but in more of a good way, shook his head. "Warned you, didn't I, as me 'Knowledge' only went as far west as 'Ammersmith? But Wales you said and Wales this is."

Spitting on his hand he held it out for the cheque. "Expect you'll be wanting picking up again some time?"

Miranda glared. There was no way the taxi driver was taking her for another ride. "Certainly not," she said, frostily. "I'll make my own way back. By train."

As the cab drove away, Miranda fell to studying Eric's cottage. Even from the outside it was obvious it wouldn't do for the *Hi There!* interview. Far too small and pokey. Not like that magnificent mansion she'd passed on the B road into the village. That would be perfect.

Picking up her luggage, she opened Eric's gate, only to find her way barred by a small person hopping from foot to foot in agitation.

"If you're looking for Eric, he's out," said Beryl, eyeing the suit and high heels of Eric's visitor.

Miranda looked at her watch. 7.15 in the evening seemed an odd time to be out, given the fabled abstemiousness of Eric's lifestyle. "Out where?"

"Um, I think he went to the pub. The White Hart. Down the street a bit, turn left. You can't miss it."

"Right," said Miranda. "And would this pub do accommodation?"

Beryl thought this over. "Only for anyone who can't stand up enough to get home."

"That'll do me," said Miranda, teetering back down the path.

***

"What did you want to tell her that for?" fumed Meryl, arriving in time to catch the tail end of the conversation. "That Eric was out?"

"Because he is."

"Yes, but we weren't supposed to tell *her* that were we?"

"Weren't we?" asked Beryl, confused. "I thought that was exactly what we were supposed to do. In fact, I distinctly remember Eric saying if a woman in high heels and a suit came along we were to tell her he was out."

"Yes, but only if he was in."

248

"Only if he was in?" echoed Beryl.

"That's right."

"Well, what were we supposed to tell her if he was out then? That he was in?"

It was Meryl's turn to look confused. "Er, no, of course not."

"So what choice did I have," persisted Beryl, "except to tell her he was out, because he *was*, wasn't he? And so were you," she finished meaningfully, "right when you ought to have been in."

"OK, OK," said Meryl, "I get the message. But what I *don't* get is why you had to tell Miranda exactly where Eric was?"

"I didn't. I told her he was in the pub, which he isn't. He's at the meeting in the village hall."

Meryl sighed. "And where's he likely to go after the village hall, eh?"

"Oh," said Beryl. "The pub I suppose." She paused as the erratic clatter of smart footwear died away in the distance. "Still, the state she's in I doubt she'll last till Eric gets there."

***

Beryl, however, had reckoned without Miranda's legendary staying power. In spite of her lunchtime session, and accidentally drinking a bottle of red, bought at the wine bar and intended as a present for Eric, she was gagging for more. She said as much to the personable young lady behind the bar of the virtually deserted pub.

"Coming right up," said Cheryl Stitch, blowing the dust of decades from a magnum of Hirondelle.

Miranda smacked her lips. "Thirsty work, mine is."

"So's mine," said Cheryl, coughing. "What line of work would yours be?" she asked, making conversation.

"I'm an agent."

Cheryl almost dropped the bottle. "An agent?"

"For my sins." Miranda extended a bangled wrist. "Miranda Barton's the name. Best tell you now, because I've been known to forget, the longer a night goes on."

"Wow. Er, I'm Cheryl Stitch," said Cheryl, shaking the proffered hand. "I've been trying to meet an agent for ages. Have that one on me," she added, her face falling as Miranda picked up the bottle as well as the glass.

"Very civil of you, I'm sure," said Miranda, glugging happily. "Whoops," she giggled, heading for the jukebox. "Getting a teensy bit tiddly."

"And why not?" encouraged Cheryl, beginning to dust another couple of bottles. "Got to let your hair down once in a while, haven't you?"

"Once in a while?" shrieked Miranda, hearing the opening bars of "I Will Survive" and shimmying over to the only other occupants of the pub: a pair of old boys playing darts. "I've let more 'air down in my time," she informed them, "than Rapunzel."

"Oh, lovely double-top," said one old boy as a dart thudded into the board.

"Ta ever so."

Chuffed, Miranda began to dance, whirling straight into the arms of her client who, along with half the rest of the town, had just arrived back from the meeting.

***

250

"Miranda!" said Eric, aghast. Ever since he'd realised Meryl and Beryl's unwitting indiscretion over his address, he'd half expected the arrival of his agent. Indeed, it had been the stuff of nightmares. None more scary, though, than this hideous reality.

"Eric," yelled Miranda. She wagged a forefinger. "Your cottage simply won't do, you know. Not for *Hi There!* I want to propose a different venue and I want you to agree with me."

"Oh yes?" said Eric cautiously. "And where would that be?"

"Fantastic house," said Miranda. "Great big place, south of the town. Much more suitable."

Eric thought for a moment. "OK," he said. "I know the place you mean. It's a hotel actually. I'll agree to be interviewed there but not in the house itself – in the field alongside."

"In a *field*?" squeaked Miranda, eyeing her shoes. "We can't be interviewed in a field. Er, I mean, you can't."

"I can, or it's no dice. And it'll have to be on Saturday. That's four days from now. Can you get the *Hi There!* team here by then?"

Miranda shook her head. "It's very short notice …"

"Yes," agreed Eric, "but think how excited they'll be when you tell them about the venue you've so cleverly found. How splendid the house is and how it'll make a lovely backdrop for the photo shoot?"

"Well, there's that I suppose," said Miranda thoughtfully. "Yes, that might do it."

"Great," said Eric. "You might also tell them I shall want lots of extra shots of the crowds enjoying themselves at our Summer Spectacular, and perhaps a little write up on the event. After all," he added, "if I'm to sacrifice my hard won privacy, it might as well be in a good cause. Do we have a deal, Miranda?"

Miranda put out a hand to shake his, missed and tried again. "It's a deal," she mumbled.

"Good on you, young Eric," cried Hetty from the crowded bar. "Pint of slurry, lad?"

"Why not?" said Eric, feeling at this precise moment that he could tackle a barrel full of the stuff. "Here's to *Hi There!*" He raised his glass to rousing cheers. "If anyone can help us get the name of this little town known throughout the civilised world, they can."

"That reminds me, Eric," said Miranda as the cheering finally died down. "Why do you keep calling this place Landoobrey when everyone knows it's called Llanrhystyddyralltarymynydd?"

"Bet she couldn't say that sober," said Mrs Jenks into the ensuing silence.

***

"There's another one," said Tony Williams, skidding the Land Rover to a halt beside a telegraph pole, upon which fluttered a Summer Spectacular poster, its colours vibrant in the gathering dusk. "The bloody things are everywhere," he added, yanking up the handbrake, "telling the world and his uncle to go to *our* field on Midsummer's Day, regardless of how we feel about it."

Terry peered past his brother. "Done it to spite us, they have, if you ask me."

"Which I didn't." Tony slammed the Land Rover into gear, lurched forwards then stopped, suddenly, cutting a sideways look at Terry. "After all, I can't be sure whose side you're on these days."

Terry peeled his face from the windscreen, straightened his cap and glared back. "What's that supposed to mean?"

"Well, who was it practically invited that Eric to steal the bar hatch back again, right at the wrong moment?"

"I didn't invite him," protested Terry, rubbing the back of his head as the Land Rover leapt forwards again, throwing him back against the seat. "As far as I was concerned there wasn't a bar hatch by then because you were supposed to have burnt it. But," he added as Tony's face darkened, "I realise now that I might have got that wrong. And to make up for it I've been having a think about other things we might do to scupper this event before the big day."

"Come up with anything have you?" grunted Tony, exhaling loudly as the Land Rover stopped again, making the gap between his stomach and the steering wheel even smaller."

"I think I've come up with a plan to move forwards … in more ways than one."

"Meaning?"

"Meaning, I've got a great idea for robbing the Summer Spectacular of its most vital asset, before it can get off the ground. Plus," he added, enjoying a rare moment of triumph, "I've worked out that the Land Rover'll go a lot better if you take the handbrake off."

CHAPTER TWENTY

The following morning, Eric crept into Mrs Jenks's shop, wincing at the ting of the shop bell behind him.

Mrs Jenks eyed the empty shelves of her "Pharmacy Department". "Can't offer you any Paracetamol, I'm afraid," she said grinning. "That Miranda bought the lot, soon as I opened, along with a bag of ice and two boxes of Alka-Seltzer."

"Ah," said Eric, "that explains her remarkable recovery."

"Seen her this morning, have you?"

Eric nodded. His agent had bounced up to the cottage first thing to admire his new piece, complete, all bar the plinth, which he'd had to return to the Market Tavern. "She's confirmed the *Hi There!* interview for Saturday."

"Be staying then, will she, till the big day?" Mrs Jenks licked her pencil, preparing to make an express order for hangover cures.

Eric shook his head. "Said she had to go home first to collect her mock croc suit and pure wool shoes. Although, come to think of it, that might still have been the drink talking."

"Mel will be sorry to see her go," said Mrs Jenks slyly. "Getting on rather well, weren't they, cwtched up in the corner like that?"

"Mm," agreed Eric. "Made me feel quite sorry for Ms Harris."

"In spite of what she put you through last night?"

"In spite of that," replied Eric. He was determined not to dwell on how the Events Secretary had milked his faux pas about Landoobrey for all it was worth.

Going on about how he'd had once suggested the raft race might be held on the River Doobrey. A misconception no one had understood, until now.

"Well, I wouldn't waste your sympathies there," replied Mrs Jenks. "Already moved on to pastures new, she has. Taken up with a fellow tuba player from the band. Seems romance blossomed when his piston valve got caught in her bell."

Eric laughed and tentatively reached for his groceries, which Mrs Jenks was holding hostage on the far side of the counter.

The shopkeeper took a firmer grip on his loaf. "Talking of romance," she said, evidently determined to do just that, "what's this I hear about you and Min Pugh the other night – gallivanting about in the moonlight?"

Eric stared. "We were hardly *gallivanting*, Mrs Jenks."

"What were you doing then?"

"We were on a mission," said Eric. Then, unable to resist the chance to talk about Min, he found himself telling Mrs Jenks the whole story.

"So there you have it," he said at last. "After all that it was just a barn full of mushrooms. Nothing underhand or illegal at all. Min and I did laugh."

He glanced at the shopkeeper. Could she tell from his voice, he wondered, that laughing wasn't all they'd done?

For once, however, Mrs Jenks had other things on her mind. "You sure they wasn't 'magic mushrooms'?"

"You mean the sort fairies live under?" queried Eric.

"No, Eric, I mean the sort that make people *think* fairies live under them. My sister in Surrey says they're all the rage down there. People grow 'em themselves from spores. Spores, which if I remember rightly, get sent down in little syringes from somewhere in Wales. Big money there is in that, according to my sister."

"Really?" said Eric, thoughtfully.

"Oh yes. Seems people'll pay a lot to get off their heads on dodgy substances."

"Good job Min and I only ate the acid drop mixture then," smiled Eric. Then, remembering their moonlight canoodle and all that puddle business, he added, "Unless …"

"Mm," said Mrs Jenks. "Unless the acid drops are being spiced up a bit as well? Good way of getting customers coming back for more, I'd say. And those sweets are being made right there, aren't they, alongside the mushrooms?" She looked searchingly up at Eric. "You told Hetty about this?"

Eric shook his head. "Didn't seem all that important when Min and I thought they were just ordinary mushrooms."

"Well, I think it's time you did tell her, don't you?" asked Mrs Jenks, finally surrendering the groceries. "The whole lot, start to finish."

***

"So there you have it," said Eric for the second time that morning, addressing the speaker-phone as he pottered about hanging some hand-washing on the sitting-room radiator. His throat was hoarse from repeating to Hetty not only the tale of his and Min's moonlit adventure, but also Mrs Jenks's suspicions about the mushrooms. "It looks as if Sid the Sweets has been up to no good with those acid drops. The name of which, according to Mrs Jenks, ought to have given us a clue all along."

"I somehow doubt," said Hetty, "that it was young Sid tampering with them. Far more likely to have been his doting uncles, don't you think? Either to ensure the success of their nephew's business or purely for devilment. After all, they've got half the pensioners in the town hooked on those sweets, haven't they? Which to a certain warped kind of mind might be rather amusing?"

Eric was silent for a moment, recalling the feeling of reckless well-being that always came over him after eating the acid drops.

"It's not only the pensioners who are hooked on them," he said at last. "Mo and Min can't get enough of them either. Er, talking of Min, shall she and I pop back up there for another look round? I've a feeling there was more to that barn than met the eye. If we could find some sort of processing and despatch area, to back up our theory about the mushrooms, we might be able to get the Twins arrested before the big day?"

There was a snort from the other end of the line. "Best leave it to the professionals this time, eh? I don't wish to be unkind but the word 'farce' does rather come to mind in relation to your last visit to the farm. What with you falling off your transport most of the way there, and the pair of you trying to conduct a search by the light of a wind-up torch."

"I like to think," said Eric with dignity, "that *farce* has no place in a well-ordered lifestyle such as mine…" He stopped as a sudden movement on the radiator caught his eye. "Hang on Hetty, my trousers are falling down."

"I rest my case," murmured Hetty.

"Pardon?"

"Nothing. Although, as it happens, I've accidentally reminded myself of an important appointment, Friday afternoon at the court house…"

"Right-ho," said Eric, who was trying to blow the fluff off his trousers and not really listening.

***

The professional Hetty had in mind set off the next day on his dawn raid, still doing up his trousers and rubbing sleep from his eyes. Not that it was actually dawn, PC George reminded himself. He'd never been that early a riser.

It wouldn't actually be a raid either, in spite of his promise to Hetty. He'd already had to upset his nephews once recently over those so-called furniture thefts, of which they denied all knowledge. His visit would therefore take the form of a social call, at the end of which he would pretend to drive away, double back on foot and inspect the barn when they weren't looking

Having parked his patrol car, PC George made for the back door of the farmhouse. Passing the kitchen window, he glanced in to see the Twins looking bleary eyed and wearing identical string vests.

The remnants of breakfast, going back weeks by the look of them, were strewn across the filthy tabletop. It was not this, however, that caused him to stare in alarm so much as the activity each of his nephews was engaged in. Terry, clipping his toenails;

Tony, snipping away at his nose hair with a pair of sheep shears.

PC George frowned. The Twins had never been big on personal grooming. Even the removal of their caps was practically a surgical procedure carried out only on special occasions. Then he remembered the grand opening of their hotel, scheduled for this coming weekend. Perhaps that explained it.

"Cuppa tea?" grunted Tony as his uncle loomed in the doorway.

"Yes, please," replied PC George, removing his helmet and wishing he hadn't as a couple of toenail clippings embedded themselves in his thinning, grey hair.

"Well you can get it yourself," giggled Terry, "and make us one while you're about it."

PC George put the kettle on, alongside a pan of what he strongly suspected to be underpants, boiling on the stove. A quick cuppa, he thought, then he'd put his plan for inspecting the barn into action. Prove Hetty and Eric wrong, once and for all, about its contents.

***

"Wow," said Eric taking a sip of his lunchtime pint as Hetty finished telling him the outcome of PC George's visit to the barn. "So he arrested them, did he, there and then?"

"Well, no," said Hetty. "It seems he didn't like to."

"He didn't *like* to?" echoed Eric. "But what about all that evidence he found? The despatch room with all those syringes of spores awaiting packaging and mailing off? The copies of all their coded magazine adverts?"

"I agree he had grounds for an arrest," said Hetty, "but, as he said, they *are* his nephews." She thought for a moment, then added, "At least he had the presence of mind to bring back a few mushrooms. He's sent them off to a proper police station for analysis. Hopes for the results any day now."

"Well that's something, I suppose," said Eric. "Depending on the upshot of that, there must still be a chance the Twins might be arrested before Saturday. Because if they aren't, I dread to think what retribution they might yet take for the Summer Spectacular going ahead exactly as planned."

***

Over the next couple of days, Eric divided his time between finalising his timetable for the parade and helping out down on the field, where things were really beginning to take shape.

By Friday evening he was more than ready for a pint and was surprised to find Cheryl presiding over the bar at the White Hart.

"No Hetty tonight?" he asked, settling himself on a stool.

"Doesn't look like it," replied Cheryl. "I only came in for a drink myself. Thought I'd best get behind the bar before there was a riot."

"You mean she didn't arrange for you to come in?"

"Nope."

Eric felt a vague stirring of unease. "Isn't that rather odd?"

"It is a bit," conceded Cheryl. "But then again, she's been running about like a bull with its balls off this last couple of days. Maybe she just forgot."

"Let's hope so." Eric buried his nose in his freshly poured pint with all the practice of a local. As he did so, a familiar figure arrived at his elbow.

"Hello, Mel," said Eric, pleased to see his friend, who'd been absent from the pub for a while, still trying to chivvy something resembling a tune from his band.

Mel subsided onto a neighbouring stool. "Hello, Eric," he said wearily. Then, perking up a little, he peered about the bar. "Not got the luscious Miranda with you this evening?" Before Eric could reply, Mel went on, "I did so enjoy meeting her on Wednesday. What a gal, Eric. And *so* interested in my *Ben Hur* production. She's rather cleverly suggested I might rewrite it as a Christmas show. Even offered to be *in* it. How about that, eh?"

Eric sighed, wondering if Mel had any idea of the damage he was doing, encouraging Miranda to visit more often. "She went back to London," he said rather curtly. Then, seeing Mel's face fall, he added, "She'll be back tomorrow, though. So you two love birds can pick up right where you left off, eh?"

"You can talk," said Mel, turning pink. "The postman's told me all about you and your little assignation with Min Pugh, planned for the crack of dawn tomorrow."

It was Eric's turn to blush, although the "assignation" was innocent enough. First thing tomorrow, he and Min would be decorating the trap together, ready for the Carnival Queen. Without Mo, as it happened, who was still away, caring for their poorly cousin.

Eric was still contemplating this delightful prospect when there was commotion in the White Hart doorway and Mrs Jenks burst in, clutching something that almost made Eric's hair stand on end.

"Where did you get that?" asked Cheryl, pointing to the Stetson, rising and falling against the shopkeeper's gingham overall.

"Off your little brother, Harry, as it happens," replied Mrs Jenks, visibly upset. "Came in the shop, he did, wearing it. The little sod won't tell me how he came by it. Said it was a secret and he'd get bashed if he told."

"Did you tell him he'd get bashed if he didn't?" queried Cheryl.

Mrs Jenks nodded. "Yes, but he won't budge. Got him outside, I have, but he's saying nothing." She twisted the Stetson in her trembling hands. "It's a real worry because, in the forty-odd years I've known her, I've never known Hetty lose her hat. Her head maybe, every now and again, 'specially round about Christmas, what with all the festivities and everyone buying her drinks, but not this 'ere Stetson, which I believe she's had since …"

"What should we do, Mrs Jenks?" interrupted Eric, sensing that she was about to veer from the point completely.

The shopkeeper considered the question. "Have to find her, won't we? Be a help, of course, if we knew when and where she was last seen?"

"I saw her on the field this morning," offered Mel.

"She was behind the bar lunchtime," said one of the labourers, whose name, if Eric remembered rightly, was Frog.

"Closed up, she did, at four," put in the other lad, known to Eric as Earwig, "Said she had something important to do and she'd be opening again six-ish."

"Which is when I arrived," said Cheryl. She glanced around the bar. "So, are we saying no one's seen her since four?"

There was a general shaking of heads, and Eric began to feel seriously concerned. Astonishing himself as much as everyone else, he stepped forward and took charge.

***

"Right," said Eric, "I suggest we get up a search party. Some of you can comb the town on foot. Anyone with a vehicle can tackle the outlying areas, taking a mountain road each. And," he added, "whoever takes the Williams Twins' road, I'll be coming, too."

"We'll do that route," said Earwig, setting off at a run for the pick-up truck, parked directly in front of the pub.

"Come along, Eric," yelled Frog. "Only two seats in the cab," he added, climbing aboard and slamming the passenger door, "but plenty of room in the back."

Eric vaulted the side of the truck and promptly disappeared in a tangled mass of builder's paraphernalia.

"What can I do?" asked Mel, hovering alongside as the pick-up engine roared into life. "Fetch the police maybe? In London they'd be our first port of call, wouldn't they, in a missing persons case?"

"Yes," agreed Eric, spitting out a mouthful of electrical wiring. "But here, that would just mean routing out PC George, whose loyalties, if you want my opinion, are suspect. You'd better come with us."

"OK." Mel hurled himself into the moving truck and landed in a sprawling heap alongside Eric. "You think the Twins had something to do with Hetty's disappearance then?" he asked, surfacing.

"Bit of a coincidence otherwise, wouldn't you say?" Eric sat down on a convenient oil drum as Earwig took the junction with the main road on two wheels. "The Summer Spectacular being robbed of its very heart and soul, the evening before the event?"

"She closed the bar, though," Mel pointed out, "apparently of her own accord. Sounds like she had something really important to do …"

"God, yes." Eric's hand flew to his forehead. "It's *Friday*, isn't it?"

"Well, of course it is. You said it yourself. We're on the eve of the Summer Spectacular, so it must be Friday."

Eric gripped the side of the bucketing truck and began inching his way towards the cab.

Mel watched his crab-like progress. "Going somewhere, old man?"

"Need to stop the truck," grunted Eric. "I've remembered where Hetty was going this afternoon and we're heading completely the wrong way."

Finally, the repeated banging of Eric and Mel on the roof of the cab caused the driver to slow down. Eric leaned round and shouted through the window. "Earwig, you need to turn round. Head for the council chamber and court house, middle of the main square."

"Is that where she was going?" asked Mel as the truck spun like a rodeo bull.

Eric nodded. "She mentioned it the other day. I wasn't paying much attention, though, on account of my trousers falling down."

"Beastly for you. And in front of Hetty, too."

"Tut, Hetty wasn't there. We were on the phone. And as for my trousers, I wasn't actually wearing them at the time. Oh, we've arrived."

With some relief, Eric climbed out of the truck, closely followed by Mel, Frog and Earwig. The four of them then held a brief powwow in the shadow of the large Georgian building.

"I'm pretty sure," said Eric, "that Hetty was coming here this afternoon. So I suggest we split up and search every inch of the place."

"We'll start upstairs," volunteered the labourers, heading for the grand staircase leading to the council chamber.

"And I'll take the court room," said Mel, hurrying down a corridor, at the far end of which stood a large, studded oak door.

Eric watched them go, before opening another, smaller door, directly in front of him. As his eyes pierced the gloom, he saw that he was at the top of a narrow, stone staircase, above which hung a rusty, metal sign bearing the legend: "To The Gaols". Flicking a light switch, apparently attached to a candle, he began his cautious descent.

At the bottom he found himself in a long, dank corridor. The subterranean passageway dripped water, making the floor skiddy and dangerous and the lighting, such as it was, grew more and more feeble the further he went. So much so that he almost missed a low, recessed doorway coming up on his right.

Approaching the barred door, his imagination conjured up images of past inmates, from highwaymen to horse thieves, pickpockets to mass murderers. It was something of a relief, therefore, to discover the present incumbent of the cell to be none other than Hetty the Hart, curled up on a stone bench, sound asleep. At least, Eric hoped she was asleep.

"Hetty!" he cried, his hand going instinctively to the large, brass lock and finding it devoid of a key. "Hetty!" he called again, beginning to bang on the door.

"Wassermarrer, Mam?" came a weak voice from within the cell.

"It's not Mam." Seizing a couple of the bars, Eric pushed his face into the narrow gap between them, feeling the rough iron rods pulling at his skin.

It was the wrong thing to do, he realised, as Hetty's eyes widened in horror. "Oh God," she mumbled, "that's all I need – being gawped at by the village idiot."

"I wasn't gawping," Eric assured her then, extracting his face with difficulty from the bars, he added, "It's me, see? Young Eric. I just wanted to see if you were OK."

"How can I be OK?" demanded Hetty, sounding much more like her old self. "Being as that bastard Terry Williams has locked me in and run off with the key. And, unless I'm very much mistaken, my hat."

"Never mind your hat," said Eric. "It's safe, back at the pub.

"You found it?" cried Hetty delightedly.

"Not me. Mrs Jenks. Turned up in her shop, it did, on the head of young Harry Stitch."

"Well, it left here on the head of not so young Terry Williams, balanced on top of his own cap, if you please." Hetty put a trembling palm to her grey curls. "Knocked it off, I did, stooping through this doorway. Gave myself a right bang. By the time I'd come to, he'd locked the door and was legging it down the passageway, laughing like a mad man."

Eric shuddered. He was all too familiar with that laugh. To say nothing of the man's tendency to misappropriate other people's headgear.

"Well, as I say, Hetty, your hat is perfectly safe." He peered again into the cell. "Bet you can't wait to get out, eh? No one's idea of fun, is it, being trapped in a cramped, windowless hole like this?"

"Oh, I don't know. It's a bit like my bedroom at home when I was a girl, except we really didn't have a pot to pee in." Hetty paused, and looked meaningfully at an earthenware bucket in the corner. "Talking of which, Eric, it'd be a help, from a comfort point of view, if we could see about getting me out sooner rather than later?"

"Right," said Eric absently. He hadn't realised before just how far Hetty had come from her evidently humble beginnings. Then, as the meaning of her last remark struck home, he blushed a little. "Right," he said again. "Well, how about I run back upstairs and get the others? Mel's up there, Hetty, and those two labourers, Frog and Earwig. Between us we could fashion some sort of battering ram and …what is it?"

"No need for all that rigmarole," said Hetty, who'd been shaking her head, vigorously, as Eric outlined his plan. "Visited another cell, I did, afore I came to this one. We could see if the key from that one fits this door as well?"

"Oh," said Eric. "Well, I'll just nip along, shall I, and fetch it?"

A moment later, Eric stood aside, allowing Hetty to step out into the corridor. "What puzzles me," he said, "is what on earth you were doing here in the first place, prowling about the gaols?"

"Thinking of buying 'em I am," said Hetty promptly. "Got a tip-off they're going on the open market come Monday. Wanted to get my bid in first if they turned out to be suitable."

"Suitable for what?" asked Eric with a shudder.

"Nightclub, young Eric. If we can get this town on its feet again, I figure it'd be good to do something for the youngsters. Love it wouldn't they? Boogying on down, down here?"

"If you say so," said Eric. Personally, he couldn't wait to get out of the dungeons and back to the blessed fresh air.

***

Back at the pub there was good news for the rescue party, returning in triumph from the court house. Young Harry it seemed, upon being held upside-down over a vat of slops by his sister, had finally admitted he'd been given the Stetson by Terry Williams. What was more, he'd agreed to say as much, in court, if needs be.

The liberation of Hetty, was then duly celebrated until, at last, it was time for Eric to think about bed.

In more ways than one, he realised guiltily, his assignation with Min being only a few short hours away.

CHAPTER TWENTY-ONE

That precious interlude with Min in the pearly dawn of what promised to be a dry, fine Midsummer's Day was something Eric was to remember for years to come. Not only had it proved to be the one sane period in an otherwise hectic day, but Min had looked utterly divine. Standing in Eric's garden, her slim arms and neck slung about with garlands of flowers, inviting him to pluck them from her, one by one, to fasten to Desmond's gleaming trap and harness.

The decorating done, Eric accepted Min's offer of a lift to the town centre car park. This was to be the starting point for his grand parade, where the seeds of triumph or disaster were yet to be sown.

***

Arriving at the car park, it seemed at first as if disaster was to be the order of the day. And not of Eric's making.

He could scarcely take two steps in any direction without someone informing him of yet another act of sabotage or wilful damage down on the field. This included all the signage being turned, overnight, to point the wrong way, and the generators, intended to power the bouncy castle, the outside bars and the fast food vans, being smashed beyond repair.

It was spiteful, last-ditch stuff, easily remedied, with the signs being quickly put right and Mrs Jenks dispatching Arnold, with his trike, to ferry new generators from the shop.

The temporary absence, though, of a fully functioning bouncy castle had already led to some families leaving the show ground disappointed.

"They were looking forward to it so much," explained one young mum, towing a glum little brood of toddlers behind her. "I can't get them to take an interest in anything else. Might as well go home, I suppose."

"Don't do that," said Eric. "I happen to know new generators are on their way to the field as we speak. Tell you what," he added, spotting Frog and Earwig careering into the car park, "how about I get you a lift back to the field in this truck? I'm pretty sure you'll find the castle as bouncy as ever when you get there."

The toddlers looked a shade less glum as Eric set off at a run towards the truck.

"Yo, Eric," shouted Frog, spotting Eric's approach. "Just dropped by on our way to the field to see if there's anything we can do?"

"There is as it happens," said Eric.

Two minutes later the children were clinging to the sides of the truck as the driver gunned the accelerator, and the young mum thanked Eric for the hundredth time.

"Don't thank me," said Eric modestly. "Thank Frog and Earwig."

"I will," said the young woman. "By the way," she added, quietly, "you do know, I suppose, that their actual names are Efrog and Eurig?"

This was news to Eric, but, before he could give the matter any more thought, his exhibits began arriving at the car park.

Tied together with baler twine, some of them, and shedding the mud and rust of decades, they rumbled in through the gates. From the impossible to the impractical, the weird to the wonderful, all had helped to shape the farming history of the town Eric still thought of as Landoobrey. And as such, he felt, all were worthy of their place in his parade.

The loudest rumble of all came from the now multicoloured steamroller driven by a triumphant Moggs Morgan, grinning through dense, black clouds of soot and steam. Defying any passing officials of the Tarmac to recognise either the man or his machine.

Floats bearing the giggling representatives of local organisations holding shaky positions in tableau after tableau then joined the agricultural exhibits.

Eric easily recognised the rugby club, frozen, mid-scrum; the Brownies, singing into the scarlet, tissue paper flames of their camp fire; the nurses from the cottage hospital, wielding giant syringes. Which as one farmer observed, massaging his hindquarters, weren't necessarily props.

Just then, the relative peace of the morning was shattered by the arrival of the undisputed Carnival Queen, Cheryl Stitch, sitting pillion on a motorbike, her frock tucked into her knickers, a fag protruding from her rosebud lips. Untucking her dress she shared a thumbs-up with Min, slapped a bashful Desmond on the rump and clambered into the trap, where she instantly outshone even the prettiest of the flowers.

"Hiya, Eric," she shouted. " 'Ow's it 'angin', mate?"

Last to arrive were the various sections of the band. The didgeridoo players formed the first ranks, with their instruments balanced on the little sets of wheels made for them by the blacksmith. Eryl Stitch and her fellow kazoo players skittered in the rear, while sandwiched in between were the woodwind, brass and string sections, who proceeded to blow, strum and pluck disjointedly.

"Do they still sound a bit rough to you?" asked a harassed looking Mel.

"Well," said Eric kindly, "any band does tuning up."

"They're not tuning up," sighed Mel. "That's a run through of their first piece."

It was chaos now in the car park and Eric spent some time breaking up chats and the occasional fight between his hill-farming exhibitors who usually only saw one another on market day. Then he arranged his procession in the order in which they would set off for their tour of the town.

Satisfied that all was well, he waved the band away. Then, stopwatch in hand, he timed to perfection the departure of all his vehicular exhibits in its wake.

It was only after he'd flagged away the last item – the elderly Fordson Major, bearing the Mann family – that Eric realised he didn't himself have any transport to the field. Desperate to accept a lift, snuggled in the trap with Min, he'd clean forgotten to bring the van.

***

"Wait," shouted Eric, as he sprinted after his parade, passing tractors and mowers, acrobats and balers, the carnival floats and Min's trap, before drawing level with Moggs Morgan's steamroller, heading up the vehicular exhibits.

Eric hadn't intended being part of the parade but, as soon as he climbed aboard the magnificent machine, he could see this was the only way to travel.

From this vantage point he had a grandstand view of the crowds, watching and cheering at every junction.

Waving rather self-consciously along with Moggs, he then braced himself as they left the town and began the steep drop south to the Bowen Field.

Nearing the field, Moggs nudged Eric. "Looks great," he bellowed.

Eric nodded. It did indeed, with dozens of stalls and sideshows grouped around the hired marquees taking pride of place in the centre.

A purist might say there was an element of improvisation in certain parts of the show ground. The beer-mat bunting, for instance, which had been Hetty's idea of a cost-cutting exercise, and the rickety tents and flimsy gazebos brought from the stallholders' own homes. But the field pulsed with locals and visitors alike enjoying themselves, which was all that mattered.

The parade received an even more tumultuous welcome on the field, filing in through the gate for what Eric liked to think of as his victory lap of the show ground. Then all the vehicles parked up in lines to be admired by one and all.

Meanwhile, the band began to regale the throng with some sing-along numbers. Grimly persisting with "Boogie Woogie Bugler Boy" as the crowd, having completely misidentified the tune, belted out "Men of Harlech".

Filled with a sense of achievement and a good slug of tea from Moggs's flask, Eric climbed down from the steamroller. His next and final challenge would be his interview with *Hi There!* magazine, scheduled for about lunchtime.

With time to kill until Min would be free to join him, Eric explored the show ground, pausing to admire everything from the ferret racing to the ever-controversial pet and pony classes. Prudently he stood aside as the Pony Show judge was rushed from the ring in the grip of her burly escorts. Moving on, he smiled to hear the distant splash of the vicar and the squeal of the human donkey.

Less gratifying were the little snippets of conversation, borne towards him on the still, summer air.

"Yes, really," said Ethel, her voice carrying from the craft marquee where she and Ivy were manning their little stall. "He thought we were knitting *hands* …"

Blushing, Eric changed course towards the WI tent, only to find himself confronted by Chopsie holding court. "Thrilled to *bits* he was with all the wood I've taken him. 'Bring me more,' he said. So I will."

Turning back the way he'd come, Eric almost cannoned into a group of chapel goers, amongst whom it appeared he was once again the topic of the moment.

"He actually asked me to *dance* with him," said a grim little woman in a hat addressing a coven of like specimens hanging on her every word. "In the *street*, of all places. When that failed he plumbed the depths of utter depravity and asked my Dilwyn instead …"

Veering away, Eric followed his nose to where Sally Stitch was spit-roasting venison

"When you going to stop picking up road kill?" asked a watching Moggs Morgan, gazing into Sally's eyes.

"When you stop leaving it where I can find it," countered Sal, who'd been wondering for some time about the bullet holes in her latest finds.

Moggs grinned as Harry and Barry ran amok in the makeshift kitchen while little Garry slept soundly in a vegetable box. "Just want to see you right, Sal. Talking of which, you thought any more about moving up to the farm with me?"

"Huh!" said Sal. "State of your cottage?"

"Not to the cottage. That's gone. Slight accident this morning with the steamroller … Big house is finished now, though, up the top. Plenty of room for you and the children. What about it, eh?"

Sally looked thoughtful. "The kids could all have their own rooms?" she queried.

"Two each if they want 'em, and I can easily build some more."

"OK," said Sal. "You're on."

***

Hearing the cheer as the Carnival Queen finished her horse-drawn tour of the show ground, Eric headed over to help Min park the trap and tether Desmond.

Together they then made their way to a stall selling miniatures of *A Deep Depression in Driftwood*, genuinely hand signed this time by the artist himself.

"How's it going, girls?" he asked.

"Brill," said Beryl. "*Everyone* wants to buy one of these."

Eric smiled to hear this, the proceeds from the stall being earmarked for the hard-up Mann family. Then, recalling the conversation he'd overheard in Sally's kitchen, he said, "I've a feeling you two might be moving on soon, from my garden."

"Has Mam finally said yes then to Moggs Morgan?" asked Meryl, rather to Eric's surprise.

"Er, yes, I think she has."

"Great," put in Beryl. "Of all the men Mam knows, he's the one I'd most want as a dad."

"And how serendipitous is that?" murmured Meryl.

***

"It's all rather marvellous, isn't it?" said Eric, moving off hand in hand with Min as together they battled the buffeting crowds.

"You can say that again," replied Min, smiling as she spied a stall up ahead manned by Sid the Sweets.

Eric eyed the crowd, crunching acid drops and laughing their heads off. "There's something you should know," he said, tightening his grip on Min's hand, "about those sweets."

Briefly he outlined the visit of Constable George to his nephews' farm and the impending results of the mushroom analysis. "I didn't tell you before," he finished, "because I didn't want to worry you until we were sure."

Min opened her mouth to say something but at that moment a cheer went up from the centre of the field. Turning, they watched as a ground crew finished inflating a balloon, in the shape of an enormous sheep, which bobbed on its cables above a rickety basket.

"Wow," said Eric. "That must be Hetty's surprise. She said she'd organised something to give people a bird's-eye view of the town."

Min shuddered. "By the look of alarm on that sheep's face I don't think there'll be many wanting to go up in it, do you? Although, it seems to be anchored to the ground by that coil of rope, tied to the Fish and Chip wagon. So perhaps it would be OK ..."

A commotion just then near the entrance to the field signified the arrival of the *Hi There!* team, who proceeded to set up their equipment in readiness for Eric's interview.

"Best go and do my bit," said Eric, walking over with Min and enquiring after Miranda, who was nowhere to be seen.

"Gone straight to the bar," grinned Steve, introducing himself, "with some theatrical type, twirling a baton. Fast worker, eh, our Miranda?"

"Oh, I don't know about that," replied Eric. "They've been old friends for days now."

In the event, Eric quite enjoyed his interview. When pressed, he admitted to having recently completed his new piece, renamed *A Goddess in Love*, which would be going on display very soon at the Tate Modern alongside *A Deep Depression in Driftwood*.

"And your inspiration for the new piece came directly from living here, did it?" queried an excited Steve, realising he was about to out-scoop every other magazine on the market.

"Oh, yes," smiled Eric, gazing beyond the lights and cameras to where little Min sat on the grass, sunning her upturned face. "Directly."

His interview over, Eric took a moment to remind the photographers of their promise to take some extra shots of the activities on the field, then he and Min set off in search of tea.

They hadn't gone far before a desperate Hetty appeared at their side.

"This is awful, young Eric," she said. "You've seen my surprise I imagine?"

Eric nodded. "Hard to miss," he replied. "Any takers yet for a ride in it?"

"Not one," wailed Hetty, pushing the brim of her Stetson away from her sweaty forehead. "It's an absolute disaster."

"Not necessarily," grinned Eric. "Once it's up, it'll make a great aerial marker for the show ground. Won't matter, then, how many road signs the Twins decided to turn round."

"They'll soon be too busy for any more of that nonsense," muttered Hetty. "Got their first guests arriving shortly, I believe, next door? Getting back to my balloon, though," she added, slyly. "All I need is for someone to go up in it, just for a little while. Show everyone it's safe."

"Mm," demurred Eric. "But who would be daft enough to do that?"

***

Floating high above the show ground, a queasy Eric did his best to enjoy his bird's-eye view of the town. It wasn't easy, especially when the town clock, which had started off miles away, appeared to be growing closer by the minute. Surely that couldn't be right, he thought. Not if his balloon was stationary.

Risking a lightning glance downwards, he was alarmed to see a thousand faces staring at something behind him. Turning, he followed their collective gaze to where the cut end of the safety rope floated in the slipstream of his basket.

***

"Shall we get the fire brigade?" yelled one bystander.

"Not if we want him down in a hurry," replied Arnold, who hadn't forgotten his own futile wait at the hands of the volunteer brigade, when he'd been marooned at the top of a ladder.

Alerted to the crisis by a *Hi There!* photographer who'd actually snapped the Twins cutting the rope attached to the Fish and Chip van, the old man was among the first to react. Groping in his pocket for his walkie-talkie, he pressed the button and made contact with Mrs Jenks, whom he'd last seen in the big tent housing the shooting range.

"What now, Arnold?" Mrs Jenks crackled in answer to his urgent summons.

"Are you still at the shooting range?" demanded Arnold.

"Yes," said Mrs Jenks, pointedly adding, "*Over.*"

"Never mind about 'over'," yelled Arnold, limping for his trike. "The time for 'over' is … well, over. Just come outside will you, and bring a gun? You need to shoot down a flying sheep with young Eric floating in a basket underneath it."

"What have I told you," whistled Mrs Jenks sternly, "about having a couple at lunchtime?"

"I haven't been having a couple," insisted Arnold. "At least, not yet. But you need to move quickly, Mrs Jenks. Drop him on the bouncy castle if you can."

Moving quickly was what Mrs Jenks did best. She was outside the tent in moments, and about to raise the gun, when Arnold's voice came again over the walkie-talkie.

"Don't forget," he yelled, pedalling furiously for the shooting range, "you'll need to aim to the left to be sure of hitting it."

"Aim to the left?" queried Mrs Jenks. "I hardly need to aim at all, do I? Something that size, I can hardly miss it ..."

"You will if you don't aim to the left," said Arnold firmly, reluctant even in the present emergency to reveal the trade secret of his uncle's barrel bending.

"Well, on your head be it," muttered Mrs Jenks, dropping the walkie-talkie, flinging the gun high and firing in entirely the wrong direction. To her amazement the sheep collapsed with a heartfelt sigh to drop squarely on the roof of the bouncy castle.

Just then, a tinkling of sirens announced the arrival on the field of PC George. Armed with the incriminating results of the mushroom analysis, he'd been on his way to arrest the Twins when the giant exploding sheep had caught his trained eye. Observation, as he was heard to remark later, being something they pride themselves on in the police.

Hearing of Eric's brush with certain death, and bearing in mind the visual evidence secured by the *Hi There* photographer, PC George resigned himself to adding attempted murder to the drugs and kidnapping-related charges, upon which he had been off to arrest his nephews. Then, after calling up reinforcements in the shape of fellow bobby, Bobby, he set off with renewed urgency to track down the Twins.

***

Watching the police contingent leap into action, Min turned to Eric. "I thought you were a goner for a minute there," she said quietly.

Eric smiled. He'd thought the same in the moments before he was shot down. And in the moments afterwards if he was honest, until he'd felt the blessed cushion of the bouncy castle beneath his basket.

"Oh, well," he said, "here I am, safe and sound. And the Twins will shortly be under lock and key, so I guess the only real losers are the guests at the prudie nudie hotel because who's going to run the place now?"

"The Twins have got tenants in," Min reminded him. "According to Frank the Mail, they've leased the place for a year so I don't expect it will matter to them what happens to the Twins." She was about to go on when a loud whinny drifted towards them over the noise of the show ground. "Oh," she said. "That's …"

"I know," interrupted Eric, "it's Desmond."

"Mm." Absently, Min drew a heart in the dusty grass with the toe of her shoe. "Well I'd better take him home, I guess. I could come back later, though, for the show dance, and bring Mo, too, as she's bound to be back by then?"

Eric grinned. "That would be nice. Er, you won't be driving down will you?" he asked.

"No, I expect Mo will drive. Why?"

"It's just that the dance finishes at midnight and I'd hate you to miss it."

Min giggled as he took her in his arms.

"Until tonight," he whispered.

***

Later, as the crowds began leaving the field, Eric turned down several offers of a lift, preferring to walk back to the cottage to get changed for the dance. There were no residents in sight in the grounds of the prudie nudie hotel. Only the back view of a couple who must surely be the new tenants, baring all as they pottered about, giving a passing tweak to the garden furniture. Suddenly, as if sensing Eric's eyes on them, the woman turned, then waved, setting far too much flesh in motion and bringing the traffic on the road to a standstill.

"Hello, Eric," she called.

"Hello, Mum," sighed Eric.

The End

Printed in Poland
by Amazon Fulfillment
Poland Sp. z o.o., Wrocław

52978860R00169